THE PRICE OF ATONEMENT

ML NYSTROM

HOT TREE PUBLISHING

THE PRICE OF ATONEMENT

THE DUTCHMEN MC
BOOK 4

ML NYSTROM

HOT TREE PUBLISHING

ALSO BY ML NYSTROM

DRAGON RUNNERS MC

Mute

Stud

Blue

Table

Brick

MACATEER BROTHERS

Run With It

Ready For It

Hold It Close

Risk It All

Give It To Me

THE DUTCHMEN MC

The Price of Redemption

The Price of Forgiveness

The Price of Peace

The Price of Atonement

For information, contact the publisher, Hot Tree Publishing.

WWW.HOTTREEPUBLISHING.COM

EDITING: HOT TREE EDITING

COVER DESIGNER: BOOKSMITH DESIGN

EBOOK ISBN: 978-1-922679-37-6

PAPERBACK ISBN:978-1-922679-38-3

To all the moms, single or married, who are the absolute backbone of the family. The world can't make it without you.

PROLOGUE

The officer handed the plastic ziplock bag to him without a lot of fanfare. Keys, wallet, watch, an unopened pack of gum, and a half pack of cigarettes stared at him through the clear material. Boots wondered if they were still any good after two years.

The rotund uniformed man behind the caged counter turned a black notebook to him and slapped a pen on top. "Sign here," he said with zero interest.

Boots signed.

It felt good to be in his own clothes again, even though the fit was different from what he expected. For the past two years, there was little for him to do in the St. Cloud Correctional Prison. He had a job in the kitchen, but other than that, he spent his hours locked in his cell or in the yard lifting weights. His body was leaner in some areas and bigger and harder in others. He'd done what he could to stay active in mind and body and simply bided his time.

He'd learned the art form of patience through forced study. The first time he went behind bars, he came out a different person. Someone he wished he'd never known or become. This time, he'd had an epiphany and was ready to make some changes in his life. He hoped he'd paid enough for his sins. The prison sentence this time was only two years, the maximum you could get for a boating misdemeanor. He was sure the reason he got the full length of it was because he'd worn his club colors in the courtroom. His past record didn't help. If the courts had done a bit more digging into his activities over the past fifteen years, his sentence would have been longer. Much longer.

The police had caught him while he was fleeing from a botched run of smuggled prescription pills. The Dark Horses MC and the Dutchmen MC stored and ran drugs over the Canadian border as their primary source of income during that time. A rival club tried to take over the route lines and attacked during the load-on at the pier close to Hastings, Minnesota. Bullets and boats didn't mix too well. One of the Dark Horses, Army, got hit and went down. Boots tossed the illegal cargo in the water and took off to draw the Tiger Clan members away and give his brothers a chance to escape. It would have worked better if the boating police hadn't shown up.

Boots tossed his gun overboard and led them on a long chase, zigzagging and flying down the Mississippi River for as long as he could to give his brothers some much needed time. The result was incarceration on a reckless boating charge. With all the truly evil shit he'd done, to be caught and jailed for what amounted to a joyride? Un-fucking-believable.

The worst part? It didn't matter that he'd gone to prison for his club now, as the Dark Horses no longer existed. Their president, Musicman, was assassinated shortly after the fuckup on the river. His granddaughter and great-granddaughter had been collateral damage. Decimated by a drug war and the death of the club's leader, the Dark Horses fell apart and scattered. Some members simply left, and some patched into other clubs. The actual person who pulled the trigger was unknown, and the authorities had filed the incident away as a cold case, but Boots knew justice had been served. Not too long after the murders of Music and his two family members, the Tiger Clan compound and almost all its members were killed in a massive explosion set up by Iceman, the former president of the Dutchmen MC. Iceman had disappeared, and the world presumed him dead in the subsequent fire from the bomb he'd rigged using his bike. Rumors abounded, though, that he'd somehow survived and was living somewhere on the East Coast.

More power to him, Boots thought. If Iceman was alive and well, Boots hoped he was happy.

The last gate clanged open, and Boots stepped out of the barbwire-topped fence. He stepped through the chain-link and instantly felt the weight release from his shoulders. The September sun glowed a little brighter, as if he were coming out of a long hibernation. He closed his eyes and inhaled the crisp tang of fresh Minnesota air. There were colors too, more vibrant than the dull grays and whites of the prison. Grasses and trees that lay just beyond the fence line appeared greener, and the sky overhead glowed in cloudless cerulean blue. Freedom. He'd never take it for granted again.

A familiar figure stood next to a black truck. Railroad leaned on the closed door, his eyes covered by sunglasses. "Good to see you, brother."

When Boots reached him, he took Rail's hand and pulled him in for a single backslap and man hug. Rail gestured to the plastic bag. "That's all you got?"

Boots snorted. "Yep. All I got left in the world."

Rail gestured to the truck's cab and opened the driver's door. "Not necessarily. I got your cut from Barker. He goes by Bob, his real name, now. Out of the life completely and drives a van for Amazon Prime. He brought your bike and some of your clothes to the clubhouse. Nothing left of the Dark Horses compound now. Damn shame."

Boots went to the other side of the truck and

opened the door. He picked up the worn leather vest with his club's logo on the back that had been. He gave a sardonic huff that might have been a laugh. "You ever meet Carmen, my woman?"

Rail got in the driver's side and closed the door with a muffled slam. He shook his head. "Different clubs back then. You know we didn't allow the old ladies or wives to be a part of it."

"She wasn't my old lady. She lived with me like she was, but I never got around to giving her my patch or a ring." Boots shrugged. "Doesn't mean shit now either. Barker told me she packed up and moved out when I got convicted. Club gone, woman gone, house gone. My tools, everything I owned—gone. The only reason I still have a bike is 'cause she couldn't sell it without my signature on the title. Really fucking glad I never sealed the deal with her."

Rail grunted. "Sucks, brother. You got plans to go back home?"

Boots traced a finger over the image of the flaming horse skeleton that had been depicted in mid gallop. Fifteen years, he'd given to the Dark Horses. Fifteen years of blood, sweat, and sacrifice for a brotherhood that no longer existed. Fifteen years of doing things for his club no one wanted to do, but he did them because they had to be done. He'd gone to prison to protect his brothers, and, in the end, none of them remained. This left a bitter taste in his mouth. "Guess you didn't hear me. I've got nothing left. I'm fucking starting over at age forty-five and don't have a goddamn clue what I'm going to do. All I know is boats, bikes, and the river. Can't do that on probation 'cause I can't get a boating license. If I'm caught, I'm back behind those walls again."

Rail climbed into the truck. "Invitation to patch over is on the table. The Dutchmen got new things going with the marina and the Harbor Bar and Grill. Between the boat garage, marina rentals, and the bar, we're doing good. The club will never be rich, but then again, we never were, anyway. We got brothers working the legit side of business now and breathing easy cause we don't have to worry about bullets finding us in the dark."

Boots followed Rail's example and loaded his big frame into the truck cab. He tossed the plastic bag onto the small seat of the extended cab and held the old cut in his heavy fist. A patch-over to the Dutchmen MC had never been on his radar, but the possibility intrigued him. What else did he have to lose? He no longer had a home or a place to be. He'd spent a lot of his life as a biker. At one time he had different plans, but now, he couldn't see himself doing anything else. "How long can I think about it?"

"As long as you need, brother. There's a cabin you can use that's not too far from the clubhouse. Iceman's old place. Not fancy, but you're welcome to use it for as long as you need it. You want work, I can find something for you, or you can find your own thing. Up to you. You had our backs for years. We got yours now."

Boots looked at the cut in his hands, one that used to be his entire world, and he made a decision. He hit the button to roll down the window, and he tossed the crumpled cut to the ground. "Long drive to Red Wing. Let's get the fuck out of here."

CHAPTER
ONE

Uff-da, not again! Janice, more commonly known as Mama J, hung up her phone and slipped it into the pocket of her apron. Her face tightened as she closed her eyes and leaned her round body over the flour-covered butcher-block work counter in her kitchen. At least Nutter had called this time. He was supposed to pick up Tad and Ian from soccer practice and treat them to dinner and a movie. She wasn't sure what delayed him. Or rather, *who* delayed him. Her ex would go through long periods of time when he showed up punctually and stayed on task. He'd take care of house repairs and updates, help with the kids they'd made, and give her money from time to time for their support. Then he'd slide back into old habits. His eye would catch on a new woman to chase, or he'd get into the party atmosphere at the Dutchmen MC compound and forget that he had obligations to fulfill. He declared loud and often that he still loved her and wanted her back, but he couldn't help himself when it came to other women.

Janice had spent years with Nutter as his old lady, wearing his patch and hoping she could build a life with him, but she got to the point she could no longer take his wandering. He had other children by two other women, and two of those children lived with her, bringing the number of her household up to six kids, plus herself, Opal, and her baby.

The ranch-style house had four bedrooms and two full bathrooms, but they were still crowded with every inch of space occupied. Janice gave the largest bedroom to Opal and little Pearl because it had the extra space needed for all the baby stuff. The next largest bedroom had two sets of bunk beds in it for the boys, and the matching one had twin beds for the girls. That left the tiniest bedroom for herself. For space reasons, she'd given her nice queen-sized mattress to Opal and bought a twin to use in her room. Janice figured it was only right, as she was the only person not having to share, and she desperately needed her privacy.

Even though she technically never got married to Nutter, she'd always considered him her husband. His club patch on her back was considered the equivalent of a ring. Unfortunately, that did not guarantee fidelity, and she grieved her breakup as any other woman would when getting a divorce.

He'd thrown that in her face when she'd gone to the clubhouse to confront him about yet another child he made with a third baby mama. Old ladies and wives had been forbidden at that time from going into the men's-only world of the Dutchmen. She had not only set foot inside the taboo place, but brought down the house with an epic breakup between her and Nutter. She could still hear his words echoing in her ears.

"You're leavin' me, eh? Just where do you think you're gonna go? The house is in my name, and there's no ring on your finger to divorce. No legal rights to the property. You leave my house, you'll go by yourself. The kids will stay put."

Of course, much of that threat was moot as there was no way he'd give up his freewheeling lifestyle to take care of his kids full-time. Nor was there a chance that Mimi, his steady sidepiece and mother of the extra two children in Mama J's household, would step in and fill the gap. She had taken off not long after announcing her third child by Nutter. She found herself another man, decided to keep and raise the newest baby, and had left the state. Kay, the latest woman to be added to Nutter's harem, was still around, but from what Janice understood, the baby she carried had turned out not to be Nutter's after all. The possibility of having three baby mamas still didn't deter Nutter from spreading his joy to as many women as would have him. Janice figured it was only a matter of time before Nutter approached her again with yet another woman's baby and asked her to take care of it.

She had mixed feelings about this. The children Mimi had by Nutter had been in her care since infancy, and when their biological mom took off, they stayed here with their half-siblings. For years, Janice kept these babies and loved them as if they were her own. They were innocent in all their parents' drama, and the only mother they knew was Janice. The thought of adding yet another baby to the brood she cared for was daunting, but also the thought of that innocent child being dumped into the foster system bothered her. Adoption might be on the table, but that bothered her as well. All these children were related with the same father, and Janice had a strong sense of family, despite her pain caused by Nutter's lack of fidelity. She didn't know what she'd do if Nutter showed up here with his cajoling words and a baby carrier on his arm.

Whatever. I can't think about that now. She wiped the flour from her hands onto the old-fashioned apron around her generous middle and walked through the kitchen into the great room. She passed by the two young girls coloring in books at the coffee table and beamed at them with a big smile. "Oh, such pretty pictures! I hope one is for me?"

Lily, the five-year-old, grinned up at her with a grape Kool-Aid-stained mouth. "Mine is!" Charlotte simply gave her a peaceful nod and continued to apply a red crayon to the paper, taking great care to keep between the lines. The two boys in the room were both four-year-olds born just months apart and currently engrossed in pulling out every block they could find in one of the many Rubbermaid tubs kept in the living space for toys. The bigger play area was in the unfinished basement, but Janice needed the kids to stay upstairs with her so she could work and watch them at the same time. She patted their heads as she approached the master bedroom and knocked on the side jamb of the open door.

"Opal? You awake?" she called softly.

"Yes, I'm here." The light voice coming from the bed sounded groggy, but there was no hesitation in the woman's response.

Opal used to be known as Peebles, one of several clubhouse sweetbutts who slept with club members or guests for favors and money. She'd gotten pregnant last year by Rebel, one of the higher-ranking members of the club, and thought her life had turned around for the better. At first, Rebel was thrilled to become a father, but eventually, his drug addiction overcame that novelty. Opal got serious about becoming a parent, got herself clean, and planned a life for her and her child. Rebel died from an overdose and never saw his daughter.

"Nutter called and can't pick up Tad and Ian from

soccer practice. I need to run over to the school and get them. You okay to watch the house for a bit?"

"You bet." Shuffling noises came from the bedroom, and the pale woman rolled off the bed. Her Walgreens uniform was rumpled from her brief nap between work and school. She had a part-time job at the pharmacy store and was taking classes at the local community college to become a nail technician and hair stylist. Both women worked their asses off, but between them, they managed to take care of the house and the kids.

The house was small, but it was rent-free. It belonged to Gabriella Viklund, who had been associated with the club for a brief time. Janice didn't know all the details of Gabby's dealings with the Dutchmen or her full relationship status with Iceman, the former president of the club, but the two women had become fast friends, bonding over childcare and cooking. When Gabby inherited this house from her deceased uncle, she promptly signed it over to Janice. This gave her some property of her own, which opened up a new world of possibilities yet to be explored.

That property still came with expenses. Taxes, repairs, updates, and upkeep—all of it took a big chunk of money. Added to the monthly budget was a long list of bills, groceries, clothes for a herd of growing bodies, toys, school fees and supplies, sports dues and equipment, doctor visits, medicines, dentists, looming braces, and more. It took both women to keep it together.

For the time being, Janice and Opal would scrape by as best they could.

"You need me to skip class tonight?" Opal asked as she rubbed her eyes. Pearl was fussy with teething, so her mother had lost a lot of sleep lately and was grateful for any shut-eye she could glean.

"No, I'll get the boys and come back with them. The kitchen is a mess, but I finished the *lefse* and *pepparkakor*. The *kalops* I put in the Crock-Pot should be ready soon. Just got to clean up a bit, and we'll get everyone fed. You shouldn't have any problems getting to class on time."

Opal ran her hands through her long gold hair and pulled it back into a messy bun at her nape. "I'll get the kitchen in order for supper. I should be able to bathe Oliver and Augustus before class. Do I need to pick up anything on the way home later?"

Janice scrunched her face. "We're good for now, thanks. I'll load up the van for deliveries in the morning."

Mama J's Old World Treats had grown from an idea to a small business that had started to turn a slight profit. During this past summer, she worked a kiosk booth at a local street festival or open market nearly every weekend. Now that school was back, and those venues dried up, several local grocery stores and restaurants now carried her baked goods, and the demand rose weekly. Janice had kept up so far, but she had to sacrifice sleep and personal time to get the work done and take care of the kids. There were days when the only break she got was a quick five-minute shower. She was only thirty-seven and already showing gray streaks in her curly brown hair. For years, she kept it short and bouncy. It had since grown long and wild, as a trip to the salon for a haircut took too much time and effort to schedule. Maybe if Opal had the energy one night, she could do a quick trim in the kitchen. Until then, Janice would scrape it back with a headband.

She removed her apron and glanced down at the long fitted tunic shirt she wore over faded black leggings. Not a fashion statement, but she didn't care about it enough to go change. She also didn't have time. The keys jangled in her hand as she grabbed her wallet and hurried out the door.

The old minivan hesitated twice before the engine caught and rumbled. *Another task to add to my list,* Janice thought as she put the vehicle in reverse and backed out of the driveway. Ten minutes later, she pulled up in front of the playing fields at the back of the school. Tad and Ian were standing with the coach and his two kids, the only ones left there to be picked up. A small jolt of guilt hit her belly, but she stifled it quickly. It wasn't her fault Nutter had canceled last minute. She reminded herself often that she was not responsible for her ex's problems, but that didn't help much when those problems bled over into her life.

She faked a bright smile as she stopped the van at the curb and rolled down the window. "Hi, Coach. Sorry I'm late."

Tad's face darkened as he spoke. "Dad was supposed to come. He was takin' us to Godfather's Pizza before home."

Janice answered back, still keeping her lips curled up. "He texted me to say he got stuck with something and couldn't make it. Maybe he'll get you a pizza this weekend."

The ten-year-old sniffed at his mother's words but didn't answer. He awkwardly climbed into the cab, all gangly limbs and shaggy hair. He still had the body of a boy, but Janice could see he would take after his father. Nutter was a big man. Handsome, tall, broad-shouldered, and strong, but with not the cut, muscled appearance of an athlete. He had a small rounded belly that didn't seem to detract from his appeal. A dad bod, so to speak. Janice could attest firsthand that his charm and expert flirtation had the power to woo into bed any woman he set his sights on.

She hoped Tad wouldn't inherit that particular talent from his dad.

Ian, her seven-year-old, looked more like her: short and stocky. He, however, didn't carry any extra weight, and if he gained any of his father's size, would resemble a football linebacker as he got older.

Both boys settled themselves in their customary spots in the van. The click of their seatbelts punctuated the dull silence.

"Good practice?" Janice trilled, desperate to fill the van with positive vibes.

The shrugs and noncommittal "it was okays" she got back held zero enthusiasm. The rest of the drive home was silent.

Janice parked under the carport and watched the boys grab their bags. "Any homework?

"I have a spelling worksheet." The monotone answer came from Ian.

"Math and an essay." Tad slung his bag and shin guards over his shoulder. Janice noticed she'd have to get him new ones soon, as he'd outgrown the ones from last year.

"Work on that after supper, yeah?"

"You bet. Mom?"

She glanced at her son as she picked up a handful of the empty juice boxes that constantly built up on the van's floor. "Yeah, buddy?"

"Since Dad didn't come get us after practice, will he come to the game on Saturday?"

Straight shot to her heart. "I don't know, Taddy. I'm sure he'll come if he can."

Tad's face showed an emotion far too old for him. "Doesn't matter. You'll be there, right?"

The never-ending chores whirled and sorted and scheduled themselves in her head. Baking, deliveries, housework, errands, pickups, drop-offs, more baking; the exponential list grew daily, and what she couldn't get done during the week, she did on the weekends. The hours she would spend watching a kids' soccer game were ones she sorely needed for all the tasks at hand. She smiled at her oldest child. "I wouldn't miss it, darling."

CHAPTER
TWO

BOOTS SUCKED BACK THE LAST OF HIS BEER AND LET OUT a soft burp. The noise in the club was jarring to his ears, reminding him of the constant drone in the prison. What he wouldn't give for just a little quiet. The Dutchmen MC's private compound had changed some since he'd been here last. The stripper pole, poker and pool tables, and the bar remained the same, but the walls and furniture had been updated to make it look more like a resort bar than an old converted warehouse. They had also built more private rooms for ranking club members and occasional guests.

There had been a time when getting or watching a sweetbutt give a blow job was a public event, as very few had any private bedrooms. He himself had sat in this very spot, conversing with brothers that had heads bobbing in their laps. Boots didn't indulge himself often with other women back then. The occasional blow job, but he always remained faithful to Carmen when it came to sex. She was no longer in the picture. Club women were still around now, ready and willing to open mouths or legs. If a sweet-butt made him an offer tonight, he had a place to take her up on it and probably would.

Rail's phone buzzed, and he opened it to look down at a text. The parallel twin scars on his face crinkled as he smiled. "My wife, Gretchen, wants me to pick up brisket sandwiches on the way home. She's up against a tough deadline and says she needs sustenance."

Duke flopped onto the sofa next to Boots. "You are so fucking pussy-whipped."

"Seen Penny lately?

"Asshole."

The bickering between the current president and his vice president held no rancor. Boots saw and heard the good-natured ribbing. Apparently, Rail was not the only man to have found something special.

A sliver of regret touched his heart. He'd thought he had that something once. Even considered putting a ring on Carmen's finger. In a way, it was good he went to jail, as he found out how committed she really was to him.

One of the club women came around with a double handful of beer bottles. The cute brunette plunked down the drinks and turned her eyes on him. "Hi, Boots. Remember me?"

He had no clue who she was. Nonetheless, he smiled at her. "Sure, baby. How could I forget?"

That seemed to satisfy her. She dropped her chin and pursed out her lower lip in a duck-face look that Boots supposed was meant to be seductive. "Maybe I can give you a real welcome home?"

He picked up a beer and took a long drink. "Sounds good to me. I have some business to talk about with the guys here. Come find me in about twenty minutes, yeah?"

She grinned happily. "You bet." She skipped away.

Duke shook his head as he watched the girl leave. He picked up his own bottle and took a healthy sip. "Good one to break the seal, brother. She's a paralegal or some sort of legal-eagle type over in Rochester and comes here on weekends to party. Goes by Bella after that vampire sparkle shit, and I do not know what her real name is. If she calls you Daddy, that's just her thing. Gets off on it. Loves to fuck but has no interest in an old man. Spider had an eye for her once, but she shut his ass down."

Boots nodded. "Sounds just like what I need. Been a long time since I got off on with anything besides my hand."

Rail leaned back. "Have at it. Should be a supply of rubbers in the guest rooms. You're welcome to stay there tonight. Cabin is still yours to use as you need it."

Boots took another long swig of his beer and got down to business. "Really grateful to you. I'm essentially starting over. Got a lot of decisions I gotta think about, but there's one I've already made." He leaned forward and put his elbows on his knees. "The Dark Horses are gone, which means my family is gone. As I see it, this club is changing, and I like where it's going. I'm not getting any younger, and going back to running illegal shit on boats is not a place I want to be. If that offer for a patch over is still good, I'd like to take it."

Duke let out a burp. "Thought you had family people in Wisconsin. Brothers and shit."

Boots's face darkened. "That bridge burned a long time ago. Nothing but ashes left."

Duke glanced over at Rail. "We gotta take a formal vote in chapel, but as far as I'm concerned, you're already a brother. We got work at the bar and at the marina if you want it. It's not glamorous, but the money is good. The club's been talking about other expansion ideas. I never thought I'd say this, but I'm happier now than I was when we ran the lines. It's nice not to spend your days looking over your shoulder for a knife aimed at your back or a gun to your skull."

Boots raised his head, his black eyes glittering as they met Rail's gaze. "Always admired Iceman and what he did to keep this club together. Strong man, strong leader. Never thought it could get better. I was wrong."

Rail pressed his lips and dipped his chin at the unvoiced compliment. "The Dutchmen have to grow with the times. We've shed blood in the past and will in the future, but always for something more than what we've got today." His eyes grew serious. "I've already said a patch over is on the table for you. But I also have to say, the club doesn't have or want the position you had with the Dark Horses. That kind of talent has no place here. You have a problem with that, then you might need to move on. No harm, no foul."

Boots spotted Bella hovering nearby with two fresh beers in her hands and a blatant invitation on her face. "The sins of my past are just that. Past, and I've paid enough for them. I'm looking forward, not behind." He stood tall and swallowed the rest of the bottle in his hand. "If the vote goes against me, I hope both of you know I have your backs, no matter what."

Duke grunted. "Same. Now go fuck some pussy. She'll be good to you."

Bella grinned big as Boots approached her and took one of the bottles. The cold beer tasted like ambrosia. "You got a room?"

She jerked her head to the back hall. "Ready and waiting, Daddy."

Nope, he didn't like her calling him that, but he wasn't about to quibble.

The room she showed him to was plain. A queen bed and a nightstand with a box of condoms, lube, and baby-wipes on the top next to an ugly lamp. There was a beat-up chair in one corner, and that was it.

Bella wasted no time once they crossed the threshold, and she rapidly stripped off her clothes, tossing them at the chair. Her body was much thinner than he preferred, but welcoming. She arranged herself on the bed, lying down on her back and propping herself up on her elbows. Her open legs revealed her pink pussy with pubic hair carefully crafted into a heart shape. She was already glistening.

Boots stripped off his shirt and saw her eyes widen a bit as she took in his elaborate chest tattoo. "That's… that's a lot of… um… detail."

"You have a problem with it?"

She shook her head, but her eyes stayed on the inked pictures.

"You already have a man's dick inside you tonight?" Boots asked as he draped the shirt over the back of the chair.

"No, just yours, Daddy."

"Good. I'm not into eating pussy that someone else just came in." Boots unzipped his jeans and dropped them to the floor. His penis stood straight out, long and thick, from a nest of dark hair. He picked up a condom and tore open the plastic wrapper. "This is the way it's going to go. I'm gonna fuck you first. Won't last long 'cause I haven't been inside a pussy for two long years. Then you'll clean yourself 'cause I don't like the taste of rubber either, and I'll eat you until you come. After that, you'll suck me hard, then I'll fuck you again. We're gonna repeat steps two, three, and four until I've come so many times, I can't get it up again or you tell me you've had enough. I'm figuring on at least three rounds. You good with that?"

Her eyes got big as he rolled the thin sheathe over his straining dick. "That's a lot."

He didn't know if she was talking about the size of his dick or the amount of times he planned to come inside her. Could be both. He lifted himself over her and place the head of his pulsing dick at her wet entrance. "You good with that?"

She stared up at him, her eyes full of desire. "I'm good."

He pushed inside and closed his eyes at her gasp as he seated himself fully. The tight clasp of her pussy felt like heaven. "Still good?"

"Yes," came her groaning answer. She squirmed under him, opening her legs further and tilting her pelvis to take as much of him as she could. "More."

He didn't go three rounds. He went four.

CHAPTER
THREE

Janice loaded up the last of the containers into the back of the van just as the kids emerged from the house. She had just enough time to get them to school and make her deliveries before Opal had to go to her shift at Walgreens. When Opal had first moved in, they'd had a long tear-filled and cathartic conversation. As Peebles, she had been one of the women Nutter slept with occasionally. As Opal, she regretted it and spent an entire evening apologizing for it.

Janice found it in her to forgive the young woman. "I can't put all the blame on you. Nutter didn't exactly trip and fall on top of you, and somehow his penis accidentally got entangled with your vagina."

They had become friends and so dependent on each other, life would have been impossible for both of them had they had to face their challenges alone.

"We need more loose-leaf paper," Tad muttered as he climbed into the front seat. Ian got in the very back, and Charlotte and Lily took the middle seats. The girls started singing one of their original songs while Ian complained and stuck his fingers in his ears.

Tad clicked his seat belt and turned to face the windshield. "Mrs. Potter said it would be good for us to have a better computer. She posts the assignments and projects on her teacher page."

Janice sighed. They had an ancient desktop that all of them used. Four kids' worth of homework, plus Opal's schoolwork, and the attempt at building a website for her baking business was more than the machine could handle at times, and crashes were frequent. "I'll see what I can do. Ask Mrs. Potter if they still have any of those Chromebooks they were handing out. Maybe you can use one until we get a better computer, yeah?"

Tad let out his own puff of air. "You bet, Mom."

She dropped the girls and Ian at the elementary school and drove her oldest to the middle school. When Opal had day classes, she would often take the kids, as the community college was not far away. Tad stayed quiet during the short drive between the two campuses. He was the youngest in his class and would graduate high school at age seventeen, but he had an air about him now that reflected a seriousness unlike other boys at his school. Janice wasn't sure if this was the first sign of puberty or if Tad had been exposed to more adult drama than he should have at his young age. She did her best to spend some one-on-one time so she could talk with each of her children, but it was hard to do with the demands of her present life. Sometimes, the only time she got with Tad was this ten-minute window.

"Something on your mind, Taddy?" she asked. She didn't look at him directly as she pulled up to a stop sign and glanced at either side of the street. It was a good thing she wasn't moving, as the statement from his mouth cut her to the quick.

"Dad's never coming home again, is he?"

Janice took in a sharp breath, and pain sliced through her. What she wouldn't give to shield her children from this hurt. "No, he's not, sweetheart." She hazarded a glance at her son and noticed his clenched jaw and balled up fists.

"I don't remember him ever coming to a soccer game even when he *was* home. He said he would come to the school play last Christmas, but he didn't. He told Charlotte he'd buy her a piano so she could take lessons. She wants them real bad, and he still hasn't done that yet. Even when he lived with us, he wasn't really with us."

Her son's not-yet-dropped voice uttered the statement, but it had the maturity of someone far older. Tears burned in Janice's eyes, and she blinked to clear them. She knew Charlotte wanted piano lessons. The little girl often pretended to play with her fingers on the kitchen table as if it was a keyboard as she sang her songs at the top of her lungs. Janice gripped the steering wheel as she fought the desire to cry. She made the turn and somehow kept going. Several responses flashed through her mind, and she as quickly discarded them as they formed. The boy made a statement, not a question, but she felt she needed to say something positive to him. She had a hard time coming up with anything. "Your father… has a lot on his plate right now." The lame excuse sounded bad in her own ears as she said it out loud.

"He cheated on you."

God, this boy was killing her! She pulled out of the drop-off line and parked the van. Conversations like this one shouldn't be rushed, and she needed to concentrate on her son rather than driving a vehicle. The engine rumbled and cut off as she turned the key and swiveled to face Tad. His hazel eyes gazed into hers, and she was struck again by the maturity in her oldest child. It wouldn't be many more years until he became a teenager. He would fill out and maybe play football in high school or continue with soccer. Either way, she'd be at every game to cheer him on. He might go to the Vo Tech to learn a skilled trade, or perhaps he'd go to a university to become a lawyer or doctor or some other white-collar profession. She would sit at his graduations and cry happy tears full of pride. Someday, he would meet a girl, fall in love, and give her grandbabies. If he asked her, she would watch them while he and his wife went to work. Nutter was not in these glimpses of the future, and with his off-again/on-again style of parenting, it was doubtful he ever would be.

Janice took a deep breath and spoke before her throat closed completely. "I've never lied to you, Taddy, and I'm not going to start now, but I will say that it's complicated between your father and me. Yes, he was with other women besides me, and that's one of the big reasons he's not living with us anymore. Another one is, I'm not sure I trust him like I used to. That's on me and not you. What you need to remember is that even if your father isn't around, that does not mean he doesn't love you or think about you. He'll always be your dad, and he's as proud of you as I am."

Tad's face gave nothing away as to what was in his mind. "Charlotte says you're one of her mothers. She has another mother. Is she really my sister?"

Janice cringed. *How the hell was she supposed to answer him? We've not had the sex talk yet.* "Yes, sweetheart, Charlotte is your sister. Another woman carried her in her belly, but you and she share family and always will."

The dubious look Tad gave her said he didn't believe her, but he nodded. "Okay, Mom. I better get inside before I get a tardy. See you later."

"I love you, Taddy."

He stopped pulling open the van's door. "Mom, can you please start calling me Tad? Dad calls me Taddy, and I... well... I don't like it much."

Janice forced a smile at her son. "You betcha, sweetheart." She leaned over and gave him a quick kiss on his forehead. The door slammed shut when he swung it closed, and she watched as he looked both ways before he crossed the drop-off lanes in front of the building. For a long minute, she just sat there, her heart bleeding for her child, and not caring if anyone saw the streams coming from her eyes. She wanted to bend over and let out the grief in her heart.

She wanted to scream her anger at Nutter.

She wanted to go home and hide in her bed.

None of these actions were options for her. She had to make her deliveries and get back in time for Opal to start her workday. Janice inhaled through her nose as deeply as she could until her lungs were painfully full and ready to burst. Then she blew that breath out into the air between pursed lips. She did this several times, enough to gain back her control and clear her head. Then she turned the key. The van reluctantly coughed to life, and she pulled out of the parking lot.

CHAPTER
FOUR

BOOTS WAS WOKEN UP JUST AFTER DAWN BY BELLA'S voracious mouth sucking on his dick. She moved over him, lining up her wet pussy with the head of his penis, and he stopped her long enough to get a condom rolled on before she slammed herself down onto him. The girl had no boundaries with anything involving sex, as evidenced by the tattoos he spotted on her back last night depicting twin arrows that pointed to her anus and stated "enter here" in a flowery script. She'd tried like hell last night to get him to fuck her there, but that wasn't something he was into.

She rode him hard until she came, then finished him off with her mouth. Afterward, she took a shower in the tiny bathroom and got ready for her workday.

"Why do you come all the way here to get laid?"

he asked as she zipped up her modest pencil skirt and blouse. Dressed as she was, she looked like a put-together career woman, a far cry from the woman who'd swallowed his cum a half hour ago. "Rochester's an hour away from here. Don't they have men that can satisfy you there?"

She smiled at him. "You've heard the saying 'don't shit where you eat', right? Rochester is a great place to live and work, and I love it there, but it would be a major conflict of interest for me to face someone in the courtroom or mediation or something of that nature when I'd just fucked them the night before. I like sex. I like it rough and hot. Turns me on big time when a man takes control and fucks me hard, but I have to be careful. One time, I had to stand in a courtroom and look the opposing attorney in the eye after having been tied up on his bed with his cock in my ass for an entire evening. That could have cost us the case if it had come up."

Boots leaned back against the bed's creaky, loose headboard and placed his hands behind his head, watching her as she held a small mirror and applied makeup. "I can see how that could be a problem."

She pulled out a tube of mascara. "Yeah, coming here to get the kind of sex I like is a hassle, but it's safe. I'm free to be Bella all night long, get fucked by as many men as I want or need, and have no obligations to anyone. I like it like that, and as long as none of the men here start chasing me, asking for more, I'll keep coming back." A cocky smile appeared on her face. "Maybe next time, I'll convince you to try the back door. It really is my favorite."

Boots shook his head as he laid back on the bed. "Sorry, baby. I'm just not into that."

She shrugged and finished applying the tiny wand to her lashes before snapping the compact shut. In minutes, she'd transformed from a woman with a hungry pussy to a sophisticated professional. She strapped on a pair of heels before straightening and lifted her heavy purse. "I have court in a few hours. Take care of yourself, Boots. I hope we can fuck again sometime. You have a nice cock."

He didn't know exactly how to respond to that statement. "Thank you. Drive safe, yeah?"

She paused in the doorway. "You bet. Have a nice day."

After she left, he listened to the quiet of the compound before getting up and taking his own shower. The pressure was shit, but the water was hot. He stood under the spray, glad to be in a private place where he couldn't see another man jacking off against the tiles. His body felt relaxed after a night of fucking, but the randomness bothered him. Bella was not old-lady material and didn't want to be. What did he want now that his world had been turned upside down? Again.

The last time his life got fucked up, he responded by growing hard and bitter. A different version of himself that had mired itself so deep in the darkness, he was surprised to find he had a way out. Very few knew his real story, and he preferred it that way. Now he had a chance to pay for the sins of his past. It was time for him to atone and climb out of the abyss he'd lived in for so long.

The sun gleamed across the river as he walked from the compound to the marina. A plethora of different boats bobbed along the piers in their slips. Cruisers, bass, sport, pontoons, big, small in an array of colors. All of them needed maintenance, and most of the people who rented space here used the Dutchmen's services for that. Boots took in the row of runabouts. These were part of the fleet the Dutchmen and the Dark Horses had used for running drugs down the Mississippi River. They'd been stripped of their hiding places and outfitted as day rentals.

Boots breathed in the air. Fuck, it was good to be free. Two years wasn't really that long compared to his first incarceration, but those months had dragged on and on for him. The daily monotony was just as much a punishment as being in a cage and unable to move. He was so fucking ready to start over.

The smooth *lug-lug-lug* of a well-timed motorcycle came into his ears, and he turned to see Rail driving up on his big machine.

"Good night?" he queried after dismounting and taking off his helmet. He stuck out his hand in a morning greeting. "Bella treat you well?

Boots clasped it. "Yeah. Had seconds this morning. I doubt I'll go for thirds. I needed last night, but you know I'm not into collecting pussy."

Rail chuckled. "She likes to party, and she's definitely into collecting dick. As long as she doesn't turn into a problem, she'll be allowed into the club. Come with me. The grill isn't officially open at this hour, but we can go in and grab some coffee. I'll tell you more of what we have going on here and what we need, yeah?"

Boots nodded and followed Rail to the outside patio part of the restaurant. A few people were in the kitchen, doing prep for the day. They wandered in and out, performing their tasks. None of them were bikers, but one of them sported a prospect patch. He looked like he should be in high school rather than in a biker club.

"Hey, Flipper, bring us a couple coffees," Rail called out to the kid.

The young man grinned. "You bet."

Rail and Boots sat at one of the worn wooden tables. The umbrellas were still down but would be spread open before the heat of the day started up. The season would change soon, as would the focus of the club's new business.

"I need a reliable boat mechanic, and I know you've got the chops for it. Duke has a salvage business he hires out for odd jobs. All of us take turns playing bouncer at the bar. Prospects do the tending and grunt work mostly, but the kitchen staff is separate. Money is tight, but it's growing and getting better. Camo does the books and says we're in the black. Not far, but enough that we can breathe easy. Most of us are happy with the new way of living. It's hard work with a schedule, but when you think about it, we worked hard with a schedule before. The biggest difference is not having to worry about staying alive or getting caught."

Flipper appeared and placed two large mugs in front of the men. "Want something else?"

Rail took a huge sip of the dark brew. "Mama J been by yet?"

Flipper shook his head. "She texted to say she's running late. Should be here soon."

"Mama J?" Boots asked as he lifted his own mug. The coffee was strong and biting. Not like the weak-ass shit served at the prison.

Rail let out a short bark of laughter. "Used to be Nutter's old lady. Ready to hear some real soap-opera shit?"

Boots raised his eyebrow in answer as he took another sip.

"They've been together a long-ass time, enough to make four babies. The problem is, Nutter made a bunch more with other women. That dumb fuck has two baby mamas, seven kids, and is still collecting pussy. He had a scare last year that he might have a third baby mama, but the DNA proved it was another man's child."

Boots frowned. "That's still fucked up. He ever heard of condoms?"

Rail turned the mug's handle away from him. "Told him that myself. Mama J has four kids by him and his club piece, Mimi, has three. Hasn't stopped him from fucking any woman interested in taking his dick. The dumbass needs to skip the condoms and get a vasectomy."

Boots winced at the thought of having that surgical procedure, but seven children by two women might convince him.

"Mama J took on a couple of Mimi's kids to raise, thus her nickname. She got tired of her man spreading his joy and got shot of him. The club helps her and Opal out as much as we can. Part of that is selling her cookies and shit here at the grill. She's a damn good cook."

"Opal?"

Rail heaved a sigh, and his face darkened. "You might remember her as Peebles. She used to… be at the clubhouse."

"Yeah, I remember her. Why Opal?"

"She got pregnant by Rebel. They tried to start a family, but Rebel couldn't stay clean. Died from an overdose. Opal is reinventing herself and doesn't want to be called Peebles anymore. Baby's name is Pearl. They live with Mama J for now."

"Fuck me, brother. That shit sounds more like a Netflix series than a soap opera." Boots snorted and swallowed the last of his coffee. He regarded the empty cup. "Any chance that Flipper guy can bring us a refill?"

Rail was leaning around to bellow at the open kitchen door when Boots heard a female voice behind him.

"Good morning, Rail. I hope your day is a fine one so far. How's Gretchen?"

Rail smiled. "Hey, Mama J. Gretchen is fine. This is Boots. He just moved here, and we're trying to figure out where he should fit in."

Boots turned around. He wasn't sure what to expect, exactly. The moniker Mama J could mean a dumpy, plain woman with a severe hairstyle that needed washing a week ago. It could mean a bitter woman with a perpetual frown on her face, mad at the world for the injustices done to her. It could mean a woman so beat down with life, she was a washed-out version of herself.

He saw none of that.

She was pretty. Not in an exotic model kind of way, but pretty. She had even features that balanced, with a cute nose and full lips that were parted in a huge friendly smile. Her dark hair was tied back in a burst of riotous curls, and if she wore makeup, it was very little. She had an appeal about her. One that radiated goodness and comfort, like a good thick stew on a cold winter night, a warm quilt covering by the fireplace, and a nice body to hold.

This is a woman who epitomizes home, was the thought popped up in Boots's head.

"Got your order in the back of the van." She held up a square box. "I made some breakfast rings last night and brought you one, special."

Her voice had that Midwestern lilt that reminded Boots of cornfields and long stretches of road where your mind could relax and just ride.

"Thanks, Mama J." Rail took the box from her and opened it. Scents of butter, cinnamon, brown sugar, and yeasty bread wafted in the air, and Boots took a big sniff of the homey smell.

"Boots, this is Janice, otherwise known as Mama J. Mama J, this is Boots."

She turned her smiling face to him, and Boots looked into the most vibrant pair of blue eyes he'd ever seen. The rest of her was not bad either. She was short and on the plump side, but she was well-proportioned. Her shoulders were broad enough to carry her heavy breasts. He could tell they were large, even though she had on a long printed T-shirt that modestly covered them. Her waist nipped in above a set of nice wide hips.

Boots wondered why the hell Nutter strayed when he had all that to come home to

"Hi, Boots. Nice to meet'cha." She stuck out her hand in a normal, friendly greeting.

He slowly took it and felt her palm grasp his. "Nice to meet you, too, Janice."

"Oh, now, everyone calls me Mama J. You can, too, if you want."

Boots thought about it for a nanosecond. Mama J was Nutter's old lady, or ex-old lady. He didn't want to know her as that woman. For some reason, it was vitally important that she had a different name. "I'll stick with Janice, if you don't mind."

He still held her hand.

"Oh, okay. I don't mind." She let out a breathy laugh. "It's been a long time since anyone called me anything else."

"Glad to change it up." Boots watched her face flush with color, and the corners of his mouth turned up. He was having fun.

Rail let out a tremendous groan as he took a huge bite of the treat. "Mmmmmm… oh, *yeah*. Mama J, this is fantastic. How hard would it be to add a few of these to the club's next order?"

She pulled her hand from Boots's and cleared her throat. "No trouble. The bakery usually takes six per day. I can make that many for you, too, but not every day. It's getting harder and harder to keep up, even with those two giant ovens I have."

"I want just one ring. For me."

"So, you won't take any back to Gretchen?"

"Maybe," came Rail's muffled voice around a mouthful of the sticky pastry.

Her laugh came out full this time, and Boots felt it in his gut.

"I'd better get these unloaded and get back home. A lot of work to do before the kids get home from school." She turned with another smile and headed back to the ancient minivan parked not too far away.

Boots watched her walk away and almost swallowed his tongue. What an ass! Nice and big, round and juicy. The kind of ass that begged for grabbing. The kind of ass that would fill a man's hands perfectly. The kind of ass that would cushion a man as he pounded in her pussy from behind. He shook his head and frowned at his thoughts. As Nutter's old lady or ex-old lady, this woman was taboo, and he should not be thinking about her that way. He wasn't patched over yet, and any hint of lust after another member's woman, even if she was an ex, would likely keep that from happening.

"I'll get Flipper to do that for you," Rail called out after swallowing the mass in his mouth. He stood up and strode to the open kitchen door to yell inside.

Boots took the opportunity to steal a section of the ring. Damn, it was good! Rich and buttery with just the right amount of sweetness. Perfect.

Nutter was a fucking idiot.

CHAPTER
FIVE

OPAL WAVED TO HER CLASSMATES AS SHE EXITED THE building and walked to her car. This was the fourth time someone had invited her to hang out over at the Liberty restaurant for a post-school drinking-and-bitching session. She wanted to go, but she had a baby at home who needed feeding and bathing. Sure, Mama J could handle it for her, but Opal's desire to be a good mother to her daughter overrode her want for booze and blow. The craving stayed with her constantly, but so far, she'd controlled it.

Opal admitted this was not easy. Her own childhood experience gave her little to go on when it came to good parenting. *"You gotta learn how to suck cock and do it well. It's the best way to find and keep a man,"* had been the advice her mom gave her. Perhaps it didn't work as well as her mama thought. The woman had been married seven times and had just as many boyfriends. She left with the last one to move to Idaho, and Opal hadn't seen or heard from her in years.

The car whirred several times before the engine caught. Opal breathed a sigh of relief. The check-engine light had been on for about a week now, but she was trying to ignore it and hoped it would at least get her to the end of the year before conking out completely. She didn't have the money to get this one fixed let alone buy a new car. Mama J's van wasn't in much better shape, but hopefully, they could keep both vehicles running a bit longer.

Opal pulled out of the parking lot and pointed the car's front bumper toward home. The sun was almost down, and a calm twilight filled the air. She was tired, but she started thinking about the tasks she had to complete at home before bed. The laundry never seemed to stop, and there were probably toys scattered in the living room. Mama J usually took care of the kitchen work and did most of the cooking. That was cool since Opal knew little more than the basics.

She was tallying up what had to be completed tonight and what she could put off until tomorrow when a set of blue lights flashed behind her car.

"Shit," she muttered, quickly glancing at the speedometer. Thirty-seven miles an hour wasn't really speeding, was it? She groaned and pulled the car over. The spot was a wooded area between neighborhoods and dimly lit. Opal cranked down the window and pulled out her license and car registration as the cop came up to the window.

"Good evening, officer. I...." Whatever she was about to say died in her throat. Lewis Canter smiled at her in his dark uniform.

This wasn't the first time he'd targeted her. He'd harassed her at Walgreens's parking lot a few times and even in the store once while she was working. *"You're only good for sucking cock and fucking, Peebles. Just another slut."* She shuddered at the memory of his sibilant hiss in her ear as he grabbed her from behind and rubbed himself against her ass. The round security mirror didn't faze him, even when the manager appeared in it.

"Step out of the car please, ma'am." He reached up and turned off his body cam as he stood by her open window. Opal didn't have to guess what was coming as she slid from her seat to stand against the back door.

"Good to see you, too, Peebles. It's been a while, eh?"

Lewis had been at the Dutchmen compound several times to gamble at the poker tables and fuck a club woman. One of those women had been Peebles. The encounter turned out to be very quick and embarrassing for him.

She swallowed and tried to play it off. "Yes, it has been. I hope you're well."

His smirk got bigger. "I'd say things are looking up about now. You know you were speeding, right?"

Opal attempted a casual laugh, but the sound came out choked. "Only two miles over. That's not enough to get me a ticket, right?"

Lewis's expression turned evil and his tone patronizing. "Well, now, speeding is speeding whether it's two miles or twenty miles over the limit."

Opal felt the first prick of tears hit her eyes. She knew exactly where this was headed, but she tried anyway. "I really can't afford it right now. I'm working and going to school and…."

He sighed and flipped open the book. "Sorry, baby. It's my job, don'tcha know. The ticket, court costs, other fines for your car registration being out of date—gonna be around four hundred dollars, I think. But maybe I'll let this one go just this once if you do something for me."

Please don't! her mind screamed. "What's that?"

"You want out of this ticket? We'll go into those woods, and you'll get on your knees."

Opal's eyes filled. "I don't do that kind of thing anymore."

Lewis closed the book and stepped close to her body. He raised his hand and seized her breast, painfully squeezing the flesh through the cloth. She jumped and cut off a yelp. "You're a whore, Peebles.

That's all you've ever been, and that's all you'll ever be."

Opal dropped her eyes at the word whore. It slashed at her, making any confidence she had left bleed out. Her past was her past, and she couldn't deny the choices she'd made once upon a time, but for her future, she was desperately trying to change her life. Still, her former life haunted her. It had already happened several times. She would be in a store or walking on the street somewhere and see a man she'd been intimate with. He would recognize her and hurry off with his wife or kids or both.

He jerked her around and shoved her in the direction of the tree line. "Be glad I'm just asking for a blow job and not bending you over so I can fuck your ass. Now get moving before I add more shit to this ticket."

Opal let the tears fall down her face as she stumbled. She couldn't afford four hundred dollars, and even if that wasn't on the table, Lewis would make her do this anyway. The knot in her belly coiled, and the serpent raised its head.

Just a little of the white powder can make this sooooo much easier.

"I don't do that anymore," she shouted back inside her head at the hissing whisper.

Lewis stopped abruptly before the evil reptile could tempt her again. "Don't get any ideas that you can report me either. Who do you think my guys will believe? An upstanding fellow officer, or a known Dutchmen club slut and drug addict? This is far enough."

In the movies, a hero like Batman would swoop in and rescue her from this bad situation. Unfortunately, superheroes didn't exist in this world. She faced him, water dripping from her eyes to her jawline. "Please don't make me do this."

His answer was to open his belt buckle.

CHAPTER
SIX

THREE DAYS AND FOUR NIGHTS HAD ELAPSED BETWEEN his release and his induction into the Dutchmen MC. Boots tipped back his beer and spotted Bella, wearing full vampire makeup, take the hand of a newly patched club member and start leading him toward the back rooms. He didn't have any qualms or jealousies about the young woman fucking whoever she wanted. She was damn good in bed, but the one night was all he wanted or needed from her.

The clubhouse was full of people tonight. Loud music pulsated through the open room, and several women had already stripped to thongs and were dancing around the stripper pole. One of them looked like she knew what she was doing. The other was so drunk, Boots was sure she would fall off the stage. The big celebration was for the prospects that had been patched in tonight. Booze and pussy flowed freely, and the newest Dutchmen were ready to party. Boots had on his new cut, declaring he, too, was a new Dutchmen member, but he didn't particularly want to party like the others. Frankly, he was ready to go crash somewhere.

"Getting old, Boots," Rail remarked as he sat on his throne in a U-shaped group of sofas. The woman he had with him was gorgeous, and she sat down next to him. "This is Gretchen, my old lady and my wife."

"Nice to meet you." Boots extended his hand.

The woman smiled and nodded. Rail had already told him Gretchen was deaf and worked as a freelance editor. They'd met during a very stressful time yet still managed to fall in love. Boots was over-the-moon happy for Rail, but the "getting old" comment needed a rejoinder. "I'm not slobbering in my beer yet, asshole."

Rail laughed as a club girl brought beers to him and Gretchen. "Valid point, anyway, brother. None of us are getting any younger."

Boots grunted an agreement as he swallowed more of his own drink. He glanced up at the new members who were toasting themselves and raptly watching the gyrations of the naked women. The drunk one staggered and fell off the stage. The freshly patched Nitro caught her and almost dropped his beer in the process. Even from this distance, Boots saw the pleased look on the woman's face and heard the whoops of encouragement as she immediately plastered her mouth to her rescuer. A moment later, a smiling Nitro was being led from the floor to the block of bedrooms. Boots surmised that before the night was over, every one of the new members would get laid as many times as they could get it up. He himself was no slouch in bed, as evidenced by the workout Bella gave him a few nights ago, but tonight, he wasn't interested enough.

Nutter came through the door with a woman under each arm. "Hey, all you bitches! Welcome to the best fucking MC you'll ever know."

The big man lifted the bottle of tequila he held in one hand and made a big show of tipping it back to drink the potent liquor straight. Then he stuck his tongue in the bottle's neck and opened his mouth wide so everyone could see him thrust it in and out of the small opening. Whoops and cheers rose from the crowd at the sight.

Boots saw Gretchen roll her eyes, and he agreed with her. He thought the display juvenile and stupid. "Be glad you're deaf and don't have to hear his bull-shit," he said as he faced Rail's woman so she could read his lips.

She looked at him in the eye, raised her eyebrows, and gave him two thumbs up. Rail laughed out loud. "Nutter is a pain in the ass, for sure. Good fun, but anything substantial, he's out the door."

Boots took another big swig of his beer. "I'm sure

that's not much help to his ex. Six kids is a fuck of a lot to take care of."

Rail leaned back in the pliant cushions and signed as he spoke to keep Gretchen in the conversation. She drank more beer herself and watched her husband. "Mama J owns the house, so no house payment, but she's still barely making it. Doctor bills for the kids, insurance, school fees, clothes—all that shit adds up. The club helps her as much as she'll let us, but she's really trying to make it on her own. I send prospects or go myself to cut her lawn and see to maintenance, like plumbing and stuff. Nutter and I put on a new roof last year, so that is one big expense she doesn't have, but she needs a new heat pump soon, and her van is falling apart. I told her the Dutchmen would take care of those jobs and she refused. She really wants her business to work so she can take care of all that shit herself."

Boots frowned. "That's a shit ton of responsibilities to handle for one person. Nutter do anything else?"

Gretchen wrinkled her nose in silence. Boots mused, *She also isn't a big fan of Nutter.*

Rail sighed and pressed his lips together. "He took it seriously for a while, but now he's off and on. He sees his kids and does some stuff for Mama J, but he's not very consistent about it. She, on the other hand, has kids around her 24/7, and whatever

Nutter doesn't help with, she has to handle. It's tough."

Boots took a swallow of his beer and grunted an acknowledgment to Rail's statement. It was tough. He remembered his own childhood as the middle child in a group of thirteen siblings all living together on the family dairy farm in Wisconsin. The work was nonstop, and there was always more of it than could be done in one day. There was never much time for conversation, games, or anything that might build relationships between them. Boots remembered his mother as being this older woman constantly cooking in the kitchen, cleaning the house, or working the vegetable garden. Rarely did she sit down, and her back had become permanently bowed from the weight of her life. His relationship with her hadn't been close, mostly because she spent very little time being a mom rather than being a domestic worker. The volume of chores she had ate up the days to the point that she couldn't be anything else.

He didn't like the idea that Mama J was on that same path.

Janice. Her name is Janice. He tipped the rest of the beer into his mouth. He glanced over at the group of new members standing around Nutter and his companions. One woman had an empty beer can between her huge breasts and showed off how she could crush it. Nutter raised a hand in the air and whooped as the hollow metal collapsed. "That's some talent, eh?"

Try as he might, Boots couldn't see the woman he'd met lining up with the man he watched.

A sweetbutt with short blue hair came by and picked up his empty bottle. She smiled at him in invitation, but he had no desire to bang a woman so young he could have fathered her. He stood up with a groan. "Partying all night isn't for me anymore. I'm heading out. See you tomorrow."

Rail stood up as well, and the two men clasped hands. "Good to have you here, brother. Always got your back."

"I swore my allegiance to the Dutchmen. I'll promise again: you'll never regret taking a chance on me."

CHAPTER
SEVEN

Opal loaded the economy-sized bottles of Tums onto the shelf, counted them once more, and checked them off her list. A couple of pharmacy techs worked in the back of the store, and the head manager sat up front behind the counter, flipping through a gossip magazine. A few morning customers walked up and down the aisles, poking at seasonal items and filling carts, and others sat back in the waiting area for their prescriptions.

Even surrounded by people, Opal felt very alone. Her recent encounter with Lewis left a bad taste in her mouth in every sense of the word. She should have figured out her past would come back to bite her in the ass, but she never thought it would have razor-sharp fangs.

It wasn't the first time she'd run into men from the club. Two other men she recognized from the

Dutchmen poker games had been in the store on occasion. One of them had his kids with him and only paid her a cursory glance. The other had recognized her. His face grew pale and scared as his glance darted between her and his wife. Opal was sure he expected her to bounce up to them and introduce herself. Opal ignored them both and kept working, just as she did now.

It's hard, she thought as she squatted to stack a row of decongestant boxes on a lower shelf. She was not proud of her past, even though at the time she thought it was a great life. A never-ending party of booze, weed, powder, and lots of sex. Men told her she was beautiful, sexy, and how much they wanted her. Sometimes they gave her money and other times they gave her gifts. They said how much they loved her and loved being with her as they sank their cocks into her body or mouth. Those same men avoided her now, as they would a leper.

It hurt. For years, all she wanted was for someone to love her, and she thought sex was the way to get it. When she hooked up with Rebel in the Dutchmen MC, she thought she'd found it. For a time, he cleaned himself up and treated her like his old lady. Then the call of the white powder took him away from her. His death from a drug overdose wasn't that much of a shock, as it was the inevitable end to the path he traveled. She would have been on that path with him if she hadn't had Pearl to pull her back.

When she found out she was pregnant, she stopped the drinking and the drugs and took a good look at her life. She'd made choices she regretted now, but she would live with them and make sure none of that shit ever touched her daughter. It amazed her that Mama J could be so forgiving and supportive, and Opal vowed she wouldn't go back to her old life, no matter what.

Except her old life still haunted her, currently in the form of Lewis Canter.

Opal's eyes watered, and she dashed away the moisture. *Stop it, dumbass. You have a goal and a way to reach it as long as you don't fuck it up!*

Gabriella, Iceman's woman, had been put into a dangerous situation with the Dutchmen. After all the shit that went down in the cities, she got her act together and left town to start a new life and a new career. Rail took a road trip last spring to see her and said she was doing really well with her new business endeavor. Her boy, Ricky, was also thriving.

Maybe that's what I need to do, she pondered as she checked off another item on her list. *Finish school, save up as much as I can, and get the hell out of here. Find a new place and a new life where no one knows who Peebles used to be.*

It would take a lot of work, but she would get there. The skills and certifications she earned at the school would help a lot. As a nail technician and hair stylist, she could find work anywhere. She still needed to save enough money to make that happen, but it would, as long as she stayed on course. There were times the stress, the fatigue, the endless workdays got to her, and she craved the release the white powder gave her. That floaty buzz offered to take her out of her body and her hard life, surrounding her in a surreal landscape. It erased all her worries and gave her peace. The trouble was that peace was a false one, and when she came back to herself, the same problems and stresses awaited her, sometimes with more intensity.

No. Opal shook her head. *I'm not going down that road. My child deserves better.* She had toughed it out many nights in the past year, crying in solitude as she rocked her daughter and fought the lure of the drugs. Sometimes the want became so overwhelming, she could feel it painfully coiled in her belly. She imagined it as a snake ready to strike. It had gotten easier, but that reptile stayed in her gut, ready to slither out at any opportunity. She hoped she had the strength to keep fighting it.

Opal finished emptying the box of stock and reached to grab the edge of a shelf to help her balance. A pair of black biker boots appeared on the floor next to her and an open hand, palm up, appeared in her line of vision. Male, broad, lined, with chunky silver rings on the fourth and pinky fingers and chain bracelet on the wrist. She knew that hand. Opal raised her eyes to meet the hazel ones owned by Camo.

He was the one MC member she had never been with in any capacity. Never fucked him, sucked him, or anything else. Camo was shorter and stockier than the other members, but still a little taller than her. She'd seen him drink his fair share, smoke a little weed now and then, but she didn't remember him getting so wasted or high, he got loud and obnoxious like Rebel. He wore his light brown hair military short, probably as a leftover from his army days. Rumor had it he saw some serious action during his time overseas, but to her knowledge, he'd never talked about it. He was the one who handled the business accounting for the club and marina now.

She'd served him drinks at the club many times in her past life and had a few friendly conversations with him. He'd never approached her for a blow job or sex, and she couldn't remember if he'd had the revolving bed partners many of the other members did. She did remember catching him observing her with his deep gaze every so often. Her stomach had fluttered then as it did now.

He remained motionless, staring down at her as if waiting for her decision. His eyes were absent of judgment or speculation. Opal's attention turned from those unfathomable orbs to the hand that lay patiently in front of her.

There were moments that snuck up and irrevocably changed the course of life from one heartbeat to the next. That organ pounded in her chest as she contemplated the offering in front of her. Some instinct in her recognized that this was one of those moments. If she took that hand, nothing would be the same.

She reached up and placed her palm against his. No lightning strikes, thunderbolts, or electric shocks hit her; something simply clicked into place like it was always meant to be there.

That idea scared the shit out of her.

"Um… hey, Camo. Thanks." Her voice was light, and she dropped her eyes as her tongue refused to work.

"No problem. I came in for a better knee brace and saw you working. Thought I'd say hi and check on you. I haven't seen you at the clubhouse in a long time." He kept his baritone voice low in volume, but it resonated pleasantly in her ears.

"I haven't been there in a long time. I got my little Pearl now, you know. Between helping Mama J with the other kids, work, and school…." She shrugged. "I don't have a lot of time or energy for partying all night anymore. I don't want that life again either."

Camo smiled, and she noticed one white front tooth slightly overlapped the other. "Yeah, I get that. Being a single mom is hard. My sister has two kids and works at a pet boarding and grooming place over in La Crosse. The only time she gets a break is when me or Mom spends the weekend with the kids so she can get away. Mitzi doesn't go anywhere. She checks into a hotel and enjoys some solitude. You know, taking a bubble bath, reading a book or two without interruption, watching movies that aren't kid related, that sort of thing. She says it recharges her batteries."

Bubble bath! Opal almost drooled at the thought. Children, in some form, surrounded her and Mama J every minute of every day. The groupings were fluid as they contained between three to seven kids, but there was always the constant presence of some little persons who needed attending. Work and class didn't count, as she was still amongst people, and those times weren't really hers to do with as she pleased. Mama J hadn't had a real break in years and was in the same boat, as ironically, the only free time she ever got was when she was working.

"That sounds amazing. I bet your sister really appreciates that help." Opal stopped speaking and took a breath. Her eyes burned with a sudden rush of moisture. "I never realized how hard this was going to be. When I carried Pearl, all I could think about were the pretty Hollywood parts. House with a nice green mowed yard, maybe a flower garden, swing set in the back, my little girl in cute pink dresses playing in a sandbox with her dog. I thought Rebel would give that to us." She closed her eyes and visibly shook off her sadness. "Now it's up to me, and I hope I get to have that someday."

Her eyes popped open as she felt Camo's hand cup her chin and raise it. Its warmth soothed her as his fingers lightly stroked her skin. His eyes bore into hers with intensity, and she found herself fascinated by their blended colors of green and brown. "You will, sweetheart. You need the kind of break my sister takes, let me know. I got your back."

His gaze shifted to her mouth, and her lips parted. He took a big breath, and Opal felt the urge to lean forward and kiss him.

He broke the stare and stepped back. "The club will too. Just call one of us. I gotta get back and finish some paperwork. I'll see you soon, yeah?"

Opal drew herself in and stood up straight. She pulled back the tears that threatened to come and gave Camo a big smile. "You bet. Have a good day, Camo, and thanks for stopping in."

He gave her a smile back and a brief nod before turning away.

She watched him leave before turning back to her next stocking task. Two more hours, then back to the house for two more, then class, and back home again. As she entered the back room to pick up the next box of items, she realized Camo left without getting his knee brace.

CHAPTER
EIGHT

Duke sat down in the booth opposite Boots with a long sigh. "Gettin' old sucks, brother. I don't know how much longer I'm gonna do this shit. Thanks for helping out."

Boots picked up the laminated menu and perused the options. "No problem. It feels good to do some lifting, but just so you know, I'm not making this line of work into a career. I can already tell my back has a time limit for working on boats, and I'm not planning on getting into the recovery business with you."

Both men, along with Camo and Nutter, had spent the morning at a salvage worksite. Several houses were being demolished, and Duke's moving company had been hired to haul off anything that could be reused in the future. Much of what they found was junk, but sometimes there was treasure in the form of reclaimed wood, windows, furniture, and other bits. Many of the pieces in the Dutchmen's compound came from Duke's operations.

"You still into that kung fu stuff you used to do?" Duke asked as he put a pair of reading glasses on his nose and looked at his own menu.

"Tae Kwon Do, and not as much as I was before. There wasn't a lot of room in the prison cell for much more than meditating." The booth bench squeaked as Boots leaned back. "If I had the option, I might have practiced on my roommate. Irritated the hell out of me most of the time."

"I always thought you were a pretty chill guy. Never let anything ruffle your feathers until you ruffled them yourself."

Boots thought for a minute and slipped the menu back between the napkin dispenser and the condiment rack. "Everyone has a breaking point—even me. That fucker nonstop farted like a machine gun. I was stuck in a cell with him for eighteen hours a day. Do I have to explain my homicidal thoughts?"

Duke chuckled. "I get it, brother. I'm surprised you didn't do something about it."

Boots frowned a little. "I wanted to, but I had no desire to stay in that place any longer than necessary. An assault charge would see me still sitting in that cell for as long as the judge could make the sentence last. Beating up the guy wouldn't do any good anyway. He was nuts, and I mean that in a mental illness way. Fucker was schizophrenic or something.

Not only did he show off his serious intestinal skills, he'd talk for hours to people he saw in the corners of the cell. Someone like that's not going to learn anything. He probably should've been in a hospital instead of a prison, but apparently he killed his mother in a rather creative and brutal fashion. That was enough to give him life."

Duke raised his head and stared. "Fuck me, was that the guy who cut up his mom and got caught when he took her head for a stroll in a toy baby carriage?"

Boots gave a slight nod.

Indignation burst from Duke's mouth, and several patrons turned at the loud words. "Why the fuck would they put a misdemeanor in with a fucking murderer?"

Boots looked up with unreadable dark eyes. "Does it matter? You know me well enough, right? You think I couldn't handle myself?"

Duke raised his eyebrows and sighed. "Yeah, brother, I do, and you can handle yourself just fine. From what I've heard, your roommate is damned lucky to be breathing."

Boots let his gaze wander. "As much as the guy pissed me off, there's no sense in punishing someone who doesn't know any better and is already in hell. Lessons have to mean something or else they don't work." He shrugged. "Besides, I couldn't figure out where to dispose of the body."

Duke let out a huff and pointed. "That right there, brother. I don't know whether you're joking or serious."

An older woman came over and interrupted their conversation. "Welcome to Randy's Wings, home of the… never mind. Whatcha having, Duke?"

"Give me the eight piece with extra hot sauce and double fries. Root beer."

Boots tipped his head back. "Same."

The taciturn waitress grunted and moved off.

"Not exactly a customer-friendly place, but the wings—" Duke kissed his fingers. "—they are divine, and the sauce will set you on fire coming and going. Randy is a fucking genius with—"

A loud voice cut through the air. "Randy! How's my favorite wingman these days?"

Boots spotted two deputies as they entered the restaurant. Both had shit-eating grins on their faces and a swagger to their movements. Randy's round face stiffened, and his perpetual smile fell a bit.

Duke huffed but kept his seat. Boots quirked an eyebrow in question at him. Duke thrust his chin at the men and muttered, "Lewis Canter and one of his merry band of assholes."

Randy invited them into the back kitchen and away from public observation, but Boots could see some of what was happening through the pass-through window. Randy was talking rapidly and gesturing with empty palms, as if in supplication.

Lewis moved in closer, and whatever he said back made the rotund restaurant owner blanch. Randy sighed and stepped out of sight for a moment. When he reappeared, he handed the deputy a padded envelope, which Lewis tucked into his jacket pocket. He patted Randy's cheek, and then both officers turned to come back into the main dining room.

"Nice to see you again, Randy," Lewis called out as the other man grabbed two baskets of wings from the counter. The man's gaze passed over the two seated bikers. He dismissed Boots as being beneath regard but locked eyes with Duke. A sneer of contempt filled the man's face, but Duke didn't back off from the stare down. Boots relaxed his body for a possible physical confrontation, but the deputies walked out without paying for the food.

"Broad fucking daylight." Duke growled. "Fuckers are getting bold."

"You know what happened in the back?"

Duke nodded. "I haven't seen it, but I've heard rumors. Doesn't take a genius to figure out that asshole is shaking down the local businesses."

"You know him?"

"Lewis Canter. Used to be a hangaround at the clubhouse, trying to join up with us. Fucker didn't even have a bike back then, and I doubt he has one now. He and Iceman got into it one night. Kicked him out permanently. How that asshole got accepted into law enforcement is beyond me."

"Rail knows what he's doing?"

Duke sighed. "Yeah, but here's the problem. We're the Dutchmen MC, former drug smugglers and dealers, and now we're trying to go legit with our own businesses. We gotta stay spit-shined and squeaky-clean to make this work. It's turning around for us, and we can't afford any screwups. We get involved in this shit, we'll get covered in it. Rail hates it, but that's the way it has to be. At least for now."

Boots watched as the waitress made up two new baskets of food to bring to them. "What do you mean 'for now'?"

Duke humphed once. "You said it yourself, brother. Everyone has a breaking point. Even us."

CHAPTER
NINE

JANICE PLACED THE LAUNDRY BASKET ON THE SOFA AND began folding the towels, stacking them on the seat next to her. Opal had washed and dried a few loads this afternoon between her work and night class. She'd done some dinner prep before she left for class and would eat when she got home.

The muted TV flashed its colored light across Janice's face as her eyes reflected her exhaustion. This was her last task of the day, and she was ready to put her feet up. The kids were in bed, and Janice hoped they stayed there. Oliver and Augustus both had major meltdowns before supper over who got the Batman plate, and Tad had waded in to separate them. She already washed the mass of dishes and set them in the drainboard. They never made it to the cabinets since they got put back on the table with such regularity, neither she nor Opal saw a reason for the extra effort.

Janice reached for another towel. *Uff-da,* what she wouldn't give for a dishwasher! One of those big stainless steel ones with the disposal built in at the bottom. With a little reconfiguration, she could fit it in without losing too much lower cabinet space. She folded the towel with a few expert flips and had grabbed another when a knock on the door caught her attention. Rail texted this morning to say he would try to run by this evening and drop off the empty plastic containers she used to transport the baked goods to the restaurant. She would pick them up when she delivered at the other places that bought from her, but at the moment, she'd had a big increase in orders and was in sore need of them.

Janice got off the sofa and felt a kink behind her left shoulder. Ugh! That spot had been bothering her off and on for weeks now. She reached behind and pressed two fingers into the cramp as she opened the door.

"Nice to see you, Rail. I apprec...." Her voice trailed off as she took in the coal-black eyes of the big man standing on the front stoop.

"Railroad couldn't leave the bar and asked if I could run these over to you." Boots filled the doorway, towering over her.

"Um... oh, sure. Uh... thanks.... Um... Boots, is it?"

One corner of the man's full mouth twitched and rose. "Yup, that's me. Want me to carry these to your kitchen? They're already cleaned."

"Yeah, sure." Janice came out of her daze and gestured for him to come in. She'd only met the man for about a minute and a half a few days ago, and she wasn't completely comfortable with a stranger coming into her house, but Rail knew him and trusted him. "Right this way."

Nutter was a big man, but Boots was big in a different way. Just his presence drew her attention to him as he entered the kitchen area. She took note of his movements as he set the containers on the breakfast bar next to the row of backpacks ready for school tomorrow morning. His aura exuded a smooth, extreme masculinity without any effort at all.

He glanced around the kitchen. The place was geared toward young children. The kids had left a pile of crayons and coloring books on the dining table. Booster seats occupied several chairs, and kids' artwork decorated the gold-colored fridge. The counter space was ample but crowded with three big mixers, a stack of giant stainless steel bowls, and another stack of plastic delivery containers filled with sweetness.

"Thanks a bunch for coming by. I'm sure you have other plans this evening, so I'll let you get to them." Janice wondered if she sounded nervous.

Boots didn't scare her, exactly, but she was on edge around him.

His dark eyes turned to hers, and she spotted several gray strands in the black of his hair. "No problem." One of his hands came up to smooth back those ebony locks. "If you don't mind, I'd like to sit for a few minutes. Noise at the marina has surrounded me all day, and there was more noise at the clubhouse tonight. The new patches have celebrated every night this week. I got one, too, but I'm not into drinking myself into oblivion with the younger guys. I could use a few minutes of quiet and calm. Okay with you, Janice? If you don't want me here, I can leave."

Her mouth dropped a little when he used her name. Very few people called her Janice anymore, as most of the time, she was Mama J. She didn't mind that moniker, but from time to time, it would be nice if someone remembered she wasn't just a mom. The novelty of having a handsome man call her Janice instead of Mama J threw her a bit, and for a moment, she didn't know what to do.

"Um…. Oh, sure, you can stay for a bit. You want a drink? I don't have any beer or anything like that here. It's not good for Opal to be around it. I have juice, milk, and diet pop. If you want water, I'll have to get it from the tap."

"Diet pop is fine," he said in his rumbling voice.

Heat flooded her cheeks as she opened the

ancient fridge and took out a Diet Coke. Her focus remained on him as he moved around the work area of the kitchen. *Janice. He called me Janice. Nutter hasn't called me that in years.*

"Pretty amazing you can bake all that stuff in this small space," he remarked with a half smile on his face.

She smiled and wished she didn't blush so easily. "Well, now, it's mostly a matter of getting organized and keeping to a schedule. It's the only way I can keep up with everything."

He took a long pull of the pop, his gaze drifting to the two-tiered drying rack full of dishes. "You don't have a dishwasher?"

She gave a short laugh. "Oh, no. Not in the budget right now, but soon, I hope. You want to go sit in the living room? I'm folding laundry on the sofa, but there's a big easy chair."

The living room showed more signs that children lived there. Toys were piled up in boxes, and a set of kids' board games and puzzles were stacked under the coffee table. Boots eased back in the worn stuffed chair and made to prop his big feet and motorcycle boots on the squat, heavy table. "Is this okay?"

Janice gave a soft laugh and waved a hand as she settled herself in the same spot she'd occupied before. "Oh, sure. This house is not a showplace. With six children, a baby, and two adults, we're lucky to keep what we have in good shape."

She reached for another towel, snapped it straight, and folded it with quick, practiced movements. *What do I say to him?* she thought. Out of the corner of her eye, she saw him take another long pull of the pop and lean his head back. He seemed to enjoy just being still. A muffled burp came from him, and he closed his eyes.

"You look tired. The marina must have a lot of work going on."

Boots let out another soft burp. "Yeah, a lot of folks are prepping for the cold now instead of waiting. There's limited space in the storage house, and boat size is a problem. A lot of people are taking their crafts up to St. Paul or Minneapolis for the winter and will be back in the spring. I've been at it since six this morning. I only stopped to get some food at the bar. This is the first time I've had my feet up all day."

Janice bit her lip. Nutter claimed he worked all day for the club's businesses, but he'd never been this kind of tired. She picked up a set of dishcloths and folded them.

"Thanks for letting me sit here, Janice. It's peaceful."

She gave another laugh. "It's not always that way in this house, Boots."

"It is now. Dark night. Calm. Easy. Kids sleeping. Pretty woman keeping me company. I needed this."

Her heart skipped at the word pretty. He called her Janice. He called her pretty. She shook it off. He was just saying that to say something. No way a man as handsome as him and built like him would think she was pretty. Especially now, when she was tired from her own workday. Her hair was pulled back in a clip at the back of her head, and she hadn't bothered with makeup. She chose her clothes for comfort, not style, and they were mostly tent-like to hide her thick body. Since her breakup with Nutter, she had lost about thirty pounds, but she still carried some extra weight and probably always would. It was nice to hear the word pretty anyway, even if he didn't mean it.

A light shuffling caught her mom radar, and she turned her head to the hallway.

"Mommy?" A tow-headed boy appeared in Pikachu pajamas. His rumpled hair stuck out at all angles, and he rubbed his eyes with one little fist. He glanced at Boots but didn't say anything to the biker.

"Bad dream, Ollie?"

He nodded and sniffled.

"Come here, baby."

She put aside the rest of the dishtowels and picked up the fussy four-year-old. He cuddled into her generous bosom and stuck his thumb in his mouth. She slowly swayed back and forth in a practiced movement, softly crooning the same lullaby she sang to all her children.

Ro ro till skären

Plocka små barnen bären
Plocka så mycket som båten bär
Skynda sen hem medan dager är
Row row to the skerries
Pick [for] the little children the berries
Pick as much as the boat carries
Then hurry home while it's day

Janice gave Boots a quick look. His eyes were open and watching them, but she couldn't read his expression. He didn't seem irritated by the interruption of his peace. If he was, she would ask him nicely to leave, as her priority was the fussy child in her lap and not the man in the room. She leaned down to kiss the strawberry-shampoo-scented head and kept up her gentle rocking.

For several long minutes, Boots stayed in place, watching her comfort the little boy and sing to him. Then he swallowed the last of the pop and stood up. Her gaze followed his tall body, and she had to lean her head back to see his face. His eyes glittered down at her. "Thank you, again, Janice. You have no idea how much I appreciate you."

Warmth bloomed in her middle, and she smiled at the towering man. "You bet. Come anytime you need the quiet, but just so you know, I can't guarantee you'll always get it."

He nodded and carefully made his way back through the kitchen to the carport exit, not making any more noise than he had to. She heard the click of the door as it closed.

"Well, now, sugar beans, think you can go back to sleep?"

Oliver didn't answer. He was already out.

Janice sighed and eased her way up from the sofa, feeling the twinge in the back of her shoulder catch again. She carried the boy to his bed and settled him in. Thankfully, he was in a lower bunk rather than the upper. She closed the door and heard Opal coming in from her class.

"Good night at the Vo Tech?" she asked as she made her way into the kitchen.

Opal didn't look right. She opened the fridge, closed it, and opened it again. "I'm… okay. Yeah, class was good." She took out a Diet Coke and put it back in, then closed the fridge one last time. The woman looked dazed, worried, distracted.

"Opal, what's the matter?"

Opal moved to the sink and filled a plastic Barney cup with water. She pounded it down and went for more. "Nothing. Just a long day. Why are you still up?"

Janice opened her mouth to tell her about Boots coming by but decided not to. The brief moments she had with him sparked a note of privacy. "Just finishing some laundry. I'll put it away in the morning."

Opal nodded. Color came back into her face, and

she took a deep breath. "If you don't get to it, I will. Pearl go down okay? Any trouble with the other kids?"

Janice answered with a negative shake. "Oh, no. Everyone got bathed and in bed with no fusses."

Opal smiled. "That's great. If you don't mind, I'm ready to crash. Thanks for all you do."

"You bet. I'll see you in the morning."

"Good night."

————

Boots's bike rumbled low as he drove away. He didn't rev and roar through the neighborhood, although that's what he felt like doing.

Mama J.

Homemaker.

Mother.

Baker.

Business owner.

Worker.

Janice.

Her house was set up to care for her kids. Her kitchen had to be a constant hive of activity, yet it was clean and neat. Cooking for that many people plus baking for the business, keeping up the rest of the household chores, and taking care of the children and a baby took up a huge amount of effort and time. The woman was a fucking powerhouse.

Boots rounded a corner and came up to a stop sign. Most people in this neighborhood were in their houses or bed at this hour. Older folks were settled in to watch the prime-time sitcom of the night. He didn't remember what was on the muted TV at Janice's house, but he spotted the collection of kids' Disney DVDs shelved below the flat screen. She couldn't hear it and didn't really watch it as she sat folding laundry. He guessed she had it on for the ambient light to help her with her task. One last chore in a sea of endless chores.

A chore she dropped when a child needed her. Fuck. The picture of her holding that little one on her lap came to his mind. The kid crawling up and curling into her welcoming lap, knowing she was there for him. Janice dropping everything to comfort and soothe the little boy. Boots noticed the kid's hair was blond. Both Nutter and Janice were brunettes. Either the kid resulted from recessive genes, or he was one of Mimi's children being raised by Janice.

It didn't matter about the child's parentage. When he sought his mother, it was Janice who answered.

Janice who crooned to the little boy.

Janice who kissed his head and put him to bed.

Anger rose in his gut as he pulled up to another stop sign. He'd overheard something Nutter said about "Mama J" letting herself go these past few years. What the fuck did that mean? She didn't do herself up like the club women? He couldn't picture the woman in that house folding laundry and seeing to the needs of a bunch of kids while wearing heels and short skirts, with full hair and makeup done. Was he referring to the extra weight she carried? Her body was heavy, but those pounds looked good on her. Real good.

Boots didn't see any particular style to her shiny hair held back in the clip thing, but it was long and clean. He bet if he ran his hands through it, the curls would be soft and springy between his fingers. Her makeup-less face was pretty. Perhaps not model perfect, but pretty. He'd seen no subterfuge in her blue-gray eyes. They showed her wariness of him when she opened her door. They showed gratitude for the simple favor of returning her containers. They showed both tiredness and resolve as she kept at the chore of folding. What really got to him was the genuine and deep love in them as she rocked and sang to the child in her arms.

Pure.

Honest.

Beautiful.

A growl rumbled in Boots's throat to accompany his bike's engine. How the fuck can Nutter say his woman was anything less? *Check that, Boots,* he told himself. *Janice is no longer Nutter's woman.*

As he rode, Boots's eyes took in neat yards, trimmed bushes, and raised beds that permeated the neighborhood. Janice's grass was cut, but there wasn't much in the way of flowers or shrubs in the bare beds. Based on what he saw in her house, he bet she would like more color in her yard. Rail mentioned that he or a prospect helped with mowing—however, he had said nothing about landscaping. There was also precious little privacy and space for everyone stuffed into that house. Boots didn't see the bedrooms, of course, but it wasn't hard to imagine the layout of the old ranch-style house. Perhaps there was a usable basement?

Ideas formed in his head as he pulled up to yet another stop sign. He was deep into his thoughts when a pair of blue lights flashed behind him.

"Fuck," he muttered as he kicked out the stand and turned off his bike. He stood unmoving while two uniformed officers exited the vehicle. One made a big show of hitching up his pants and putting on his hat before approaching him. The older one reached him first.

"License and registration?"

Boots gave him a quick chin lift as the younger one sauntered up. "In my pocket. Mind if I reach for it?"

"Go ahead, but go slow."

Boots complied and handed the man the requested documentation.

"Kinda late for a ride, isn't it?" the younger one said. He was grinning, but not in a friendly way.

Boots glanced at the man. This area was poorly lit,

but there was enough moonlight to see and recognize him as one of the two involved in the shakedown at Randy's place. Lewis Canter. Boots filed the picture away as he faced the deputy.

"An errand for a friend. I'm on my way home."

The other officer stood behind Lewis and used a heavy flashlight to examine the two cards. Boots couldn't see the name on his badge, but his posture wasn't cocky like his partner's.

"You sure about that? We know you guys are on the wild side of drinking and partying and fucking." Lewis smirked at him. "Maybe you're on your way there with some special favors?"

Boots's jaw clenched. He'd been through the drill before. "You want to search my bike? Pat me down? You don't have a warrant, nor probable cause. I wasn't speeding, or driving recklessly, or any other moving violation."

The other man spoke. "You're right. However, seeing a biker wearing Dutchmen colors in this particular residential neighborhood sends up flags. You're not under arrest or charged with anything. We just want to know why you're here."

"As I stated, I was on an errand for a friend. I'm done, and I'm heading home."

Lewis spoke again. "Maybe you stayed a while with your... friend. Shot the shit? Had a drink or two?"

The man's tone grated on Boots's nerves. Lewis

was fishing for something, any crumb he could use to slap cuffs on him and put him in the back of the squad car. In another life and another time, Boots would have punched the man in the face and driven away.

Or done something worse.

No way would he risk his probation like that. "You got a breathalyzer back there? I'm glad to blow in it. Only thing I've had to drink is a Diet Coke. You wanna check my saddlebags? You'll find them empty. Not even a tool kit. Check me for a gun?" He raised his hands slowly. "Have at it. I have nothing on me that's illegal."

Lewis wasn't done. "There's a woman who lives near here. An *associate* of the Dutchmen MC. Maybe you were paying her a visit?"

Boots saw red at the thinly veiled insinuation. He clamped his lips together as he stayed in control. The vision of blood running down the smirking man's face was appealing, but that would be a sure way for him to get thrown back in the slammer. He kept his mouth shut.

"Knock it off, Lewis." The other officer stepped forward, and Boots could see him more clearly. He was older than his partner, probably closer to Boots's age. "I'm officer Milton Tarnaski. No need for a pat down. I can tell you're not drunk or high, and you didn't break any driving laws. It's just odd to see a biker in this neighborhood at this hour. If your errand had to do with Mama J, just tell us, and we'll be done."

Boots slowly lowered his hands to his sides. "You know Mama J?" He'd rather use her real name, but since the officer called her by her nickname, he thought it best to follow suit.

"My wife buys her breakfast rings every week from the grocery."

Boots relaxed a bit. "I dropped off some of her containers. She needed them back quick, and I was doing her a favor."

"Is that the only reason you paid her a visit?" The singsong voice of Lewis dripped with implication.

Boots wanted to answer the fucker with a kick in the teeth, but Tarnaski lost his patience and got there first. He flashed his light right in the younger man's face and barked, "Enough, Lewis! There's no cause here, and you trying to make something happen doesn't help."

Lewis's tight face blazed with fury, but he backed off.

Tarnaski turned back to Boots. "I appreciate your cooperation. There's a lot of older folks in this neighborhood, and a lot of them are widows. We've had some calls about disturbances from some scared old women, and we increased patrols to help them feel safer. I know it's profiling, but the Dutchmen are not known for being choirboys. Seeing a biker in an odd place at an odd time—" He shrugged. "I get it's not fair, but I hope you understand why we stopped you. If you want to file a complaint, you're free to do so."

Boots met Tarnaski's gaze and stayed silent for a moment. He felt this officer was genuine, and frankly, he understood the preconceived idea. He didn't like it, but he got it. "No, officer. No complaints. But if you see me or another Dutchmen in this area, more than likely we're helping out… Mama J."

Lewis sneered. "Puh, Mama J. Sure you weren't here visiting that other biker whore?"

Tarnaski exploded. "I told you to knock it off! Keep it up, and I'll write *you* up. You've already got a nice list of infractions you do *not* want to add to!"

Boots saw anger boiling in Lewis's face, but the man held back. Boots wondered how long the list was that the seething man had accumulated.

Tarnaski gave Boots one last look. "You're free to go, and you have my word, you won't be bothered again if we see you in the area. Right, Lewis?"

Belligerence radiated from the younger man, but he bit out a "Yessir" as Tarnaski walked back to the patrol car. Boots noticed with some amusement that Lewis attempted to get into some sort of stare down with him as a last-ditch effort to assert his dominance. Boots laughed at the man before turning away to mount his bike and leave.

CHAPTER
TEN

The Dutchmen chapel meeting that day held a lot more excitement than other ones in the recent past. After the mundane profit-and-loss reports from Camo, discussions of more boats for their rental fleet, and future expansion of the marina, Boots brought up the subject of Janice's neighborhood and his encounter with Lewis and Tarnaski.

Nutter, who had been falling asleep at the table, perked up. "Shit! I know that guy! He used to be a regular hangaround here, hoping to prospect. Remember when he tried to best Ice in poker a few years ago and win a night with Ice's old lady? Cocky little bastard lost, and Ice beat the shit out of him for thinking he could fuck Gabby." Nutter threw his head back and guffawed with deafening volume. "Peebles named him Minuteman. He tried to fuck her once and blew his wad before he ever made it to her pussy. Fuck me, that asshole is now a cop? Fucking hilarious!"

"Opal."

Nutter wiped his eyes and his laughter kept going, but he turned to face the man who'd said the word. "What's that?"

"Opal. She doesn't go by Peebles anymore," Camo stated. His face was serious, without a hint of a smile.

Nutter dug himself deeper. "Whatever, man. I don't care who you are, that shit is fucking funny."

Rail piped up from his seat at the end of the table. "At another time it would be funny, but today it's not." He drummed his fingers on the smooth wood of the meeting table. "Bothers me there's a cop with a vendetta against the Dutchmen near Mama J's place. She say anything to you, Nutter?"

The big man answered between chuckles and waved a meaty hand in the air. "No, but I haven't spoken to her in a few days. I'm supposed to pick up the kids and take them for bowling and pizza on Saturday afternoon. I can ask her then."

"Why not now?" The cold question came from Duke. Boots was glad he asked it. Nutter was a ranking member. Boots was too newly patched to say anything, as they would consider it a sign of disrespect. *Not that I have a lot of it for the assclown,* he thought as he watched the man squirm.

Nutter attempted to lighten the sudden seriousness that hit the room. "I suppose I could call her, but you know how she is. Always busy with something. Besides, my old lady can take care of herself."

Duke crossed his arms as he leaned back in the creaking chair and frowned at the man. "Far as I know, your dick's been in every pussy in the city but hers in the past couple of years. Seems to me, she stopped being your old lady a long time ago."

Nutter's expression sobered at Duke's statement. Boots saw the animosity between the two men shimmer as they faced each other. "She knows the score. We got kids together. I'll always be in her life, whether or not she's taking my dick."

Duke's lip curled, but Rail stopped him from saying anything else. "Old lady or not, Mama J and Opal have ties to this club, and this cop Lewis may target them because of it. We need to keep them on radar, but on the down-low. I don't want to give him any more ideas than he already has. Boots, you're on grass-mowing duty from now on. I want you to do regular drive-bys, visits, that sort of thing. Keep it business related, but be visible."

Boots nodded and pursed his lips to keep from bursting into a shit-eating smile. He'd already planned to do just that, but it was better that he had Rail's permission and orders.

Nutter didn't show any happiness at this declaration. "What the fuck, Rail? Shouldn't I be the one to do that shit?"

"Tarnaski met Boots and said he wouldn't get harassed again. From what I've heard, he's one of the few cops who's a stand-up guy and keeps his word. If they see Boots around there regularly, mowing grass, picking up deliveries, more people will get used to him. Besides, when was the last time you were at Mama J's?"

Nutter shut his mouth.

Rail leaned back in his own chair. "Anyone else have anything to add? Good. Meeting adjourned."

———

Thwack! Thwack! Thwack!

Three knives hit the target board in quick succession, all within a three-inch circle in the middle. Boots walked over to pull them out so he could throw again. He was outside the cabin, spending some much-needed alone time to gather his thoughts. After the chapel meeting, he made a stop at the marina, but Flipper had already caught up the work for the day. Rather than go hang out for an afternoon of drinking at the clubhouse, he decided to get some laundry done and do some throwing.

Thwack! Thwack! Thwack!

Sweat was beginning to form on his brow as he retrieved his knives again. Some people found this type of repetitive practice boring and would lose patience with it. Boots found this quiet solitude comforting. He'd shared his childhood bedroom with three brothers in double bunk beds, but even with the constant list of daily backbreaking chores, he found some alone time for himself. It was his oldest brother that showed him how to throw knives, and when he could, Boots had spent hours hurling the thin pieces of metal into the side of the barn. A memory came up of his father's anger at discovering that hobby.

"What the hell are you doing?"

Ten-year-old Boots jumped in the air and dropped the knife in his hand. His heart raced and adrenaline surged through his veins at getting caught doing this instead of mucking out another row of barn stalls. "I'm done with my side. Jarrod is supposed to do the rest."

"I don't care whose side is whose," the thin bent man said gruffly. "I need those stalls done. Get your ass in there and take care of it. I got a cow to butcher this afternoon. You're helpin', so I'd better not catch you lazing around again."

"I was going to go to the library this afternoon."

"You heard me. There's work to be done."

Boots hated butchering time. It was messy, bloody work and took a long time even with everyone pitching in. "But Dad, I—"

The slap across his face stung, and he dropped the rest of his knives in the dirt.

"Don't talk back. I said get these stalls finished. You

want to play with knives so bad? There's plenty of cutting to do later. Get to work."

Boots sniffed as his face swelled. His father would get angrier if he saw tears. "Yessir." His voice cracked only a little.

The man grunted, then strode off toward another barn.

As Boots bent over to retrieve his knives, he spotted Jarrod, his younger brother, peeking around the side of the storage shed. A nasty smirk lifted the corners of the boy's mouth.

Thwack! Thwack! Thwack!

Boots let the knives fly, and the points pierced near the center of the target. He needed to put Jarrod out of his mind. Old life. Old sins. Old and buried a long time ago. Best to leave it that way.

"You ever miss?"

Boots glanced behind him. Rail stood next to his bike, helmet in hand. Boots'd been so focused on his thoughts, he hadn't heard the motorcycle pull up. "Not in a long time." He went to pull his knives out and make another throw. "Something on your mind, or are you just visiting?"

"A little of both. Duke and I want you to know we appreciate you jumping in and seeing to club business. We're all still raw from the shit that went down up in Bloomington and the cult discovery from last year. I don't know how we got caught up in all that crap, but I'm hoping we're done with it."

Thwack! Thwack! Thwack!

Boots threw in rapid succession as Rail moved to stand beside him. "I get it. I've been through my own hell, and I'm not planning on doing it again."

"You talking about your recent prison experience or something else?"

Boots recognized a fishing expedition when he heard it. He couldn't blame Rail for taking his pulse. Patch over or not, he still had history, one the Dutchmen knew about. He yanked out his knives and turned to face the club president. "You having second thoughts about me in the club?"

Rail pursed his lips and shook his head. "You became a part of us when you took your oath. I'm not gonna lie and say there aren't a few concerns, but no one is against you being here."

Boots tested the tip of one knife against the ball of his thumb. Still sharp, but he could detect a slight burr starting to form. "I swore an oath to the Dutchmen, but if there's a problem, I'd like to know so I can explain, atone, or leave. The last thing I want is to cause trouble."

Rail's gaze wandered to the target board and the many chips gouged from the center. "No problems. If anyone has something to say, they can say it to me first. You handled the shit with Canter and Tarnaski well. We're not looking for trouble, but it has a habit of finding us."

Thwack! Thwack! Thwack!

"By the pricking of my thumbs, something wicked this way comes."

Rail looked back as Boots uttered the strange words. "What's that?"

"Phrase from *Macbeth*, the Shakespearean tragedy." Boots faced Rail and met his eyes. "Like I said, the past is in the past. It's no secret to anyone the sins I've committed. I sacrificed the life I wanted so fucking badly and paid for my crimes in blood and bone. I could be twisted up with anger over it, but there's no point, and I'm done with that now. It's time for me to move on. I like where the Dutchmen are and the direction we're going. I don't plan to fuck it up."

The two men stared at each other, unmoving for several seconds. Finally, Rail spoke. "You always throw darts with that kind of accuracy? Spider wants to set up a tournament at the bar. You'll be on that project with him, yeah?"

A weight lifted from Boots's chest, and he let out a breath he hadn't realized he was holding. "Yeah, that would be fine with me."

CHAPTER
ELEVEN

IT WAS GOING TO BE A BAD DAY. OPAL'S MIND HADN'T
changed since she made that prediction this morning.
It started last night, when Pearl would not fall asleep.
The baby was cutting more teeth, which made her
whiney and irritable. Every time Opal tried to put
her in the crib, she started crying and wouldn't settle
until her mother picked her up. Opal rocked her for
hours, but the baby would not go down.

By dawn, Pearl finally drifted off exhausted,
leaving Opal gritty eyed from lack of sleep. Tired or
not, there were house chores that had to be done and
other kids to get off to school. As much prep work as
Mama J did the night before, there was still a certain
amount of chaos in the mornings, and this one had
more than usual. Ian spilled milk and cereal on
himself and had to go change clothes. Charlotte and
Lily got into a fight over who got to use the spoon

with the pink princess handle. Augustus had a meltdown. Over what, was a mystery. A flustered Mama J tried to get all the kids sorted, and she finally got them loaded into the van. Normally, there was a two-hour window where Mama J took the kids to school and made her deliveries before returning to the house while Opal watched the younger three kids. Today, Mama J was late leaving the house and got caught in a major traffic delay caused by a road accident. While Opal cleared the breakfast bowls, Ollie and Augustus tag teamed in an effort to overturn every toy cube and storage box in the living room. In the meantime, Pearl woke up and demanded Opal's attention again.

The chaos cut out her shower time before work. Opal slathered on deodorant and scraped her hair back into a ponytail. She made it to the store just as her shift started but discovered she'd left her packed lunch in the fridge. Mama J would probably take the time to bring it to her, but that would take time out of her own schedule, plus she'd have to load up all three children into the van for that one simple errand. Too much trouble, so Opal bought a pack of Nabs and a pop, which hopefully would stave off hunger until she got home after class.

The worst part was the craving circling her mind, and today, their voices spoke strongly to her. Very strongly. *Just one hit. Just one to get through the day. Take it.*

Her fatigue put her in a fog, and she made several mistakes on the inventory count. At the register, her eyes had trouble focusing on the buttons, and twice she'd had to call the manager to make corrections.

I'm failing, Opal thought repeatedly. Her head hurt, and she was hungry, which didn't help the constant temptations that called to her. They started in the morning. Every morning. Sometimes they were soft little whispers she had no trouble ignoring. Occasionally, they pushed a little harder, talking in the loud voices of irate, demanding customers. Then there were times like these when the only thing she could hear was the screaming in her ears for the temporary relief only the white powder could give her.

She clocked out under the eyes of a frowning manager and walked stiffly to her car. Hopefully, the pressure in her head would quiet once she got to class. Opal loved her cosmetology work and reveled in the transformations she could make. Haircuts, color, style, facials, nails—she'd learned so much, and her instructors said she had a knack for it. At the school, she smiled a lot, and chatted with the other students about jobs, family, all the mundane chores of life. She was happy there. Happy enough at this chance for a solid future for her and Pearl that she could beat back the pushing voices with no trouble.

I'll be good once I get to campus, she thought as she unlocked her car with shaky hands. A text beeped on her phone. Opal checked it in case it was Mama J needing her to pick up something on the way home later tonight. It was a notice that class had been canceled for the evening.

Opal's palms sweated in the falling temperatures of night, and the pressure built in her head. She had three free hours, and the structureless block of time ate at her brain with possibilities. Yes, she should go home and help Mama J. There was always something that needed to be done at the house. She could ask for a few more hours at work, as she always needed money. Or she could go visit the special house on the east side of town and lose herself in whatever pills or powder she could afford with the cash in her pocket.

Tears poured down her face, and she leaned against the car door. The need for that blessed oblivion was more than she could handle. She didn't want to call Rail or Duke for help. Her addiction was something she wanted to fight on her own terms. Mama J would do what she could, but at this moment she was caring for her six children as well as Pearl.

Opal typed in a desperate search. Her schedule was so thick, she hadn't been to a meeting in ages and didn't know if there was one on a Tuesday night. It took her five tries before she got the words typed in, but a notice popped up that there was an NA gathering at a Presbyterian church on the other side of town.

Opal sobbed in relief when she saw the address. She hadn't been to this one, but it started in fifteen minutes. She could make it there. She *would* make it there.

The church itself was dark, but there were lights on in the back lot. Opal spotted several cars parked near a side entrance. She closed the car door, turned to face the building, and froze as the demons spoke to her.

You don't know these people. The special house is not far. You know them much better.

Yes, she did. She knew the people that lived in that house and what they dealt. "I can't," she whispered out loud. "I can't go back to that life."

You're hurting. You're in pain.

"I'm always in pain."

You can go there and make it all go away.

"No."

One pill will make it stop. Or one line of the white powder. Just this once. What harm will it really do?

The temptation pushed at her with its promise of escape. She wanted it so bad. Opal shook her head and muttered "no no no" over and over again, but try as she could, she could not force her feet to move toward the building.

Weak. Soooo weak.

She pressed her hands to her face. "Help me!" she softly cried.

"Opal?"

She heard her name spoken in a different voice than the one hissing in her ear. She lowered her hands, and she saw Camo walking up. His hands were in his jacket pockets and his expression showed concern.

"C-Camo," she gasped.

He took in her face and cursed softly. "Fucking hell. C'mere, baby." He opened his arms and took her into them, wrapping her up in his secure embrace. "I got you. I got you. Hang on, sweetness. Stay with me."

She clung to him, and he took her weight as she sobbed against him. He simply held her, and she drew strength from him. The demon in her ear fell silent at last.

"You heading to the meeting?" he asked, his voice low and rumbling in a comforting way.

"It's.... It's been a long time s-since I've been to one. T-Today was bad. Real bad."

He squeezed her tight. "I get that, baby. I under-stand more than most. The white dragon got its claws in when I was overseas. Still chases me."

"White dragon?"

"That's what I call it. I read lots of fantasy books growing up, played some D and D, that sort of thing. Some dragons were really cool, and others were monsters. The white one is both."

She sniffed. His warm male scent brought comfort

to her mind. He didn't smell like strong perfume—just clean. The kind of clean she wanted to be.

His hands rubbed up and down her back. "I'll tell you my story if you want to hear it, but let's do that another time, yeah? I think you need this meeting worse than you need to listen to me talk about myself. Want to walk in together?"

Opal pulled herself together and stepped back. Her spine straightened from the infusion of borrowed strength, and she wiped at her eyes. "I'd like that."

Camo took her hand and began walking toward the lights. "Just to remind you, the club's got your back. I need you to know, I've got it too."

CHAPTER
TWELVE

Boots slammed the engine hood closed and called to Flipper. "This guy is heading to dry dock, right?"

"Yep."

"How many more we got today?"

"That was the last one on the schedule. The rest are staying in the harbor. Got a bunch more for flush and antifreeze seeded for the rest of the week, but there's some cheap bastards who do their own and fuck up their whole system. They'll start showing up soon. Two words for those fuckers. Cha. Ching."

Boots responded with a grunt. Yes, there were people who preferred to do their own maintenance. Some of them knew what they were doing, but he expected there were those who didn't and ended up with locked up engines needing repair or replacement. Oh well. That meant more money in his pocket.

He stood up and stretched his spine, hearing the bones crack and realign. Christ, bending over for so many hours a day irritated the fuck out of his back. There were diehards who ran their watercrafts until the first snows, so he would have work for a while longer. "I'm heading to Janice's place to get her yard done. Should be the last time this year."

Flipper wrinkled his nose. "Janice? Who the hell is Janice?"

Boots rolled his eyes. "Mama J."

The younger man barked a laugh. "I've always heard everyone call her Mama J. Never thought about her havin' a real name.

Fuck. Didn't anyone know this woman? It bothered him a lot that no one saw her as anything else but a mom, a worker, or a caregiver. Not even her old man. *Ex old man,* he reminded himself.

He was dirty and sweaty from dealing with boat engines all day, and he planned to get dirtier and sweatier while doing yard work for the woman. Still, he wanted to be clean for her, at least in appearance. With his past, he'd never be totally clean on the inside, but he at least could make the effort on the outside. He took a quick shower at the cabin and bound his wet hair back in a tie before putting on his nicest pair of jeans and a black T-shirt. He put on his rings and his chain, then took them off again. *I look fucking ridiculous for mowing grass.* He changed into stained work jeans and a faded green T-shirt with little holes all over the front. A glance in the mirror had him wanting to change back. With a strangled curse, he stomped out his door and mounted his bike.

Fuck. Get your head out of your ass, Boots. It's grass. You're mowing her grass. That's all now, and that's all it will be. She's not the type of woman to go for someone like you, so don't go there.

———

October in Minnesota was deceptive. Some days were cool and fall-like, and others resembled summer. Today was a summer day, and it was hot. Janice had been in the kitchen all day, baking breakfast rings, *lefse*, *papperkok*, and tiny tarts. Orders were coming in like crazy, and she was behind in her housework. Tad, Ian, Charlotte, and Lily were doing homework in the living room. Ollie and Augustus were napping, and Pearl sat in her bouncy chair on the big table where she could watch all the action and coo. Janice was forever grateful that the baby was happy just observing life and didn't demand to be held at all times. When Charlotte was an infant, she screamed incessantly until someone picked her up. Since her bio mother wasn't around much, it fell to Janice. She often wondered if that was the reason Charlotte never bonded with Mimi. When she called out for Mommy, the little girl meant Janice. Whenever Mimi came around, she was Mimi—never Mommy.

Janice lived in dread that one day, Mimi would come and claim Ollie and Charlotte. Legally, she could, and Janice would have little leg to stand on. Nutter mentioned that Mimi had moved on and started a new life with a new man and had a third child by him in the process. Another boy, named Rupert. The likelihood of Mimi returning for her two children was slim in that she probably would have already come and got them before leaving Red Wing.

Perhaps she would follow Mimi's lead. She'd started a new life but hadn't thought about a new man. She missed it. The companionship and the intimacy of having a partner in her house and in her bed. When she and Nutter first got together, it was brilliant. She loved being a housewife and had no desire to start a baking business empire. The cooking and cleaning was something she treasured, as she felt it was her contribution to a solid relationship. When the children came along, that was even better. Yes, she might be viewed as old-fashioned or out-of-date in her thinking, but that was the life she always wanted, one as a stay-at-home-mom and housewife. Janice had hoped Nutter would put a ring on her finger someday, but he insisted she was his woman and that a patched old lady was just as good or better than being a wife.

Maybe this was true with some couples.

Gradually, Nutter started spending more and more time away from home. The first time she woke to his empty spot in the bed, a little dart stung in her heart. More lonely nights followed, but he would come home and act like he'd missed her so much, she forgave his absence and welcomed him back.

Then he brought her Charlotte, and those tiny darts turned into arrows.

Still, she stayed with him. He'd cried and begged her forgiveness, claimed he loved her more than any other woman, told her how sorry he was, and promised never to stray again.

The babies kept coming.

Janice lifted a stack of dirty bowls to the sink, and the spot under her left shoulder cramped viciously. *"Uff-da!"* She grimaced and reached over to awkwardly pressed two fingers into the knot, a gesture that was becoming more and more common. Pearl giggled and clapped her baby hands together.

Janice blew her a raspberry. "Oh, you think that funny, do you? Little monkey butt. Yes, that's you. Little bittie monkey butt."

The baby giggled more, and Janice grinned at her. "Monkey butt, monkey butt, cutesy little monkey butt," she sang as she played with the baby's toes with one hand while digging into the knot with the other.

"Mom! Someone's here!" Tad called from the living room. "He's gonna mow."

Janice assumed it was Rail or a prospect. Her lips thinned. She didn't enjoy taking what she thought of as charity from the club, but as much as the Dutchmen had cost her, and with all she had going on in her life, she needed the help.

Janice lifted Pearl from the bouncer and expertly put the baby over her shoulder. "Homework done?"

"Almost. Ian's done. Can we go outside?"

"Not while the mower is going. Finish up and you can watch some TV if you want."

Janice bustled with the squirming baby to the carport door and through to the backyard. The man pulling the old mower out of the shed wasn't Rail or a prospect. It was Boots.

Janice's heart sped up and her face flushed. Not with pleasure, but embarrassment. It seemed every time she'd been around this man, she was at her worst. Frazzled from morning deliveries, worn out from a long workday, or covered in flour from a marathon of baking. It shouldn't matter to her, but it did.

"Oh, hi, Boots. Nice of you to come out and do this for me."

He stood up to tower over her. "No problem, Janice. I'll get the trimming done while I'm at it. This is probably the last time you'll need lawn care for the year. Anything else you want done?"

She shook her head and jiggled the baby, who had

started fussing. "Oh, no, thanks. It's so nice for you to do this much."

"I'm glad to do it."

His dark eyes were unreadable, and Janice found herself mesmerized by them. There was no doubt in her mind that this man could be dangerous, but she didn't see that when he looked at her. His gaze never wavered, and she swayed toward him a bit.

"Mom, can we have a snack before supper?" Ian called out, effectively breaking Janice's concentration.

Boots's eyes shifted then to the boy standing on the carport. "Guess that's your cue to get back inside and mine to get to work."

She gave a laugh that sounded both high and nervous. "I suppose so. Thanks again."

The TV was on some superhero cartoon when Janice made it back to the kitchen. She set Pearl back in her bouncy seat and tickled the baby's toes again. Janice moved to the sink and started the laborious task of cleaning the buildup of dishes that never seemed to get done. Dinner tonight was her personal recipe of plan-ahead tacos. The meat was simmering in the Crock-Pot, and the tortillas and other toppings were in the fridge. She could have the meal on the table for the kids in ten minutes or less when the time came.

She rinsed out a mixing bowl and raised her eyes at the growl of the mower as Boots passed close to the kitchen window. *Uff-da*. She let out in a puff of breath at the sight of him shirtless and pushing the mower. The weather today was warmer than normal, but that would soon disappear as winter invaded the area. Sweat glistened on his back, and she saw the long slabs of muscle flex as he walked behind the rumbling, spitting machine. His torso tapered into hips that sat above a nice beefy rear and long sturdy jean-covered legs.

Oh, he's gorgeous! Janice thought again as water splashed over her from the oversized bowl. Nutter wasn't bad looking, and she always thought he had a decent body, but Boots was prime grade-A male. A ping hit her heart as an unexpected dart hit it. There's no way a man like him would ever see her as a possible love interest. There were so many women out there with young, firm bodies that did not have any obligations in life other than to keep themselves looking beautiful at all times. What would a man like him ever see in a dumpy mother of six who didn't have time to get a regular haircut or put on makeup?

"Nothing," she said out loud. "You can fantasize all you want, Janice. Just don't forget what's real and what's not."

"Did you say something?" Opal entered the kitchen and slumped in a chair. The woman looked wiped, but she grinned at the chortling baby and picked her up for a cuddle. "How's my girl? How's my little Pearl?"

"Oh, she had a good day today. Ate a lot, so I

expect she's getting ready for another growth spurt." Janice stacked the bowls in the drainboard and dried her hands on the dishtowel draped over her shoulder. That pesky spot pulled but didn't cramp. "Tacos tonight. Simple and easy clean up, don'tcha know."

Opal smiled. "Simple is great. What do you need me to do?"

"Nothing at the moment. Just see to your little one. They grow up so fast, and you need to treasure every moment you can get with them."

"Who's that outside? He looks familiar, but I can't place him."

Janice glanced out the window at the man turning the mower to make another pass. "He's a new member to the club. Used to be from the Dark Horses. Goes by Boots."

Opal's lips fell a bit as she pressed them together. "I remember him now."

Janice turned to the former club girl. The tone of her voice and her expression gave Janice pause. "Should I be worried about him around the kids?"

Pearl let out a big *"Gah!"* and grabbed a handful of her mother's hair and stuffed it in her mouth. Opal gently extricated the strands. "I don't know anything other than a few stories and his reputation. The Dark Horses said if the club had problems, he was the one to clean them up."

Janice frowned. That sounded rather ominous, but it didn't fit the image of the man who'd sat across from her in the living room sipping a pop and enjoying the quiet. The club also said Rebel was a stand-up guy and Nutter was a good father. Or at least they used to say that. Both reputations had changed once the truth came out. No telling if this was true about Boots.

She shook herself, focusing back on her never-ending tasks. "Well, now, it really doesn't matter. He's only here to mow. I'm going to take him a glass of water. Would you tell the kids to get cleaned up for supper?"

"You bet."

Janice filled a tall plastic cup with ice and water. She thought about making a quick run to the bathroom to comb out her hair, but it was full of little bodies washing their hands.

Fantasies and realities, Janice. Don't confuse the two. She armed herself with that thought as she walked out to meet Boots as he finished up the yard. That dart pinged again. He really was magnificent. She put a smile on her face to cover up the heat in her middle and handed him the water. "Thanks again for doing this, Boots. Hot work, eh?"

He smiled and her breath seized. "No problem, Janice." He took the water and tipped it back to gulp the entire contents. Rivulets ran over his jaw and down his chest, and she watched them run over his tattoo. This one was vivid, jarring, and more frightening than the club one on his back. A set of black axes crossed above a detailed black-and-white skull on his stomach. The curved blades dripped red over his thick pecs and broad shoulders in long rivulets of blood. There were words printed in elaborate script across the cracked, weathered forehead of the skull.

"**Vivamus, Moriendum Est** – Let us live, since we must die."

A second line of script traveled under his belly button.

"**Permitte Divis Cetera** – Leave all else to the gods."

It was a stunning piece of art, but its sinister appearance was also frightening. It was a reminder to anyone who saw it that Boots, despite his calm Zen-like attitude, was still a biker with a violent past.

"You got a lot of empty flower beds up front and a bunch of overgrown bushes. Rail ever say anything about taking care of those?"

Janice tore her eyes away from Boots's chest and gave a little hand wave to dispel the uneasy feeling she got from his body art. "Oh, no. The boys just come and take care of the mowing. I'd love to plant some tulips. They're my favorite because they grow back every year. I'll get to the bushes myself when I have time."

He fished a piece of ice out of the cup and crunched it between his white teeth. "When's that gonna be? When Ollie graduates high school?"

She grew flustered at his teasing. "Oh, well… I…. Uh…."

"I'm kidding, baby. I'll catch these tomorrow after work, yeah?"

Baby? Her skin flushed with heat. It had been ages since anyone called her baby or anything other than Mommy, Mom, or Mama J. "Sure, sure, that would be great. Um… are you… hungry? I've got tacos tonight. My favorite quick and simple supper."

Why did she ask him that?

He shook his head. "Thanks for the offer, Janice, but I need to get to the bar. Rail's got me on bouncer duty from time to time. Raincheck?"

"Oh, sure. I always have plenty." *Stop it, Janice. You're dorky enough without adding more.* "Come by anytime."

His smile never left his face. "I'll keep that in mind." He handed her the cup, and to her surprise, leaned in close as if imparting a secret. He smelled of cut grass, sweat, and man. On someone else, it might not be a good scent, but on him, it was wonderful. "I know you spend all your nights here taking care of everyone, but if you ever get a chance, come to the bar. I'll buy you a drink."

Her stomach leapt into her throat, flipped over, and sang a round of hallelujahs. She had to concentrate to keep her breathing steady. She forgot all about the scary tattoo. She forgot all about the club. She even forgot about Nutter. His lips were so close to her that all she had to do was turn her head just a bit and….

Opal called from the carport. "Hey, Mama J, kids are at the table."

Janice rallied. "Okay, then. First night off I have, I'll come to the bar. That will be when Lily graduates."

He laughed, his head tipping back and genuine mirth coming from his mouth. Janice was struck again by the contrast between the handsome, easy-going man and the brutality of his tattoo. "Go take care of your kids, baby. I'll clean off the mower and be on my way. Have a good night."

"You too."

CHAPTER
THIRTEEN

Boots backed his bike into the line just outside of the clubhouse. The sun had already made its descent, and cooler air had fallen with it. Still wasn't quite jacket weather, but there was a definite nip in the air that indicated winter was on her way.

The Dutchmen compound wasn't rocking out tonight. There was music in the background from someone's playlist, but most of the members were simply hanging out, shooting pool, or playing cards. A few sweetbutts roamed around, serving drinks, but no hangarounds were present.

Boots joined Rail, Duke, Camo, and Nutter in the inner circle of sofas. A cute blonde came over to him with a big smile. "Something you want tonight?"

He looked at her with a tired smile. "Beer. I don't care what it is as long as it's on tap and cold."

"You bet. Anything else?"

Boots ignored the speculative twinkle in her eye. "No. Just the beer."

She clomped off in her cowboy boots and short skirt. Nutter watched her swaying ass as she left. "Brother, you're missing out. That one is a sure thing. Mouth like a fucking vacuum."

Irritation grew in Boots, but he didn't respond. He learned a long time ago from the art of silence that people who had to fill empty space with words often gave away their secrets. That skill served him well while he was in the Dark Horses and in prison. He loved the quiet, and he yearned to have more of it.

Noise had surrounded him all day long. The grumbling boat engines, screaming power tools, deafening blasts of the air compressor, blaring barge horns. Most times, he could turn it off and ignore the cacophony, but from time to time, he craved the peace he found in Janice's living room.

The blonde set a large foaming beer mug on the table in front of him, making a show of bending over and thrusting her butt in the air. "You want anything else, just ask me."

Boots picked up the mug and took a long sip. He wasn't that much of a connoisseur. To him, beer was beer. He'd heard Duke wax poetic about IPAs, different varieties of hops, and a bunch of other shit he didn't care about. All he really wanted was to drink a cold one after work and reset his brain. A vision of what Janice was doing right now crossed his mind. Was she putting the kids to bed after cleaning from their taco dinner? Puttering around her kitchen? Sitting in the living room, folding laundry to a muted TV and decompressing after her own workday?

"I could use a refill, gorgeous." Nutter's voice cut across Boots's thoughts. "What else you got to tap?"

The blonde grinned. "Be glad to get you anything you want."

Rail waved her off. "Later. Duke's got some news, and it can't wait for chapel."

Duke leaned forward and placed his elbows on his knees. "Boots and I went for wings last week. Randy Shaw owns the place and has been a good friend of mine for years. Saw some shit going down that bothered me. Couple cops came in and pulled Randy to the back for a talk or something. One of them was Lewis Canter. They left with a couple big takeout bags with some extra sauce. I saw it again today while Penny was here."

Nutter chimed in. "So, they decided on wings instead of donuts for a change. What's the problem?"

Duke frowned. "The extra sauce came as a sealed envelope."

Rail picked up his own mug and took a healthy swallow. "Cort told me he gets regular visits at his gas station convenience store. Mentioned something about some cops asking for 'gifts.' Said he has to stock certain brands of cigarettes as 'giveaways' for them. I'm not sure if there's money involved. He got real tight-lipped when I asked him. Either way, it's extortion."

"Heard a couple of other businesses are getting targeted," Camo added. "Not just here, but down in Lake City and Wabasha. Seems to me, Canter is starting a network."

Nutter scoffed. "Even if he is, what are we supposed to do about it? We're the Dutchmen MC, not the fucking saviors of the world or some such shit."

Duke leaned back. "I hate to say it, but Nutter's right. It chaps my ass, but it's not our problem or our business what happens outside of the bar or the marina. I don't think this requires a chapel vote. Still, I think we need to be aware of what's happening so we can protect our own. Some cop comes in here to shake us down, we need to know how to handle it."

"Chances of that happening are pretty damn low. I doubt there's a cop in town brave enough to walk into the marina and demand something from us." Rail pondered. "Our problem is those associated with us by extension or business, like the cooks in the restaurant, waitstaff, businesses we work with. People that have ties to the club but aren't members."

"They know where Janice and Opal live and their past connection with the club. Remember, I mentioned it? If anyone is vulnerable here, it's them."

Boots ran a hand over his head. "I don't think they're in life-threatening danger, but if Officer Dickwad and his buddies find the opportunity to harass either of them, I'm betting they probably will."

Camo audibly growled. "That shit does not happen."

The chair creaked as Rail leaned back and steepled his fingers, invoking the presence of Iceman with the similar gesture. "I don't know what we can do other than stay vigilant. We've got a good thing going here and can't afford to fuck it up. Anyone hears anything, keep it tight and bring it to chapel. All we can do right now. Boots, you need to do more drive-bys at Mama J's. Camo? Heard you were into Opal. That true?"

Camo's face still showed his fury, but he took a breath and replied. "She's into me too. If this goes the way I want it, I'm makin' her my ol' lady."

Railroad nodded in approval. "Good. She needs a good man behind her."

Nutter abruptly slapped his hands on his thighs. "Nothing else to say about it, eh? I gotta take a piss."

The big man got up and left the ring of bikers.

Boots had a lot of ideas about what they could do, but none of them would be acceptable in their current circumstance. The club was transitioning into something better, and any wrench thrown into that would not be welcome. It frustrated him that he had to sit on his hands when he could do something about these problems, but he'd already said goodbye to that part of himself. Past sins needed to stay in the past, and his focus should always be on moving forward. Calm, logic, long-term thinking and planning were needed for both the club's future and his own.

He took another swallow of the cold beer and let the liquid slide down his throat. "You know what I used to do for the Dark Horses, right?"

Rail's gaze darkened, and he slowly nodded. "Yeah, we do. Already told you we don't need that kind of talent."

Boots put the empty mug on the table. "I'm not looking to get back into that unless it turns out to be necessary. All I'm saying is, I'm here if you need me."

Duke frowned. "I hope it never comes to that."

Boots stood up. "Me too, brother. Me too. I'm gonna hit the head and get over to the Harbor Bar for bouncer duty. Have a good night." The pressure in his own bladder had built up, and he made his way through the main room to the bathrooms in the back hallway.

"Hey, Boots."

He turned to see Bella in full vampire makeup, wearing a short black dress.

"S'been a while, Daddy. You ready for another round?" she purred.

He smiled at her. "No, thanks. I appreciate it, but I'm good."

She gave him a coquettish look and stuck out her lower lip. "You getting some on the regular from another woman?"

"No. I'm too old to play games, Bella, or whatever your real name is. I had a great time with you, and I appreciate it, but I'm not fucking you again. You're a beautiful, smart woman who likes to party and be free. That's cool, and you have that right to live your life, sweetheart. It's simply not for me. You need help with your car or boat or whatever, I can do that, but anything else just isn't going to happen."

She dropped the character and laughed. "I understand. Every once in a while, I think about it, but I can't see myself ever settling for that toothpaste-ad husband and raise two-point-five kids in a suburban McMansion. I like fucking and I like variety." She shrugged. "I come here to avoid getting flack from friends about my lifestyle, but I still get judged. There are men who can fuck a different woman every night of the week if they want to, and no one bats an eye. I have to dress up and play a role for that same right. Pisses me off sometimes."

Boots grunted an acknowledgment of her words. "I learned a long time ago, there's no one without some dark in their past. I have more than most and no rights to judge anyone. I have plenty of my own sins to atone for. We make choices and live with them. That's it. If you're happy, it doesn't mean shit what other people think."

She cocked her head to the side and smiled at him. "You're a really cool guy, Boots. If you ever change your mind, you'd be welcome anytime."

Boots chuckled and nodded. "Go find Nitro. I heard he's been a big hit with the ladies."

She grinned at him and visibly switched back into her club character. "Thanks, Daddy! See you around."

Boots watched her ass as she sauntered off, presumably in search of Nitro or some other entertainment for the evening. He made his way down the hall, passing by several closed bedroom doors. One stood partially open, and he was treated to the sight of Nutter's thrashing ass as he stood behind the blonde. She was yelling and putting on a good show as the big man pumped wildly.

"Yes, baby! Oh, yes! More! Harder!"

Nutter grunted with every thrust and added his own voice to the mix. "So fucking good, baby!"

Boots pondered two thoughts inside his head. First, he wondered if Nutter was smart enough not to be on his way to another baby mama. Second, Janice was better off without this ass clown. He went into the hall bathroom to take care of business and found himself alone. Anger welled up as he pictured Nutter taking Janice the way he was taking the blonde. No finesse. No care. Not even affection. Just animal rutting at its most basic level. When Boots had his one-nighter with Bella, he took care of her, and even though that act would not be repeated, he continued to show the woman some respect. Boots didn't think Nutter even knew the name of the woman he was currently ramming his dick inside.

Disgusted, Boots left the bathroom and walked quickly past the open door and back to the ring of bikers working on their next round of drinks. Nitro was leaning on the pool table, practically drooling as Bella talked to him. She reached out a finger, trailed it down his chest, and didn't stop until her hand slid between the man's legs.

Nutter was fucking a nameless blonde. Bella was about to fuck another one-nighter for the hell of it. Every one of them was a consenting adult, yet the whole scenario bothered Boots. He had a restlessness in his gut over the randomness of it all. Why it bothered him so much, he couldn't say. He just knew he didn't like it.

You have no right to judge anyone, Boots. Not with your past.

He left the clubhouse with a wave to the other Dutchmen who were still seated in the inner circle and rode the short distance to the bar. The place was full of noisy people, but nothing sparked any warning bells or other problems. *Too bad,* Boots thought as he finished out the night. His gut was churning with the need for release, and a good fight would get out some of the tension. In the past, whenever his temper flared, he had plenty of ways to let his demons free. He felt them now, bubbling below the surface of his new façade, and he prayed for the strength to never let them go again.

The ride to his cabin was cold but brief. He stored his bike in the garage and went straight to the master bedroom. Normally, he would drop his clothes on the floor and crawl into the bed, but tonight he stripped off his shirt and tossed it into the round white laundry basket in the corner. He frowned as he took in the room's state and drew a finger along the top of the dresser. A long clean line showed in the thick dust. A picture of Janice washing dishes at her sink came up in his mind. He pressed his lips together and strode into the kitchen to grab cleaning supplies and rags.

CHAPTER
FOURTEEN

OPAL HELD THE MIRROR AT AN ANGLE, AND THE WOMAN in the chair twisted her neck to see the reflection.

"That looks fantastic! You did a great job. I love it!" Erica declared. "My boyfriend is going to be so excited. He's been asking me to go blonde ever since we started going out."

"Boyfriend? I didn't think you were seeing anyone."

Erica sighed. "It's only been a few weeks, but he's so great. A real man, you know?"

Opal wiped off her station and dumped the used foils into a plastic bag. "That's a pretty big change for someone you've only known a few weeks."

Erica shrugged. "When you know, you know, right?"

Opal had no answer for her friend and fellow student. When Erica asked her to do a bleach-and-color job, she really didn't know why. Erica's natural color was a deep warm honey-and-caramel mix. Her present pale color wasn't nearly as vibrant in Opal's opinion. Still, she was learning, and Erica seemed pleased.

"As long as you're happy with it. That's what counts."

The instructor came by and let her keen eye roam over Erica's shining head. "That is excellent work, Opal. The best I've seen in a long time." She ran her hands through Erica's shining curls. "Perfect color balance, texture, natural style. I didn't think I'd like it, but you pulled it off. You have a real knack for this. Bravo."

Opal smiled and soaked in the praise. "Thank you."

Erica preened at herself in the mirror. "We really need to go get a drink some night soon. I hear that place over at the marina is really cool. The Harbor Bar? We should totally go."

Opal was younger than Erica by a couple of months, but she felt so much older than the exuberant woman. "Most nights I have to take care of my daughter, but maybe sometime."

Erica tossed her head and fluffed the curling mass. "Don't take too long, girlfriend. Life happens while you wait."

Opal cleaned up her station and put away her scissors and combs. Erica had no idea of Opal's past life, only that she had a child and was completing her cosmetology license. Opal had no intention of sharing it either. "Right now, life includes diapers and strollers. If I get a free night, I'll let you know."

Once the floors had been swept and the lights turned off, the class dispersed into the cold dark. The night was crisp and held a note of frost in the morning. Opal stepped carefully into the parking lot in case any ice might have formed from the earlier rain sprinkle. She waved at several of the other students as they did the same shuffling walk.

This is nice, she thought, still riding the high from the instructor's praise. Other kudos had come to her for style cutting and framing. She loved hearing the admiration for her work. Many of the skills taught in the classes seemed to come to her naturally, and the instructor had remarked on how easily she'd picked them up.

Life may happen while you wait, but I'm not going to settle for anything less than my dream, she decided as she reached her car.

Two headlights suddenly came on, and blue strobe lights flashed across her vision, blinding her. Icicles formed in her belly and panic filled her mind. *No, not again. Not here!*

A squeal sounded behind her, and Erica skipped across the lot to the squad car as Lewis emerged from the door. He caught her lithe body and pushed her away from him, twirling his finger. She laughed joyously and showed him her new hairdo, prancing in a circle and fluffing the shiny mass. Whatever he said to her made her happiness fade as she stopped bouncing and stood still. He pointed at the car, and she went to the passenger side. Opal saw his head turn toward herself, and she quickly slipped into her car, locking the door. She could almost see the smirk across Lewis's face as she turned the key in the ignition.

"Please, please, please start," she chanted out loud. The car hitched once but fired up, and Opal thanked every deity she could think of. She waited a few minutes to see if Lewis would leave first. He didn't.

As she pulled out and passed by his car, she couldn't help but glance over. She was close enough to see him and glimpses of blonde hair as it bobbed in his lap. A sneer crossed his face as he met Opal's eyes. He put a hand on Erica's head and roughly pushed down. Opal tore her gaze away and fought the urge to stomp on the gas. She was afraid Lewis would use any excuse to come after her, even if he had Erica with him.

Her hands shook all the way home, and the cravings hit her with vicious intensity.

You need me.

No, I don't.

Just one hit.

Stop.

Only one.

STOP!

Tears flowed down her cheeks. She pulled over, as the shaking was making it impossible to drive. She fumbled for her phone, and she couldn't control her fingers long enough to text. After the third attempt, she finally hit the pre-programmed number.

A voice answered, low, smooth, and full of concern. "Opal?"

"C-Camo?"

"Where are you, baby?"

Just hearing his voice brought her peace. "At the bottom of my street."

"I'm on my way."

CHAPTER
FIFTEEN

THE ENGINE CLICKED AND SPUTTERED BUT DIDN'T TURN over. At all. Janice huffed and turned the key again, with the same results. "*Uff-da.* Please, just one more day, and I promise I'll get you fixed. Somehow."

She had no illusions that the van was living on borrowed time and that the grace period had just run out.

"What's wrong with the van, Mom? Why isn't it starting?" Ian piped up from his spot in the back.

Janice glanced in the rearview mirror at the boy. He had inherited Tad's old shin guards and was wearing the new-to-him-gear proudly. "I think the battery finally gave up the ghost."

"How are we going to get to the game?" Tad crossed his arms in irritation. To him, being late was not getting any warmup time with his friends before the game started. "Can Opal take us?"

Janice sighed. Yes, Opal would have stepped in, except two of her tires were flat. They'd been fine a few nights ago when Camo had followed her home from class. Opal had been pale and shaky, but Janice hadn't pushed her. She and Camo had gone into the living room, and Janice went off to bed to allow them some time. Janice hoped there was a budding romance there, as Camo was a good man. Opal needed someone like him in her life.

The small carport was only big enough to house the minivan. Therefore, Opal parked her vehicle on an angled side area to the house. Some Friday-night vandal must have come through the neighborhood and slashed her tires while everyone was asleep. Janice noticed the damage earlier this morning as she cleared the back of the van of yesterday's containers and brought them in the house. They sat on the counter next to the mound of unwashed dishes in the sink. She didn't know if anyone else had been vandalized, and maybe she would check later, but at the moment she was racking her brain to figure out how to get the two boys to the soccer game.

Janice opened her phone and dialed Nutter. His cheery voice came on.

"Voicemail suckers! Leave me a message."

She took a breath. "Nutter, I know it's early on a Saturday morning, but I've got a problem. The van won't start, and the boys need to be at a soccer game in less than an hour. Can you come take them?"

She hung up and tried the van again. More clicking.

"Dad's not going to come," Tad said with a bitter tone.

The chances of Nutter getting the message and showing up were low, but Janice had few options. Ubers were possible, but that cost money she didn't have in her budget. Maybe one of the other mothers could help out, but she didn't have many of their phone numbers. She dialed Arris and got another voicemail. Then she tried Monica, but the woman was already transporting a vanload of players and had no room.

"We're not gonna make it, are we?" Tad spat belligerently. "Stupid van. Stupid battery. Stupid Dad."

Janice took another glance at the back. "I'm trying to fix this, Tad. The attitude isn't helping."

Another mother and another voicemail. Desperation tinged her thoughts as she pressed the numbers for Nutter one more time. *Please answer, please, please please....*

"Voicemail suckers! Leave me a message."

Janice sighed. She thought about calling Rail for help, but more than likely, he was all the way down in Wabasha with his wife. No way could he get here in time. Maybe one of the other Dutchmen could help? A picture of Boots appeared in her mind's eye. Yes, she thought he would help her if she had his number, but how many unrelated handsome single men would be available on a Saturday morning to come rescue a dumpy mom and her two soccer kids?

Janice sighed and called Nutter again.

"Voicemail suckers! Leave me a message."

Another grimace crossed her face. She could download the Uber app, make an account, fetch her credit card, and….

The lugging sound of a motorcycle hit her ears. Did Nutter actually get her message and come?

She exited the van and spotted a big black Harley pulling into her driveway, followed by an old Ford truck. It wasn't Nutter on the bike—it was Boots.

Thrills hit her stomach as the man dismounted and removed his helmet. He was gorgeous enough to be on a book cover, but at the moment, his eyebrows scrunched together and his mouth turned down in a frown.

"What happened?" he asked, gesturing with his chin at Opal's car.

Janice swallowed and shook herself out of the attraction fog. She had other priorities to take care of, and her libido-induced fantasies weren't one of them. "I'm not sure. It happened last night is all I know. Probably some kids celebrating a winning football game by making trouble. It's the last thing I need right now."

She laughed, trying to fake a cheery mood. "Actually, that's not it. My van conking out is the last thing

I need right now. The boys have a game, and I can't get Nutter to answer the phone."

Boots's face relaxed. "How much time do you have?"

"About a half hour. Even if I got Nutter on the phone now, we'd never make it in time."

Her throat quivered and threatened to close. She fought the sensation, determined not to break down in front of this man. It meant something to her for him to think she had everything under control, even when it was obvious she didn't.

He turned to the driver of the truck. Camo had exited the cab and now walked up to them, staring with anger at the damaged tires. The two men exchanged an unhappy look.

Boots spoke first. "You got a helmet with you?"

Camo nodded. "Brain bucket. Not a full face one."

"That will do. Let's get that thing off the back and onto the carport. Janice, get your boys and your stuff for the game and put them in the truck. Camo will take them, and you'll ride with me."

Janice blinked and electricity sparked in her belly. "Um… on your bike?"

"Yeah. Camo only has two spots in the cab with seatbelts. You'll wear my helmet 'cause it's got the full face shield. I'll take the smaller one. We'll get you to the game and deal with this sh… stuff later."

Tad had climbed out of the van and stood next to

his mom. "Who are you?" he asked with his belligerence showing in both voice and posture.

Boots didn't miss a beat. "I'm Boots. I brought something for your house as a surprise, and now I'm going to take you to your soccer game."

"What did you bring?"

"Dishwasher."

Janice let out a small cry as another shock flooded her senses. "What? That's not.... I'm...."

"Argue later. Let's get the boys going."

His authoritative voice wasn't harsh, but it was firm, and Janice didn't have time to waste. "Ok, then. Boys, grab your bags and get in the truck. I'll be... uh... right behind you."

Ian complied with a grin as the two men lifted a large tarp-covered appliance onto a hand truck and wheeled it behind the van. Opal appeared at the carport door and stepped out, wearing ripped leggings and a baggy gray sweatshirt. Pearl laid in her arms with a pink binkie in her tiny mouth, and a toddler clung to Opal's knee.

"What's going on? Oh!"

Camo raised his head, and Janice noticed the woman blushed from head to toe in her sloppy house clothes. "The van died, and the guys are helping me get the boys to the game." She didn't mention the other gift. She was still wrapping her head around it.

"How long will we be at the soccer field?" Boots asked as he handed Janice the helmet.

She took it and popped it over her pony-tailed head. The word "we" rang in her head. "Ian's is first. There's about a half hour break before Tad's."

Boots nodded and turned to Camo. "Drop the boys with us and come back here. You can start the prep work, measuring and cutting. I'll text when we're getting close to the end, and you can come get them. Yeah?"

"You bet."

Janice's head still reeled a bit. "There are chairs and a cooler in the back of the van."

Boots nodded again, and both men transferred the items to the truck bed, securing them with bungee cords. "Let's go."

Tad's mouth turned down in a huge frown. "Mom, are you sure?"

Janice's voice came out muffled in the huge helmet. "Yes, sweetheart. We can trust these men. I promise."

The boy made one more warning glare at Boots before climbing in next to his brother. Camo got in the cab and started the engine.

"Ready?"

The word was directed at her from Boots, and he held out his hand to her. Janice looked at it once and took a large breath, steeling herself for what was to come. *Uff-da!* "You bet."

Boots mounted the bike, and she got on behind him, stretching her legs around his hips and wrapping her arms around his waist. The scent of motorcycle and man drifted to her nostrils and assailed her senses. It had been a long time since she had been on the back of a bike. Years ago, Nutter would take her riding through the bluffs, over to Lake Pippin, or wherever they wanted to go. Those trips dwindled over the years, becoming fewer and fewer until they didn't exist anymore. Janice wondered if any of those other women rode with Nutter now. She didn't have time to think about it much as the bike took off, and she gripped Boots harder as they followed the truck.

Wind blew around them, but the helmet kept it from biting into her face. She didn't notice it much, anyway, as her focus remained on the man in front of her. The play of his muscles as he shifted gears. His strong command of the machine was evident as he moved with precise control. Her old instincts revived as she leaned smoothly with him into the turns, and the slight inertia pulled at her stomach. She missed riding, the rumble of the bike, and the adventures it brought. Nutter took her to the giant Sturgis rally before Tad was born, and she loved the long stretches of road with nothing but her man, the bike, and herself. Those days were long gone, but the memories reignited the fire in her for that time in her life. She'd been younger, thinner, and beautiful back then. Nutter had told her countless times how much he loved her and that they would be together forever. It seemed like a lifetime ago, built on broken dreams and broken promises.

Stop it, Janice. You have two boys whose games you've got to cheer through. The stern thought came as they pulled into the parking lot of the Y's soccer field complex, but the ache stayed in her heart.

Boots held the bike while she dismounted before getting off himself. Streams of other parents were making their way to the grassy areas, loaded with coolers, folding chairs, blankets, and bags. The weather was unpredictable this time of year. Sometimes the games were sunny and warm, and other times they could be windy and cold.

She took off the helmet and handed it to him. He walked around back to toss both pieces into the truck bed and pull out her game-day gear. "Tad, Ian, come get your bags, will ya?"

"You don't have to stay for this if you don't want to," Janice said, giving him an out.

"I'm staying."

The two gentle words made her stomach flutter, but when she glanced over at him, she saw he wasn't speaking to her. He was speaking to Tad.

Man and boy locked gazes. Tad wore a challenging expression, as if daring Boots to change his mind. Boots hefted two chairs over his shoulder and lifted the wheeled cooler to the ground. "Grab the blanket, yeah?"

Tad stood still for a moment until Ian ran over and picked up the folded bundle. Tad moved then and took it from his brother. "I got it."

They joined the caravan of people heading through the gates. Voices drifted around them as they set up next to the first field. Conversations about who won last week, which kid would be a starter for what team, when the playoffs began, and who would make it in. Janice spread the blanket on the grass and let the voices drift around her while Boots unfolded the chairs. Ian plopped down and rummaged through the cooler for a juice pouch. Tad announced he was going to find his friends.

"Okay, sweetheart," Janice called as the boy turned and ran off to join a group of boys his age. The coach called for his players, and Ian jumped up, dropping the empty pouch on the blanket.

"Trash, kiddo," Boots's voice rumbled.

Ian grinned. "I forgot." He picked up the crumpled silver plastic and tossed it in the bag Janice had hooked to the side of the cooler.

Once the boys left, Janice's awareness focused on the man standing next to her. His presence filled her senses with color. He didn't wear any cologne, but there was a clean scent to him. The warmth from his body touched her even though they weren't standing that close together. She could see the surety in his hands as he finished the task and settled his large frame into the canvas chair. "Um…

I have a thermos of coffee in the bag if you want some."

He smiled at her. "That'd be great."

She poured him a plastic cup of the dark brew. "I hope black is okay."

"Perfect, baby."

More flutters erupted within her at hearing "baby" come from his lips. A little dart pinged her heart as well. Nutter used to call her baby.

She sat in her own chair and sipped at her coffee. The day was cool but not so bad as to be uncomfortable. She'd sat through a number of cold or wet game days, wearing a big plastic rain poncho and a thick jacket. Almost always by herself.

"I really appreciate all your help."

His gaze moved from the field of young soccer players to hers. "I got your back, Janice. Always."

She wanted to kiss him. She wanted so badly to lean over and plant her lips on his. To taste their coffee flavor and find out if they were as soft as they looked.

"Give me your phone."

It took a minute for his words to penetrate. "What?"

"Give me your phone. I'll put in my number and text myself. You need something, you call me."

Her belly skipped the flutters and dove straight into trapeze flips. "I… I'm…."

"Babe. Phone."

She handed it to him, and moments later, his back pocket buzzed.

"I mean it. You need something, anything, you call me, and I'll be there."

Tears pricked the backs of her eyes. "You don't have to do this. You don't have to do any of this."

He fixed his gaze on Tad on the far side of the field. The boy was bouncing a ball expertly on his knees. "I'm probably stepping over the line here, but I'm going to say it anyway. Your boy is pissed. He hasn't had a lot of promises kept to him by the men in his life, and by that, I mean his father. He's very protective of the one steady person in his life, and that's you. I looked your boy straight in the eye and told him I was staying. I'm not breaking my word."

Janice swallowed. "You're right. Tad hasn't been happy with his dad lately. You still don't need to…."

His gaze met hers, and the intensity in his eyes made her take a breath. "I'm not breaking my word."

The soft declaration had the impact of a sledge-hammer, and it was all she could do to keep from bursting into tears. "Okay."

A whistle blast pierced the air, and the first game started with cheers and applause from parents as they called out encouragements. Janice brought her attention to Ian as he ran down the field with a pack of other boys after the black-and-white ball.

Just before halftime, Ian ran hard down the field and kicked the ball into the net. The poor goalie dove for it and missed. Janice jumped up and whooped with excitement. "Yes! Way to go Ian! Score!"

She turned to Boots with a huge smile on her face. "That's the first goal he's ever made."

He smiled back. "Glad I was here to see it, baby. I hope I can see his second, third, and fourth."

CHAPTER
SIXTEEN

CAMO MEASURED THE SPACE ONE MORE TIME TO CHECK his marks. The Sawzall lay on the counter above his head, out of reach for the curious little girls staring at him from the open door of the living room. He saw one of them stick her thumb in her mouth as she watched him with wide blue eyes.

When he arrived back at the house, Opal had changed into nicer clothes and combed her hair. Her appearance was a far cry from how she used to dress at the club, but he thought she still looked amazing. He'd spent more than one night at the compound watching her laugh and flirt with the men of the club. Did it bother him she had been with so many other men? A little. But it was more about the downward spiral she'd been coasting on rather than the number of bed partners. He'd recognized the addiction pathway she traveled as it mirrored his own experience. Rebel's death was no surprise to Camo, and of all the brothers in the club, he was probably the happiest to be out of the smuggling business. Now, he hoped Opal would see him differently, as more than just another Dutchmen member. He felt a strong connection to her that was more personal than attraction only. He hoped she felt it too.

Pearl sat in an angled bouncy chair on the wide kitchen table, gurgling and cooing. Opal cooed back as she brought up a basket of clothes from the basement and started folding them. Camo bet laundry was a never-ending task with this many people in one house.

He cleared his throat. "I'm gonna start cutting in a minute. It's pretty loud."

Opal bit her lip and nodded. "Thanks for telling me. I'll get the kids to stay in the living room. You need any help?"

"Not right now. I'll call if I do."

She picked up Pearl and hustled the girls back from the doorway. Camo picked up the electric saw and began cutting through the cabinet shelving to make room for the dishwasher. The noise filtered through his earplugs as he removed braces and carefully widened the area. This part under the counter was the easiest spot to get to the back wall plumbing and had no drawers to relocate, so the cuts were minimal.

Once the extra pieces were removed, he took a

disk sander to smooth the edges. A movement caught his eye, and he spotted one of the boys peeking around the doorjamb. The kid giggled and jumped back, then slowly peeked out again. Camo made a game of it, ignoring the curious kid, then jerking his head at him and making a funny face. The boy laughed at him and darted back to hide again and again.

Opal stayed hidden in the living room where a medley of children's songs played from the TV. Camo finished the detailing and heaved himself off the floor. His back popped as he stretched from the cramped position before he strode to the doorway.

"I can't do anything else without Boots's help. I'm not sure where all the hoses have to go, and he does. I can look at the van and patch your tires long enough to go get new ones."

She glanced quickly up from her half-folded basket. "I'm sure Mama J would be really grateful for any help on the van. I can't afford new tires right now."

"You don't need to afford new tires. I'll afford them."

This time her eyes stayed up. "I can't pay you back anytime soon. I don't have a lot of extra money."

He held up a hand. "I'm not asking for payback of any sort."

"But—"

"Take the help, sweetheart. I promise there are no strings attached."

Her face started to crumple. "I don't know what to say. The dishwasher, my tires, coming to get me when I'm.... Camo, it's too much."

He went over to her and gently took the half-folded thermal shirt from her hands. "There's no such thing as too much, sweetheart. You have to know by now where I'm coming from." He placed his hands on the balls of her shoulders. Her eyes dropped again as she tried to hide from him, but he noted with some satisfaction, she didn't run away. He took a large breath and opened himself up to take a chance. "I used to watch you in the club."

She flinched and tried to pull away, but his hands tightened their hold. "No, sweetheart—please just listen to me. I am not judging you. Believe me, I've made plenty of my own mistakes to worry about let alone point fingers at someone else. All I'm saying is I get it. I get you. Rebel was my brother, but he was too far gone with his addiction. I know he loved you as well as he could, but the white dragon was too much for him. That's no excuse for leaving you and Pearl all alone."

She blinked a few times before raising her watery eyes to meet his. The vulnerability in them sledge-hammered his gut. "I can't tell you how many times I saw you with *him* and wished it was *me*."

Her breath hitched.

He lifted one hand to frame her cheek and stroke the soft skin under her chin. "I used to dream of being with you. I wanted that house with a nice green yard to mow every week, a flower garden, swing set, a sandbox, and a big goofy dog to chase the kids. I still want those things, only I see those pictures with you and Pearl in them. If it's too soon, tell me and I'll back off, but I'll always be here for you and your daughter when you're ready. I promise if you let me in, I'll never give you cause to regret it."

"Camo." She sighed.

He wasn't sure who moved first. Maybe they both did. He found her lips under his, and he dove in deep. She molded to him, slanting her head and allowing him full access. He took it and proceeded to put his mark on her. Joy made his head giddy, and he wanted to pump his fist in triumph. Instead, he held her close, wishing there was a way to take her to her room and physically make his claim.

The giggle behind him was the reason he couldn't. That and the hope he hadn't just over-whelmed Opal. He had no doubt he'd just thrown her a big curveball, and he prayed she would be able to catch it.

He released her mouth and folded her close so their bodies were fully against each other.

"Is this real?" she whispered in the folds of his shirt. Fear tinged her voice, but there was something else. A small micron that had the power to heal and find better. Hope.

"As real as life can get, baby. Give me a chance, and I'll prove it to you."

He felt it then. It was almost imperceptible, but it was there. A slight relax in her body as she accepted him. He rested his chin on her shoulder and couldn't help the happy smile that burst across his face.

CHAPTER
SEVENTEEN

Boots exited the garden center with a cartful of supplies and a head stuffed with more information than he thought he could possibly need. The family-run business had been around for decades, and the staff really knew their way around plants, bulbs, growing seasons, harvests, heirloom vegetables, soil nutrition, nitrogen deficits, and more. He glanced down at the bags of topsoil, trowels, seeds, and bulbs and wondered how he ever thought this was a good idea.

His goal was to clear out the messy flowerbeds at Janice's house and plant flower bulbs so she'd have color at her house. It was supposed to be a surprise, and he'd planned on getting the work done while she was out on her errands, but he was pretty sure she'd catch him in the act. He had no idea that planting flower bulbs would get this complicated, but he'd already bought the stuff, so he might as well follow through.

He lifted the bags of topsoil into the bed of Camo's truck. The only vehicle he owned was his bike, and he would ride it as long as he could, but very soon, he would need something with four-wheel drive and a roof for when the snows came. A shovel and rake clattered as he tossed them in next to the bags. Duke's girlfriend, Penny, had an older Jeep Wrangler for sale. Maybe he could work a deal between her and Duke to pay installments, or work off some of the price.

His thoughts were interrupted.

"Looks like you're getting ready to bury a dead body or two."

Boots felt a myriad of emotions flash through him at the sarcastic voice, the primary one being rage. He ignored the man standing behind him and continued to load the truck.

"I'm just kidding with you, Boots. Met you back a ways when Milt and I stopped you in that old neighborhood. Remember me?"

Boots lifted the tailgate shut with a hard clanging slam. "Yes, I remember you. Officer Cantrell."

Lewis's lips parted in a smarmy grin. "It's Canter. Officer Canter. A bit late to start a garden, isn't it? I guess growing up on a dairy farm doesn't teach you a lot about plants. Just how to shovel cow shit."

Another flash of seething rage flew through

Boots. It was so strong that he felt his forehead break out in a sweat from the heat. He clamped down on his anger with iron chains as he tried to ignore the dick in uniform.

The other man leaned on the tailgate and gave his head a single back toss. "Yeah, I looked up your record. Pretty impressive. What was it like, finding out both your parents died while you were locked up? You know. The first time."

The knife slid into his heart, and he fought to keep control. Visions of Lewis's face, bleeding from a broken nose, swam in his head. The sound of cracking bones as the man's ribs caved in rang in his ears. He imagined the satisfaction of hearing Lewis gasping for breath, coughing blood as he crawled away on broken legs, desperate to escape. Wrath filled Boots until his hands shook with the need to tear something apart. He held himself rigid, not moving one centimeter. If he did, he would descend back into the darkness he'd fought to escape so many years ago. This time, there would be no mercy. No second chance.

Lewis took the silence for acquiescence. "I guess it doesn't matter anyway. You can't go back home now, since there's no home to go to. Shopping mall or houses? What did those developers put on your family farm once your brothers sold it?"

Red skimmed Boots's mind. His heart raced and the control he had on his body was slipping. He turned and stood tall and met the other man stare for stare.

Lewis's face fell a bit, and his cockiness depleted slightly. Fear glinted in the man's eyes, and they dropped down quickly in submission. Boots saw the bullish attitude change to one of cowardice. He recalled a time when people spoke of him as the stuff of nightmares. The kind of predator far worse than the boogeyman used to scare children into obedience.

If he gave into his instincts and descended back into that black abyss, he'd lose any chance of atonement.

Boots lifted his chin to stare down at the diminished man. "Officer Canter, I'm not parked in a handicap spot. The tags and inspections are up to date. I have a current license, as you well know. There is nothing illegal about purchasing dirt or yard supplies. You have no reason to detain me. Therefore, I'd like to go about my business."

Lewis made an attempt to regain his footing. "Make sure you put that cart back. I'd hate to arrest you for property damage."

Boots nodded stiffly and turned his back to the man as he wheeled the awkward flat cart to a close-by corral. Lewis moved back to his squad car as a perky blonde girl bounced out of the store and hurled herself into his arms.

Poor girl has no clue, Boots thought as he climbed into the truck's cab. His phone read just after two thirty. Janice would be out picking up the kids from school. He might get the beds prepped before she got home if he hurried.

The tightness in his chest lessened, and some of the rage leaked out of him. He imagined himself in Janice's arms as she crooned to him, easing his mind, calming his raging pulse, soothing the beast that resided in his soul. If she only knew.

He started the truck and left.

———

The sputtering sound of the van caught his ears just as he finished laying out the last bag of dirt. The beds at the front of the house were clear of debris and now filled with the rich black color of new soil. Boots took one empty bag and stuffed the rest of them into it, along with other trash.

Instead of Janice, it was Opal who emerged from the van with Pearl in a carrier slung over one arm, followed by all the school-aged children.

The kids immediately flocked around him.

"Whatcha doin'?"

"How come you have dirt in bags? Did you buy it?"

"It smells funny!"

Tad approached warily, but not with the same aggression he'd showed in the past. "Mom's got Augustus and Ollie with her for some shopping and then the grocery store. She won't be back for a while."

Boots stretched his back. "Good. That gives me time to finish this and leave."

The boy looked at the pile of spread dirt. "What is it?"

"I'm making a surprise for your mom. See those bags?"

Tad nodded.

"Those are different colors of tulips, hyacinths, gladiolas, daylilies, and some other flowers that will appear in the spring. There's a lot of different colors, and if what I read is correct, there should be something in bloom all spring and summer next year. They're bulbs, so they will come back every year."

Tad kept his eyes on the bags. "How come you're doing this?"

Boots picked up a trowel. "Because your mom works hard and deserves something nice. I thought it would be a cool surprise for her to see things growing in her flower beds next year."

Tad suddenly grinned. "So, it's a secret?"

Boots grinned back. "Only if this gets done and covered up before she gets home."

"Can I help, then?"

"Sure. The boxes are marked with what season they bloom in. I was thinking of planting row by row instead of in groups so there's always something coming up. Make sense?"

"Tad, you need to come inside and leave Boots alone," Opal called. She'd taken Pearl from the carrier and put the baby on her shoulder. The woman's eyes were nervous as she walked toward them. "Kids, come inside, now."

Boots saw her half-turned stance as if she was braced to run. "If they want to stay outside, I'll keep an eye on them for you."

Opal licked her lips. "They need a snack and to get started on any homework."

Boots glanced over at Tad. "You have homework?"

Tad shook his head. "Not today."

Ian ran up. "I wanna help too!"

Boots turned back to Opal. "They will be fine with me."

She licked her lips again. "Um… I'm responsible for them."

"I know that, sweetheart." Boots locked stares with her and called on his patience. Being nervous around him was par for the course, and he understood her concern, but if she was a part of Janice's life, he needed her to trust him. "For the record, you do not have to fear me. I will protect them and you. Camo is my brother, and from everything he tells me, you're his woman. I swear you have nothing to fear from me."

"Please, Opal!" Ian begged.

She looked uncertain but gave in. "An hour, then

you have to come inside, yeah?"

"Awesome sauce!" the boy crowed and ran over to poke at the boxes.

Tad was more sedate as he looked at the selection of bulbs. "Purple iris. Mom likes purple."

"Glad I picked something good. Let's get to work. Ian, you get the glads and the daylilies and line them up like this. Tad, you do the same for the tulips and the irises. We'll put them on top of the soil first. When we like the arrangement, we'll bury them and cover the area with straw. Sound like a plan?"

"Yeah! Mom's gonna be so surprised!"

Tad scoffed at his younger brother. "Not until spring, doofus. God, you're so annoying." He picked up a box of red tulips. "Do you have a brother who bugs you to death?"

Boots took a sharp breath. "I have several brothers and sisters, but one died."

"What happened?"

The innocent question sent a shard of ice through Boots's heart. "He was killed in a farming accident."

"I'd hate for any of my brothers to die, even if they are annoying. I'm sorry," Ian added as he carefully laid a bulb on the ground.

"Thanks. It happened a long time ago, and a lot has happened since. We gotta move on, and that includes getting these flowers done."

Tad dug his fingers into the soft dirt. "Mom really

is going to be surprised. She hasn't been happy in a long time. Maybe this will help."

Boots's ears perked up. "Why do you think your mom isn't happy?"

Tad shrugged and pushed an oblong bulb into the ground. "She cries sometimes at night when she thinks we can't hear her. I just want… I just want…." He slammed a hand down on the buried pod. "I just want her to be okay. Not be worried all the time."

"Look at me, kid."

The boy raised watery eyes to meet Boots's.

"I can't promise life won't be tough, but I can promise I'll do everything in my power to make it easier for your mom and you. Your job is to do the best you can in school and help her whenever possible, yeah?"

"Dad doesn't help much. He comes around once in a while, then he leaves again."

The prick of a dart hit Boots's heart. This kid was hurting, and the last thing Boots wanted to do was add to that. "That's not on you, kid, nor is it on your mom."

Tad tucked another iris into a hole. "If I was really super good, do you think he'd stay?"

Boots felt the heartache and confusion coming from the boy as if they were palpable things. He pushed the trowel into the dirt as he spoke. "I don't think that's the answer. I'm not an expert, but I can tell you from my own experience that people as individuals are responsible for their own decisions. What your dad does isn't something you or your mom cause, so neither of you two should own that problem. Like I said, your job is to go to school and help your mom as much as you can."

Ian bounced up. "I'm finished!"

Christ, the kid has only two settings. On or off. "Sounds good. Let's get the straw spread and clean up the mess."

"Are you staying for dinner this time?" Tad inquired.

Boots hesitated. He wanted to see Janice, but he had to get to the bar for bouncer duty. "I can't tonight, but maybe sometime later, yeah?"

"Promise?"

So much emotion in that single word. "Yeah, kid. I promise."

CHAPTER
EIGHTEEN

Her head was going to explode.

Janice loved that Opal and Camo were now together and growing a new relationship, and she didn't begrudge them their time alone, but that left her as one adult herding two witches, one Power Ranger, a Darth Vader, and two Ninja Turtles through the annual sugar festival known as Halloween trick or treating. She'd simplified the process by driving to the various churches that held Trunk or Treat events and let the kids roam through the parking lots of decorated trunks. It was easier to keep track of them as they were contained, and she didn't have to worry about August and Ollie running off to strange houses while she hurried the girls along. Three churches later, the kids' pillowcases were brimming with candy, and they were begging to start sampling.

The ride back to the house was loud as the children recounted what they'd seen.

"My favorite was the big dragon's mouth."

"I liked the candy shop one."

"Mine was the Ghostbusters car."

Janice placed two fingers to her throbbing temple and pressed. "How 'bout we play the quiet game and see who can make the least amount of noise before we get home?"

"That's no fun!" one witch (Charlotte) screeched.

"Yeah! No fun!" a Ninja turtle (Ollie) answered in like volume.

Janice gripped the steering wheel. "Okay, then let me put it this way. Everyone be quiet or I'm taking all the candy away for a day."

"A day?!"

"Make that two days."

"*Two days!*"

"Stop talking," Tad whispered in a hiss. "She'll just keep going if you say anything else."

The van's decibel level begrudgingly decreased, and Janice was able to get home without any more incident. The peace lasted just long enough for them to get into the house. The piles of candy were dumped on the kitchen table in one big mess as the kids started sorting it. Chocolate and candy bars went in one big bowl, Laffy Taffy, jelly beans, and the like went into another one, Sweetarts and other sour candies into a third, and the last bowl held the ones nobody liked or wanted. Janice would keep that bowl until Christmas, then throw it out during her New Year's purge.

"How many Snickers did we get?"

"I like Milky Ways better."

"Who got all the candy corn?"

"Oooh, look at the squishy eyeballs!"

"Gross! I'm not eating those!"

Janice filled a water glass at the tap and took two Tylenol caplets. "You can have two pieces each, then you need to get ready for bed."

"Only two? That's not fair!" Augustus yelled with his Turtle mask hanging down his back.

Tad as Darth Vader stepped in. "Two is plenty. We have lots of candy for weeks if we play it right."

Gratitude filled Janice at her oldest son's help, but she was still the adult in charge. "I can make it one or none if you keep it up. Pick one of your favorites and one of your least favorites, then go brush your teeth. You still have school in the morning."

The kids grumbled, and a fight broke out when Charlotte and Lily wanted the same princess marshmallow piece. Janice was about to lose her mind when a familiar rumble echoed outside the house. Camo had taken Opal and Pearl in his truck, and there was only one person who would dare ride a motorcycle in this cold weather.

Boots knocked on the door before coming inside. The kids swarmed him to show their treasures.

"I got a Ring Pop!"

"These are my favorite Nerds!"

"Look at my Twix bars!"

Boots's presence in the house had become a common enough sight that all the kids knew him by name. He smiled down at them. "Looks like you guys got a good haul tonight."

"What's your favorite?" a chocolate-covered Ollie asked.

"Reese's Peanut Butter Cups."

The boy dashed back to the pile. "I saw some of those!"

Janice winced at the volume of Ollie's yell and placed her fingers over the familiar knot forming in her shoulder. Between her head and her back, she wasn't sure which one bothered her the most. Probably her nerves.

"Mama, look! I found one! I'm going to give it to Boots." Ollie held up his treasure.

"That's wonderful. Let's use inside voices, please."

"Okay!" he yelled back with only a fraction lower decibel.

Boots took the candy as the boy dashed back to the pile. "I've got your containers in my saddlebags." His eyebrows came together. "You okay? You look like you're in pain, and it's not a costume."

"*Uff-da.* My shoulder is acting up again, and I

have a headache. I took some painkillers already, and as soon as they kick in, I'll be fine."

The two girls ran by. "Can we have some juice boxes?"

"You can have some water."

"Juuuuuuuice!"

"No more tonight." She filled two plastic cups with sparkles on their sides and handed them to the girls, who grabbed them and walked/ran to their room. She turned back to Boots with fake drama. "I'll toss a couple packs of Twizzlers to distract them while you make your escape." She laughed and winced at the same time. "I expect the big crash in about a half hour. I just have to make it till then."

Ian heard the "T" word. "I want some Twizzlers!"

"I think you've had enough sugar for the night. It's time to get cleaned up and ready for bed."

At the "B" word, the kids rebelled as one.

"Nooooo!"

"I don't want to go to bed!"

"I'm not tired!"

"I haven't had my second piece of candy!"

The cacophony pierced her brain, and she was about to lose it completely.

"Your mom said it's bedtime." The words were spoken in a gentle voice, but they held a note of authority.

Tad was the only one who didn't complain. He

fixed Boots with a questioning look. "Are you staying long?"

Janice held her breath but let Boots take the lead.

"I'm only here to run your mother's stuff back to her, but I'll stay if she needs my help."

Tad scrunched his face up but was interrupted from saying anything else by the noise of a loud engine echoing on the street. A moment later, Nutter came in the house with a booming voice. "Where's all my ghosts and goblins?"

Janice felt her eye twitch, and her shoulder cramped further. "Nutter, what are you doing here?" She forgot about the screaming sugared-up kids and focused on the whimpering box held in her ex's arms.

The big man turned belligerent. "Something wrong with a man coming to see his children all dressed up in their Halloween best?" He burped and finally noticed Boots standing in the kitchen area, and the man's attitude dropped further south. "What the hell is he doing here?"

Janice reached up to press her fingers into the painful muscle knot that throbbed in tandem with her head. "He's dropping off my containers, like he does every night. You can talk to the kids for a few minutes, but it's still a school night. No more candy."

Nutter grinned as the children ran into the kitchen, screaming, "Daddy, Daddy, Daddy!" Janice felt her right eyelid twitch in a rapid tattoo. *Uff-da!*

"I got something better than candy." He set the large box on the counter and opened it to reveal a scraggly puppy. The volume of the kids' yells of excitement was deafening, and Janice had to put her hands over her ears as the noise knifed through her head. *Uff-da, no!*

Two arms came up behind her, and two hands rested on her shoulders, and her heart immediately calmed as if a heavy warm blanket had surrounded her. *Boots is here.*

The thought was somewhat comforting amid the chaos, but at the moment, she had other priorities that didn't include her sanity. "A dog? You didn't talk to me about getting the kids a dog."

Nutter blinked as the children danced around him. "Why should I? All kids ought to have a dog."

Janice was floored. "Where did you get it?"

Nutter blinked again as if her questioning him made no sense. "I found it on the side of the road. Thought the kids would like a pet."

Incredulity filled her brain. "So, you picked up a stray dog on impulse that might belong to somebody and brought it here as a gift on a night when I've been herding the kids through candy mazes and dealing with sugar highs?"

Nutter frowned and turned nasty. "Who do you think you are, telling me I can't bring my kids a gift? You took his gift without any protest." He flung a hand at the silent Boots behind her. Janice felt the fingers tightening into her shoulders, but Boots maintained his control.

Janice lost it. "A dishwasher, Samuel! Boots brought me a dishwasher to make my life easier. You have no idea if that dog has had its shots, or has fleas, or something else wrong. Who's going to pay the vet bills? Buy dog food? I have nothing here to feed it with. No dog toys or beds or...." Frustration flowed with the tears down her cheeks. She grabbed for her control—

And missed. "You don't think! You never have when it comes to me and what I need. I... I... I can't deal with this. You need to leave."

Nutter started in. "You can't keep me from my kids!"

Janice sensed the escalation coming but couldn't stop it. "You're supposed to have them every other weekend and one or two supper nights during the week. I've never stopped you from coming to any school events or their soccer games. It's you who doesn't show up. It's you who calls last minute to cancel. It's you who skips out on the plays and the teacher conferences and the report cards and the book fairs and trick-or-treating and... and..."

Nutter looked as if he'd been struck. Janice bit off her tirade. She'd vowed never to air their dirty laundry in front of the kids, nor criticize their father, yet she had done just that.

One of the girls started crying, and the youngest

boys followed. Opal and Camo showed up at that moment with confusion on their faces. Pearl was, thankfully, asleep and could stay that way through a tornado.

"Go to your bedroom and lie down, baby. I'll get this sorted." Boots's rumbly voice was tight but calming in her ear. The weight of his hands on her shoulders anchored her and brought her back to some semblance of control.

She protested, but he firmly directed her down the short hallway to the bedrooms.

"I'm here. Let me help you."

Janice closed the door and let herself go. She grabbed her pillow and screamed into its muffled softness. What would she do with a dog? If she made Nutter take it with him, it would more than likely end up back on the street to fend for itself. If it stayed, it was another mouth to feed, clean up after, and care for. She was already stretched thin on time, money, and now patience. The kids would consider her the bad guy for getting rid of the pet. Her brain tumbled through its usual gymnastics of sorting, planning, and budgeting, but she kept coming up short.

Sometime later, she heard Opal's soft voice as she directed the sniffling kids to bed. Janice wanted to get up and go take care of business like she always did every night, but her body wouldn't move. Guilt ate at her for the scene she'd help throw, and she prayed her slipup wouldn't cause the children any more stress than they already had. Tad worried her the most. He was such an angry boy. Angry at the world, at his dad, at life, and now, probably angry at his mom.

Her mind spun over and over again, pulling up memories to torment her more. The first time Nutter cheated on her. Then the second. Her slow but steady weight gain. Her lack of job skills and only a high school diploma with no secondary school for a trade or degree. Her loneliness.

Tears steadily coursed down her face and soaked into the pillow. She needed time, but that was a luxury she couldn't afford to have.

The house gradually quieted, and a soft knock roused her from her doldrums. She sat up and found Tad standing next to her bed, with the dog by his side. "Dad's outside with Boots and Camo. The other kids are in bed. Opal said Boots said he will go get dog food tonight once Dad leaves." The boy's eyes dropped, and he bit his lip. "I know it's a lot, but can we keep him? Please? I promise I'll take care of him and go for walks and stuff."

Janice's heart cracked and bled. This was her oldest son who had stopped asking for things a long time ago. He was the one who sat between his brothers in the van's back seat to keep the peace. He ate the grape popsicles so his sisters could have the cherry ones. He gave up his TV shows so his siblings could watch their cartoons. "Come here, sweetheart."

She folded him into her embrace. "I need you to know I appreciate all the things you do to help me. I'm so sorry you saw the mess between your father and me. You shouldn't ever have to go through that. You and the other children don't deserve that."

More tears fell from her eyes as her son's arms came around her neck. "It's okay, Mom. I love you."

Her chest heaved, and she sniffed. She'd do whatever she needed to in order for Tad to have his one request. "I don't think it would be fair to take the dog without checking to see if he belongs to somebody. Tomorrow, after school, you can take some pictures with my phone, and we'll put up some flyers and Facebook posts to see if anyone owns him. If no one comes to get him in, let's say a week, then we'll take him to the vet and get his shots and stuff. Okay plan?"

He grinned against her neck. "Thanks, Mom."

"You're welcome, precious. Go on to bed. We have a full day tomorrow and the rest of the week. I'll see you in the morning."

The dog whimpered and perked up his tangled ears. He followed Tad into the bedroom but came back when Janice went into the kitchen. She looked down at the quizzical face. "You are a mess, aren't you? Let me get you some water for now. Food is coming soon."

Her heart had settled back into its normal rhythm when a soft knock at the kitchen door caught her attention. Boots opened and entered as quietly as he could. "You okay?"

She sighed and looked at the bag of dog food and bulging shopping bag in his hand. "You bet. I should be used to this by now. I'm sorry for losing control earlier."

"You're allowed to get pissed, Janice. Bringing an animal into someone's home should have been talked about first." He glanced down at the scrawny, unkempt canine who was staring longingly at the bags. "If you can't keep it, I'll see what I can do to find it a good home."

Janice took the bowls from him and filled one with water. "I'm going to try. Tad asked me to keep it, and he never asks for anything." She blinked back more tears as they formed and sniffed. "*Uff-da*, I'm more of a mess than Mr. Mutt over there. What do I owe you?"

"You don't owe me anything, and don't try to insist. The Mister is a Miss and needs a bath and a name."

"Tomorrow. I've made all the decisions I can stand today." Janice sighed as she poured kibble into the second bowl and set both down in a spot next to the fridge. The dog eagerly explored both. Janice's shoulder cramped again, and she winced as she stood up, grabbing at the spot to dig in her two fingers. A hand gently removed them and replaced them with four. Boots pressed into the knot, firmly massaging it. It hurt like hell for a few seconds, but then the troublesome area released, and Janice let out a soft moan of relief. "That feels really good. I've had back and shoulder trouble for a long time."

"I'm not surprised. You're a lot like Atlas with the weight of the world on his shoulders."

"Atlas? I thought that was a book of maps."

His chuckle buzzed her ear and sent thrills down her spine. Both of his hands moved to her shoulders, massaging and forcing the tight muscles to relax. "Atlas was a Titan who was forced to hold up the world in the heaven on his shoulder for eternity. Comes from Greek mythology. I had to study it in college."

She jumped a little. "You have a college degree?"

His hands kept up their movements. "Bachelor's only. I did a double major in History and Literature with a concentration on European classics. I started my master's but didn't finish it."

"Why didn't you finish?"

His fingers tensed and the temperature dropped a little. Janice was afraid she'd trespassed on something private. Then he took a long breath and the moment passed.

"Plans change. Life happens. My dad and mom needed me back on the dairy farm. There was an... incident."

Janice heard the unspoken request. He didn't want to share this part of himself with her. She was mildly disappointed, but with the earlier drama still lingering in the air, she let it go. She tipped her head forward as he moved his hands to massage the rough spots between her shoulder blades. "History and literature? That's a long way from milking cows."

He pressed and rotated on another knot. "Yeah. I wasn't suited for farm life. My brothers and I didn't get along too well. Too many generals and not enough soldiers, if you know what I mean. Some things happened…. It got rough. This was not a great time in my life. I was… someone else. I couldn't go back to academia and was searching for my place when I met Musicman and the Dark Horses. Their lifestyle appealed to me, or to the person I was then. I found a niche I was good at, and they needed me for it. The rest is history."

Janice felt his hands move lower to her mid back. She braced as his fingers gripped her ribs from behind and his thumbs rotated around her spine. "That is incredible. You could have a career in massage therapy if you wanted it."

He chuckled again. He moved his hands again to press against her lower spine in the most fatigued area of her body.

A sharp dart hit her heart as she realized he could feel the love handles on either side of her waist. She suddenly became aware of his close heat behind her, the slow languid pressure of his hands on her body, and the awareness of him as a man that bloomed in her middle. It had been such a long time since she'd been touched, and here she stood, sweaty and frazzled from her day as the most perfect male she'd seen in her life was putting his hands on her. Self-consciousness assailed her mood, and she stepped away to make some space between them before she could make a bigger fool of herself in front of him. Thankfully, the dog chose that moment to whine.

"You might have lucked out, and she's already housebroken. I'll walk her while you do what you need to do, yeah?"

She turned and faced him, raising her eyes to meet his gaze. "You know you don't have to do this. You don't have to do anything for me or the kids. I'm very, very grateful for all your help, but you have no obligations to me."

His eyes darkened, but not in anger. He seemed more reflective, which piqued her curiosity even more about this mysterious man who was slowly working his way into her life.

"There is a mountain of sins laid at my door. People I've hurt, things I've done, too many regrets to count. Rail and the Dutchmen offered me a chance to change all that. I've paid for a lot of my transgressions, but I still feel the need to atone for my past. In truth, I'm being selfish when I'm helping you, because, sweetheart, you're helping me more."

Janice had no other words to add. The night had been physically and emotionally draining, and her energy reserves were fast depleting. Her head dropped as fatigue engulfed her. "Thank you for being here and for taking care of the dog. I'll walk her myself since we have to get along and I need some air. I guess she'll get a name tomorrow."

Boots studied her for a moment, and his eyes grew heavy. She thought he had something else to say, but he gave a sharp nod instead. "I'll leave you to it. I'll call tomorrow and see how you're doing. Good night, sweetheart."

"Good night, Boots."

He turned and she watched as he left the house without looking back. An ache radiated from her middle. She wanted to call him back to her, but she kept her silence. Too many emotions had already passed through her in the last hour that adding anything else would be dangerous. Even so, she yearned to have him close again.

The sound of his motorcycle starting up had her shaking her head to get herself back on track. The rumble faded as he drove away and she bent to strap on the new collar on the dog. The canine frantically licked the food bowl in an effort to get every last crumb and ignored Janice when she snapped on the leash. "Come on, puppy. Let's get your business done, so I can get my business done."

CHAPTER
NINETEEN

Boots twisted the screwdriver to tighten the last retaining screw and slipped. The point of the metal tool gouged across his index knuckle, opening a small gash. Blood poured from the wound, and he cursed as he moved his hand so he wouldn't drip the red stuff all over the customer's boat. The last thing he wanted to do today was add to his workload. Temperatures had taken a nosedive, and this winter's predictions were that it was going to be rough. Snow was imminent, and the boat owner holdouts had been calling all morning to get their crafts winterized and stored immediately. Of course, the problems were time and demand—not much of the first and plenty of the last.

Rail, Flipper, Boots, and one town mechanic had been busting their balls all day to get as many done before the big freeze started. Only a few were left in the lineup, and Boots was debating on staying out on the pier until they were done. Once they were done, he could concentrate on other tasks for the upcoming weekend. He reached for a clean shop towel and pressed it against the wound.

Perhaps if his mind hadn't been on other events, he might not have hurt himself.

"Looks bad, *brother*," a voice called out.

Boots turned to see Nutter heading toward him. He had no trouble seeing the aggressive swagger in the man's long strides and how he held himself tall in order to look down on his opponent. Boots found it more amusing than intimidating. Nutter and he were close to the same size, but where Nutter had the big manly dad bod going, Boots was cut and lean.

"I've had worse and lived to tell about it. What's up, Nutter? Coming to work the marina for a while?"

Nutter stopped and crossed his arms. "No, I came to see you, brother. I don't like it when men sniff around my old ladies."

Boots pressed the towel harder. "Old ladies. I didn't think plurality was acceptable."

Nutter looked confused. "What the fuck? Don't start giving me fancy words and double talk. I'm talking about you being over at Mama J's a few nights ago."

Boots kept quiet and waited. Many times, silence was more effective than bluster.

"I come by to see my kids, bring them a present, and you're there, confusing her."

Boots took the cloth away from his knuckle and looked at the gash. Not bad enough to need stitches, but it would leave another scar; one among many.

"We been together a long time. Too long for some yahoo to come in and interfere."

Boots picked up a bottle of superglue from the open box of tools and supplies behind him. One-handed, he managed to pinch the skin together and squeeze out a small drop of glue onto it. It burned like hell, but fused the wound shut.

"That's what you're doing. Interfering. She and I are working things out, and I'm telling you, you need to back off and quit making her more confused than she already is." Nutter waggled his fingers around his temple. "She's not the brightest bulb and has trouble sometimes."

An angry burst of heat erupted in Boots's middle, which distracted him from the pain in his knuckle. "Not the brightest bulb," he repeated as if to confirm what he just heard.

Nutter dug himself deeper. "Yeah, she's not that smart, ya know."

"Not that smart."

"She got good grades in school, but when it comes to life, she needs a man to take care of things."

"Take care of things."

Nutter's arms dropped to his sides in frustration.

"Yeah, asshole! You gonna stand there and keep repeating everything I say?"

Boots kept his cool but was boiling mad. He put the tiny bottle back in the toolbox and stood straight to meet Nutter's eyes. Another effective technique he had learned was that it was seldom that a guilty man could hold a direct stare. "She wasn't the one who came to visit sugared-up kids when they were about to go to bed and riled them up even more with some random dog."

Nutter blustered some more. "That mutt was a gift for my kids."

"That you picked up from the street with no knowledge of temperament, or medical records, or supplies."

Nutter pointed an angry finger at Boots. "You don't get to tell me what I can and can't give my kids."

"No, I don't. By that logic, you don't get to tell me not to see Janice."

"She's my old lady, Boots. Back the fuck off!"

Boots braced himself. If it came to blows with Nutter, he had no intention of holding back. The urge to see blood flow burned in his gut. "Your old lady? What about the woman sitting in your truck when you were dropping off the dog? Is she your old lady too?"

Nutter paused. "Mama J knows the score."

"Are you sure?"

Nutter blinked and shook his head. "What the fuck are you talking about? Of course I'm sure."

"Ever wonder if 'the score' is why she left you?"

The big man sputtered like an angry engine. "Doesn't matter. I love her and she knows it, but I can't be held to just one woman. It's just taking longer than I thought for her to come to her senses."

Boots shook his head, trying to come to terms with the man's thought process. "So, you're saying, she'll come around to your way eventually and accept that you'll never be completely faithful to her. Is that what I'm hearing?"

Nutter crossed his arms and gave a bit of a satisfied smile. "That's it exactly. She'll get there as long as you stop messing with her head. That's why you need to back off and leave her alone."

"No."

It was Nutter's turn to shake his head. "What?"

"I said no. I'm not backing off. I'm not going to stop helping her. I'm not leaving her to deal with everything on her own. You might have been with her for years, but you don't know the woman."

"What the fuck? I've known her for years, asshole!"

"What's her favorite color?"

Nutter stopped. "Why the fuck is that important?"

"Purple. What is her favorite dinner to cook?"

"I don't—"

"Tacos. What flowers does she like?"

"What—"

"Tulips because they grow every year. What is the main focus in her life?"

Nutter's face flushed red, but he remained silent.

"If you don't know, you're not paying attention. Everything in her life revolves around the kids—hers and the ones by another woman. Everything. From the moment her feet hit the floor in the morning to when she finally goes to bed at night, she's working for her kids. Her time is more precious than gold, and if you were any kind of man to her, you'd be the one getting her a dishwasher instead of another mouth to feed."

Nutter roared and swung a meaty fist. Boots let it connect with his jaw, and the blow staggered him back. Pain exploded, and he tasted coppery warm blood as it filled his mouth. He spat on the floor and stood straight. "My turn, asshole."

The fight started with wild punches and yells from Nutter. Boots stepped around and evaded the man, taunting him with near misses and landing punches on the man's ribs and back. Nutter's movements became more and more frenzied as he tried to hit his opponent but couldn't get close enough. The big man lost his temper and grabbed a random work stool. He flung it at Boots's head and charged him like a bull. Boots batted the stool away but didn't make it in time to avoid Nutter barreling into him. Both men went down, dangerously close to falling in the frigid river water. Nutter was sitting on top of Boots and raised both fisted hands to bring them down in one big hammer blow on his back when Boots rolled over and struck out with a whipping motion to throat punch the big man. Nutter grabbed his neck as he choked, falling to the side. Boots jumped out from under the man and stepped back, his lungs heaving.

Pounding footsteps sounded behind him. Boots didn't take his eyes off the gagging, gasping Nutter, but he spotted Rail running up, followed by Duke and Flipper. He sucked in lungful after lungful of the cold air, letting the sting in his nostrils burn off some of the killing rage he fought back.

"What the fuck? You two assholes ain't got nothing better to do than fuck each other up? Stupid fuckwads!" Duke yelled as he stepped between the two combatants.

"The club has enough shit going on without war between brothers," Rail added. "Whatever it is, work it out."

Nutter pointed a finger at Boots and managed to garble, "That motherfucker is trying to take my woman!"

Duke swatted down Nutter's arm. "Which one, motherfucker? You've had dozens!"

"Mama J!"

Duke threw his hands in the air. "Oh, for fuck's sake!"

"Well, well, well. Got a call from a concerned citizen that there was a fight going on at the docks."

The new voice cut through the tension, and all four bikers stood down. Duke helped Nutter to his feet as the man continued to cough. "No fight here, officer. My friend just fell down, and we're helping him up." He brushed off Nutter's shoulders as if cleaning dirt off of him. "See? No fights here."

Boots sucked at his swollen lip and kept silent. The deputy wasn't Canter this time, but one of his buddies. He looked barely old enough to be out of high school. Boots was tempted to tell him to run along so the men could finish their discussion. Blood sang in his veins with the need for violence. The rush of adrenaline had his hands shaking and his breath sawing in and out of his chest as he fought to keep hold of his control.

The brash young deputy hitched up his pants and sniffed. "No fights, eh? What happened to that guy's face?" He jerked his beardless chin in Boots's direction. "Little too much blood, I'd say, for no fighting."

"He fell down too." Rail said in menacing monotone, daring anyone to contradict him.

The kid didn't take the hint. "I think you people are lying to me. It's not a good idea to lie to an officer of the law." He smacked his lips together. "Maybe I could overlook some things, but I'd have to have a good reason to."

A visible change came over both Rail and Duke. Boots himself stood up straighter as he met the eyes of the Dutchmen MC president. Nutter was still swaying, but the three other bikers moved to surround the smaller, younger man.

"Did you just call me a liar?" Duke's growl made the deputy blanch.

"I… uh…."

"I believe he was asking for a bribe to forget anything he heard or saw here, brother. Maybe he doesn't know who we are." Rail towered over the pale-faced kid in uniform. "Perhaps we should introduce ourselves. You have heard of the Dutchmen MC, right?"

The deputy swallowed. "My mistake." He backed away, only to bump into Boots. The cop whirled around and was frozen to the spot. One look at the hard biker's dark expression, and the kid lost any color he had left. Terror was reflected in his face as he gazed into the abyss of Boots's eyes. What he saw in them shook the deputy to his core, and he stumbled back to escape the menace. With a scared cry, he all but ran back down the dock.

Rail watched him go before turning to the two warring bikers. "I'm sick of this shit. Nutter, you gave up your claim on Mama J a long time ago. As far as the club is concerned, she can choose whoever she wants, and she may not want anybody right now. Leave her the fuck alone. You, too, Boots. Her yard won't need cutting till next year."

"But my kids!" Nutter started.

"I didn't say abandon your children. I said leave her alone, and let the woman have some peace for a change. She's fucking earned it, putting up with this shit."

Boots kept his silence. He agreed that the yard work was over for the season. Rail didn't say anything about shoveling snow.

CHAPTER
TWENTY

MIRACLES HAPPENED OCCASIONALLY. FOR THE FIRST time in months, Nutter came to take his kids for a rare weekend. She was suspicious that his motivation was seeing Boots at her place, but regardless of the reason, she had a glorious night to herself.

And she had no idea what to do.

It had been such a long time since she had this kind of freedom, the possibilities were endless. She could take a bubble bath and not be interrupted. She could read a book. She could go shopping. She could go to a movie that didn't involve cartoons. She could…. She could…

She could break down and cry because she had no identity or life outside of her kids.

"Mama J? What's wrong?" Opal said as she came into the kitchen, holding Pearl. The younger woman had this Saturday off for a change and would be spending it with her daughter and Camo. This would be the first time they would be together as a unit. The baby was napping at the moment and should be all smiles and giggles later. The plan was for them to take her to the mall for shopping and dinner at the food court, then spend the night at Camo's place. The park was out as the days were getting too cold, and it wouldn't be too many more weeks until the weather morphed into full-blown winter. Snow was not unheard of in November.

Janice sniffed. "Oh, nothing. I'm just having a moment."

"Is it Nutter? I saw him just pick up the kids. Did he say something to you?"

Janice shook her head. "No, I'm just feeling sorry for myself. Never been without a child in my house for over ten years now." She huffed a laugh. "I have no idea what to do with myself."

Her laugh ended in a sob, and her face crumpled.

Opal hurried over to the woman and hugged her. "You wanna come hang with me and Camo and Pearl?"

Janice swallowed her tears and patted the younger woman's thigh. "No, thanks for asking. You need to have time with your man and your little girl. It's important. It really is." She took a big breath. "I'll be fine. I just have to figure out what I should do right now."

Opal's eyes shone and her mouth lifted in a

conspiratorial smile. "I have an idea, but you have to trust me."

A few hours later, Janice looked in the handheld mirror at her new haircut. Opal had tamed the wild curls and trimmed them to layer around Janice's face. She also added some mahogany color with copper highlights. The effect was stunning.

"This is wonderful, Opal. Thanks so much." Janice turned her head this way and that. She couldn't remember the last time she had her hair actually styled. It seemed she never had two hours to rub back-to-back to get it done.

Opal's eyes glowed. "Now all you need is something nice to wear, and you're ready for a night out."

Janice scoffed. "Oh, now, that's not necessary."

Opal pushed back. "Yes, it is. I heard Boots invite you for a drink at the Harbor Bar. You should go tonight."

Janice huffed again. "Oh, that's a place for young people. Not old women like me."

"That place is open to anyone."

"I won't know anyone there."

"Yes, you will. Rail and Gretchen will probably be there. Duke and his woman, Penny, usually come too. All the prospects, and of course, Boots. You know who won't be there?"

"Who?"

"Nutter. He'll be the one at home with the kids.

This is your best opportunity to go out and remind people you're more than just Mama J."

Janice's stomach knotted up. "I don't know."

Opal took the woman's hand and met her eyes in earnest. "You've been the anchor that held me together when I was ready to fall completely apart. I know you have some nice clothes in the storage bins down in the basement. Ones you haven't been able to wear in a long time. I can do your makeup, and you can get a chance to be Janice tonight and be treated like a woman for a change."

Janice held back the tears. It had been a long time since she was treated as anyone other than a mother. So far, Boots had never seen her wearing anything other than what she termed "working" clothes or with full makeup. He was the first man in a long time to recognize she was a woman as well as a mom. The idea of him seeing her dressed up had her holding her breath. Would he like what he saw? Would he truly find her attractive? It would be a risk, but it was one she found herself wanting to take. "Okay, then."

CHAPTER
TWENTY-ONE

JANICE HELD HER BREATH AND WATCHED ANOTHER group go into the bar. Bright light spilled from the windows into the parking area where she sat in her van close to the back. She could hear the thumping music from the band that was playing tonight. The place had gone from a so-so bar to one of the hottest spots in town. Rail should be proud of what the MC had accomplished under his leadership. If Iceman were here, he would feel the same way.

That knowledge still didn't help Janice's nerves. She and Opal had dug through several of the Rubbermaid bins in the basement for the clothing she had once worn when she was younger and had a life outside of motherhood. With the weight she had lost, many of them would fit again. Opal found a pair of bootcut jeans that hugged Janice's body and shaped her rounded butt into something a Kardashian would be proud of. She discovered her old bone-colored cowboy boots with stacked heels in a bin of dressy shoes she no longer wore. They were cute and not too high, as Janice didn't think she could handle any spiky heels. The blouse was a wraparound style that tied off at one corner of her waist and had floaty three-quarter bell sleeves. The muted purple color had a touch of metallic sheen that set off the copper highlights of her hair. Opal insisted on doing her makeup. Janice almost cried when she saw the results. The smoky look to her eyes and the gentle contour the budding cosmetologist had created on her cheeks—all of it was subtle but impactful. Janice hadn't felt this confident in herself in years.

Opal had shooed her out the door. "Go, have fun. Enjoy a real night out."

Easier said than done. Janice sat in the van for a few more minutes. She assumed Boots was in there since his bike was in the line of motorcycles against the dock fence. Perhaps she could just sit here a few more hours, then go home.

To what? The house was empty. Camo had come by dressed in biker chic to pick up Opal and Pearl. The care the man had for the two females showed such tenderness that Janice had wanted to weep in happiness. Now she wanted to weep for herself.

Is this what I am now? she thought as two more people entered the bar. *A woman too scared to go out by herself?* So many other parts of her life, she did by herself, or mostly that way. When she took a kid to the doctor, she did it by herself. When she went to Tad and Ian's soccer games, she did it by herself. When she gave birth to them, she'd been by herself. *Damnit, I'm a thirty-eight-year-old woman. Why* couldn't she go in that bar by herself?

Boots is there.

He would see her. He would see her as different from the mother and the worker everyone else knew. He called her Janice. He called her baby. He spent time at her table. In her house. In her company.

What if he didn't like what he saw? What if she was mistaken about him? He might be in there right now, with his arms around a tall thin blonde more suitable to him than the thick-bodied Mama J.

Then again, he might not.

No place I'd rather be, baby.

There's only one way she would know for sure. She would walk in, order a drink, and find some unobtrusive spot along the wall out of the way to people watch for a while. She would see Boots and simply deal with it if he was with someone. No harm, no foul. The next time he came to her house, she would be over this ridiculous idea that he had any type of regard for her other than friendship.

She screwed up her courage, exited the van, and walked up to the bar's door. The music was louder here. She took a big breath and opened the door.

Sound blasted her ears, and the change from the

cool outside to the warm interior startled her. People were talking, shouting, laughing, and singing with the cover band on the small stage. It was overwhelming, and Janice felt the urge to run back outside to her safe van. She almost did it until she spotted Rail and Gretchen at the crowded bar. Seeing the two familiar faces helped, and she inserted steel into her spine before making her way across the room to greet them.

One drink. Just one, then I'm going home.

Rail gave her a cursory glance and then snapped back. "Mama J?" he mouthed. If he said it out loud, she didn't hear it over the music. Gretchen turned her head and smiled in sheer delight. Janice smiled back as the woman waved her over for a big hug. God, she needed this boost in confidence, thrilled she found a welcoming spot.

Rail continued, signing as he spoke so Gretchen could keep up with the conversation. "Almost didn't recognize you. You look fantastic."

She smiled and flipped her hand. "Oh, now. Opal just needed a guinea pig for practice. Did a nice job, eh?"

"You bet she did. I don't ever think I've seen you here at the bar."

"Never been before. Always too busy with the kids. Nutter has all of them for once and all night too. I need to take advantage of any free time I can get, don'tcha know."

Rail laughed and gestured for a bartender. "You picked a great night to come. This is a hot band we've been trying to book for months. Full crowd. What are you drinking?"

She hesitated. It had been so long since she'd had an adult beverage, she didn't know what to order. She didn't know any sophisticated drinks, and her mind blanked.

"Rum and diet is a safe bet," a voice behind her rumbled.

Her heart jumped on her stomach like it was a trampoline at the kiddie park. She half turned and looked up to see Boots right behind her.

———

He spotted her the moment she walked in, and a fifty-pound anchor thudded in his stomach. He thought she was pretty before, but with her hair and makeup done, she was gorgeous. The top she wore showed off just enough of her cleavage to be enticing, and those jeans. Fuck, those jeans showed off the magnificence of her ass to absolute perfection. Big, round, womanly, it was the kind of ass that jiggled and swayed naturally when she walked. The kind of ass some women had to add padding to their behinds to achieve. The kind of ass he wanted to grab with both hands while he sank his dick into the wet pussy that came with it. The kind of ass he could bang all night long and never get enough.

Boots drank a beer here and there throughout the evening but stayed away from the stronger liquor. The beer wouldn't affect him enough to cause a problem if he had to wade in, but doing shots like some of the other bar patrons was a bad idea. If something went down, he'd need all his faculties to take care of it. Nutter was usually the one to oversee this job, but he was out tonight, for whatever reason. Boots didn't know why. Rail told him Nutter was getting more and more unreliable and tended to drink and flirt with the women rather than keep an eye on things. The more Boots learned about Nutter, the more he concluded the man was a fucking moron.

Especially if he let go of that scrumptious ass.

Boots moved up behind Janice, taking in the round shape of her behind, and caught the last of her statement.

"Never been before. Always too busy with the kids. Nutter has all of them for once and all night too. I need to take advantage of any free time I can get, don'tcha know."

He watched Rail wave to one of the prospects manning the bar. "You picked a great night to come. This is a hot band we've been trying to book for months. Full crowd. What are you drinking?"

Boots saw her indecision. This was a woman who had apple juice and Capri Sun pouches in her fridge.

"Rum and diet is a safe bet," he said as he reached his destination. Janice turned to look up at him, and that anchor settled firmly in his groin. "I told you I'd buy you a drink whenever you came."

She smiled at him. "Hi, Boots. Yes, you did."

The prospect set a short glass filled with ice on the bar and drizzled some clear liquor into it followed by a blast from the drink gun. Boots handed it to Janice. He leaned in, and the scent of jasmine teased his nose. *Fuck, he was getting hard.* "I'm glad you came. You look fantastic, baby."

He noted the flush to her skin as she accepted the drink that had been poured in front of her. One of his two sentences threw her off. Maybe both.

She took a sip of the drink and her eyes widened. "Oh, my. I haven't had anything this strong in years."

Of course not, Boots thought. She was not the type of woman to take chances by drinking during her pregnancies, and he had already learned she didn't keep alcohol in the house around her kids or the recovering addict who lived with her. "You're welcome to have as many as you like. If you don't feel safe driving later, I'll take you home."

She smiled nervously. "That's very nice of you, but I'm sure I'll be okay."

"Janice."

Her eyes met his.

"I said I'd take you home. You can trust me."

Those blue eyes of hers changed slightly. "I do trust you, Boots."

He felt that anchor lodge deeper in his gut. His gaze caught the amused expression on Rail's face and the happy one on Gretchen's. Boots ignored them and kicked out a barstool. "Have a seat, sweetheart. Tables are full, but I'll clear one for you if you want."

Janice blushed again and took another sip of her drink. "Oh, no, you don't have to do that." She lifted a hip to slide onto the stool and faced the band sideways to the bar. Boots positioned himself right behind her. He laid his arm on the bar next to her shoulder so he could keep an eye on the crowd and still be close to her. All he had to do was lean over so he could talk to her without shouting. The tantalizing scent came from her hair, and he wanted to bury his nose in those soft springy curls.

Rail signed and spoke. "Business is good?"

Janice nodded. "Oh, yeah. Lots of orders coming in now. Good thing I had Carson Knilling put in the two big ovens, don'tcha know. I'm thinking I need to do a better website and the Facebook page. Tad loves working on the computer, and I bet he could help with that."

Rail chuckled. "He's a fine boy."

"Oh, that he is." She fell silent. Boots wondered if her thoughts had drifted to Nutter and what he and the kids were doing at this hour. Sleeping, most likely. At least he hoped so.

The band started the opening riffs to AC/DC's "Thunderstruck", and the crowd ramped up with them.

Rail shouted to Boots, "Looks like we're close to capacity."

Boots yelled back, "About twenty away, from my count." He took the opportunity to put his hand on Janice's shoulder right where the cloth of her shirt ended and her skin began. His fingers encountered warmth, and he felt her jump at the contact. He didn't move.

"Since when did you go from being a badass biker to someone who worries about the fire marshal?" Gretchen signed as she teased her husband. Rail interpreted to keep everyone in on the conversation.

He grinned at his wife and answered back. "Since I got put in charge of the club's interests and keeping them safe. Speaking of which, did you hear what happened down in Wabasha?"

Boots shook his head.

"I don't know all the details, but there was a fire set at the Bait and Tackle store. There's some suspicion about how it started, and I got a bad feeling about it. We'll talk about it tomorrow at chapel. Need everyone there, as this is serious business, yeah?"

Gretchen bounced with the pulsing, loud music.

Her deafness didn't prevent her from enjoying the music or dancing. She gestured to Janice to come join her.

"Oh, no—it's been so many years, I don't think I can anymore."

Gretchen wrinkled her nose and signed. "If I can, you can," Rail interpreted her words and added to them. "Go live a little, Mama J. You're among friends."

She gave a quick glance back at Boots before swallowing the last of the drink and giving in to Gretchen's insisting hand.

Boots watched the woman as she moved stiffly at first and then opened up like a flower. She smiled and laughed, and Boots swore he heard it from where he stood. She was flushed, but now it was with delight.

Good, he thought. *That woman deserves every happy moment she gets in her life.*

He scanned the crowd periodically, but his gaze always drifted back to the dancing woman. Her movements looked looser and freer, like she didn't care who watched. Happiness was reflected in her face. Boots wondered how long it had been since she had this experience. She didn't seem to be unhappy in her life, but the elation he saw in her now was something he was sure she'd not felt in quite a while. When he watched her with her children, he saw the way she treasured them. When he watched her now, he saw pure joy.

He thought she was beautiful when she held and comforted Ollie on her lap. He didn't have the words to describe her splendor now.

"What the fuck are you doing here!" a voice exploded across the room.

Nutter stood inside the entrance of the bar with a petite brunette woman under his arm. He stared at Janice with a dark scowl on his face as he stormed over to her. The music stopped and the crowd parted to let the big man through. Anger bloomed in Boots's gut. He already knew where this was going.

Janice stopped dancing and stared at her thunderous ex. Boots watched her visibly wilt under Nutter's scrutiny. He frowned deeply as he made his way over to them. His intent was to get between Nutter and Janice. Out of the corner of his eye, he spotted Rail moving in that direction as well.

"I said what the fuck are you doing here?"

"I'm… um… dancing," Janice sputtered.

"You're not supposed to go to bars!"

Janice blinked. "Why not?"

Nutter flung his hands out. "You're a goddamned mother. That's why not!"

Gretchen's face got tight, and she gestured sharply as Rail joined the grouping. He read her signs aloud in a firm voice. "What does that have to do with dancing at a bar?" Rail turned his frosted gray eyes to Nutter. "I'd like to know that answer myself."

"Mothers don't go to bars. They stay home with the kids. They don't go out dancing or—" He pointed to Janice's V-neck blouse. "—show off their tits like that."

Boots reached the group that had drawn the eyes of every bar patron in the place. He deliberately stepped between Nutter and Janice. "I suggest you aim that hand in another direction, brother." His volume was low, but the tone of his voice ate through the tension like acid.

Nutter sneered at him. "Who the fuck do you think you are? That's my goddamned old lady."

Boots stood nearly toe-to-toe with the senior Dutchmen member. "*Was.*" He emphasized the word. "Was your old lady. She's a free woman now and can dance any fucking time she wants."

Nutter blinked, and Boots could smell the alcohol on him. Apparently, the big man had done a considerable amount of pregaming before coming to the bar. *Did he drive that way? Fuck, did he drive that way with the kids in the car? This was supposed to be a night he spent with them, not fucking some random woman he picked up.*

Janice must have wondered the same thing. She sidestepped Boots and asked, "Where are the kids? You were supposed to be with them tonight, which is why I decided to go out and be with people around my age for a change."

Nutter huffed a breath. "They're fine at my mom's house."

"Your mom's? Samuel, this was supposed to be a weekend for *you* to spend with the kids. Not your mother."

He waved her off as if batting away a mosquito. "They're fine at her place."

"She has a two-bedroom bungalow. Where are they sleeping?"

Nutter's face got hard. "I said they're fine."

Janice drew back. "You don't have anywhere to take them, do you? You're living at the clubhouse or spending the night with whatever woman you happen to be with. What happened to your house?"

The big man huffed and rolled his eyes to the ceiling. "None of your business."

"It is when my kids are sleeping piled up on a floor. What's wrong with the house?"

"Nothing's fucking wrong with the goddamn house."

"Then why—"

"Because you're not in it!" the man roared. "I can't stand being there. It's too fucking empty! Too fucking quiet! I miss the fuck out of you and the kids, and it kills me to walk into that place alone. I miss my family. I miss having a home. I miss my woman, and I want her back more than anything in this world."

Boots felt Janice rear back as if she got hit. Rage

built in him as he quelled the desire to punch Nutter in the mouth. If he was so goddamned remorseful, why the fuck did he have another woman on his arm at that moment?

The brunette thought the same thing.

"What the fuck, Nutter?" She raised her nose in the air. "You were screaming how much you loved *me* while I sucked you off in the parking lot a few minutes ago. Everything you said to me was bullshit. I'm outta here!" She huffed off with angry strides.

Nutter wasn't done. He ignored the woman's exit and focused on Janice. His voice softened. "I love you so goddamn much, I can't be in that house without you."

Janice started to shake as she stood next to Boots. His fists doubled, and he fought for control. Incredulity filled him at the man's words, and the rage in his gut boiled. *Yeah, I can see how much you love her,* he wanted to say, but Rail stepped in first.

"We've had enough of this shitshow for tonight. Nutter, go to the clubhouse and sleep it off. Boots, take Mama J home."

Nutter's bleary gaze fixed on his club president. "Rail…."

"I don't care. Get your ass out of here, or I swear, brother or not, I'll have it thrown out." Rail turned to Janice. "I'm sorry, Mama J, but I think it's best you go home. You're always welcome here, but tonight I need you to help me keep the peace. Yeah?"

Janice wiped at her eyes, unaware of the black streaks left on her face. "You bet. I'm so, so sorry."

"Nothing to be sorry about," Boots found enough control to say. "Let's go." He took her hand and led her outside.

Nutter's forlorn cry followed them. "I love you, Mama J!"

Boots heard a fresh whimper come from Janice's throat.

Once they were out in the parking lot, Janice headed to her van. "I can't leave it here. I have stuff I need to do tomorrow."

Boots reached out a hand, wiggling his fingers for the keys. "I'll drive you home and have one of the boys come get me. I don't want you behind the wheel right now, and I only have one helmet."

"That's very sweet, but you don't have—"

"Janice, look at me."

Her watery gaze met his as she fell silent.

"You do trust me, right?"

Janice stayed quiet for a pregnant moment. Then she sniffed and answered in a clear voice. "Yes, Boots. I said I did, and I do."

Her words settled in his gut. "Let me take care of you."

She sniffed again and stiffly nodded.

He took her hand and led her to her van. The engine started and he let it run for a moment, taking in the check-engine light and the rough sound. It needed some serious work, but there wasn't anything he could do about it now except pray it got them to her house.

He didn't try to talk to her during the ride home, but he glanced over several times. She kept her head turned to the window and raised a hand to brush away falling tears, further smearing mascara under her eyes. He wished she would speak, but he understood her need for silence.

The house was quiet, but Opal was home, as indicated by her car parked to the side of the carport. The big light was off, but the covered bulb over the side door was on. Its yellowish glow did very little to pierce the dark, but it was enough.

Boots got out of the van and walked around the back end with the intent of opening the door for Janice, but she'd already exited. He was glad the dark covered his frown.

"Thank you for driving me." She sounded tired and dull. "It's been an… interesting night."

"That's one way of putting it." He opened the screen door and inserted the key in the doorknob. "You should have a deadbolt on this too."

She gave a little laugh. "We don't have anything a serious thief would want."

"Anything precious needs to be kept safe. There's a lot of precious in this house." His thoughts churned. Anger still flowed inside him, but it was tempered with desire and a touch of desperation. He turned to face Janice. He brought his hand up and placed two fingers under her chin to raise her face to his. "It's been a fucked-up night. I get that your head is full of Nutter's shit. You got a lot on your plate, and I'm adding more, but I need to do this. I'm staking my claim."

He lowered his head and took her mouth.

He meant for the kiss to be light, but the moment he touched her, he couldn't stop. He drew her in, sucking her lower lip into his mouth and stroking his tongue over its fullness. His hand slid from her chin to her neck, and he tilted her head so he could deepen the kiss further. To his surprise and satisfaction, she opened to him. Her tense muscles relaxed under his fingers, and her tongue tentatively touched his. He kissed her over and over again, pouring everything he had into it. Admiration, desire, care, need—he projected all of it as he gently and thoroughly plundered her mouth. His groin tightened, and he wanted to grind himself against her, but he held back. She'd already been devastated by the night's events, and the last thing he wanted to do was overwhelm her to the point of scaring her off.

The low rumble of a motorcycle reached his ears, and he lifted his head, ending the kiss. Her erratic breath pleased him as it puffed against his lips. "Consider being with me before you think about going back to him."

The dim light couldn't hide the sparkle of tears in her eyes. "I don't know what's happening."

"I get that, sweetheart, and I'm sorry you're dealing with all this shit at once."

"M-my children are probably sleeping on a floor right now."

He moved back a little but didn't release her from his arms. "Are they safe?"

She blinked. "Yes, they're at their grandmother's."

"Did they eat tonight?"

Her nod was stiff. "I'm sure someone made them supper or at least ordered pizza."

"They're coming home tomorrow afternoon?"

Another nod. "Nutter's mom makes them go to mass with her in the morning, but they should be here after lunch."

"They're safe, they're fed, and they'll be home tomorrow. That tells me they are fine. If you're worried and you want to go get them now, I'll take you, but I know you get very little time to yourself. It's not a bad thing for you to have a little space now, and no one walking in your shoes would blame you if you took a night off. It's up to you, but I think you should take it. What do you want to do, baby?"

He felt her shaking, her need to let out everything inside in a long crying release. His heart ached for her and the temptation of what he could do to make her feel better. "Do you want me to stay with you tonight?"

The question was loaded. There was no doubt she knew what he'd want to do if he walked into her house. The real query was, did she want the same?

She swallowed. "Ollie and August like to go 'pretend' camping. I bet they are having a good time and made it into a game."

He took her cue. "They ever go real camping? Tent, campfire, s'mores, and all that shit?"

She shook her head. "Nutter said he'd take them sometime, but it hasn't happened yet."

"This goes like I want, we'll take them on a trip next summer."

Her gaze was sharp. "I'm…. I don't know what to say to that."

He wished he could say what he was really thinking. About how much he wanted to take her inside the house, strip those jeans from her hips, and show her how she should be treated. He imagined if he went down on her, she'd come on his tongue within seconds. Then he'd take her again and again until the memory of Nutter's attentions was erased.

"You don't have to say anything. Go inside. Relax as much as you can. Read a book, take a bath—whatever you want."

He kept his dark gaze on hers and tipped up her chin so her eyes met his. "Every fucking fiber of my being wants to walk into this house and make you mine in every way possible. The hair, makeup, clothes—all of that was for me, wasn't it?"

She trembled under his fingers. "Yes."

"Don't ever doubt for a second that I want you. If tonight had gone differently, you'd be in my bed right now, and I'd be making us both very happy. The only reason I'm not is because the timing sucks. I'm afraid you're in the wrong headspace to share any kind of intimacy with me, and I'm not going there until you're ready for that."

She stared up at him silently. Her eye makeup was slightly smeared at the corners. "I'm so sorry." Her broken whisper cracked his heart.

"Baby, you have to hear me now. You've got nothing, not a goddamn thing, to be sorry for. If anyone should be sorry, it's Nutter, the club, me, and whoever else has let you down. You're the strongest person I know. Not many women would take on another's children to love and support and comfort. The night I saw you rocking little Ollie back to sleep, you took my breath away." He brushed his fingers lightly over her cheek. "You deserve all the good this world can give you, and I'm praying like hell I get to be a part of it."

He kissed her softly once more, and her lips quivered under his. A scratching sound came from the door followed by a high-pitched doggy whine.

"Go now, baby."

Her movements were stiff as she entered the

house with the puppy dancing around her feet. Before she closed the door, she turned to him. Her face was full of uncertainty, but her voice was sure. "Thank you, Boots."

He placed a hand flat on the cool wood as his body and his head wrestled over control. The need to make this woman his in every sense pulsed through his veins, and it took every ounce of his iron will to keep from raising his fists to pound on the door for admittance. He forced himself to turn away.

"Heard about what happened at the Harbor." Flipper sat on his growling bike and handed Boots the helmet he brought with him. "How's Mama J?"

Boots cursed as he stiffly mounted behind the younger man. The bike was a Road Glide with an extra seat that wasn't built for men of his size. His riding position and weight would be awkward handling for Flipper, but they weren't going too far. "She's fine for now. Let's get the fuck out of here."

Thankfully the talkative man didn't ask any more questions as he put the Harley into gear and pulled away. Boots was fine with only the road sounding under the bike's tires, and he silenced the thoughts in his head.

CHAPTER
TWENTY-TWO

THE ROLLING PIN MADE ITS THUMPING NOISE AS JANICE shaped a mass of dough into a rectangle. Her motions were on autopilot as her mind went somewhere else.

He kissed me. Every time she thought about Boots, a thrill hit her belly and she recalled that kiss. He was on her mind constantly. His taste, his words, his... everything.

A sound came from her throat that was more of a whimper as she picked up the bowl of filling and began spreading it over the thinned dough. The sweet scent of cinnamon, brown sugar, nutmeg, crushed walnuts, and cherries filled the kitchen.

He kissed me. Me! What could he possibly want with someone like me?

She began rolling the rectangle, taking care not to

tear a hole in it as she turned the oblong shape into a log.

Sunday night, he texted her.

Boots: Kids get home all right?

Janice: Yes, they are good.

Boots: Good. Been thinking about you. I'm gonna come get the van for a tune-up. You want to pay me? Make me one of those breakfast rings.

She pinched the seam closed and bent the log into a ring, pinching again to seal it. Nutter had brought the kids home from his mother's and hung around instead of taking off like he usually did. He played Candyland with the younger kids and teased Tad until the boy joined them. Nutter even held baby Pearl while Janice made a shepherd's pie for dinner. His boyish grin still charmed as he blew bubbles and entertained the tiny girl.

"I miss this part the most," he'd said with a big smile. "Always loved rocking my babies."

Janice's heart tripped. Yes, he did love that part. The rocking, the bathing, the cooing and playing. He'd made trips to the pharmacy to get children's Tylenol when they were sick and spent time at the toy store buying dolls, hockey sticks, and skates. Did that make him a good father though? He regularly missed birthdays, school plays, and other activities.

Tad had noticed, and his attitude toward his father had worsened quite a bit.

Janice was sure it was finding out that Boots had been at the boys' game that prompted Nutter's extended visit yesterday. If he knew about the kiss….

She used her knife to make uniform slashes in the ring and slid the baking sheet into the upper oven. The dishwasher beeped to signal the end of the cycle. She was forever grateful for the gift. It cut cleaning time in half and allowed her to end her workday sooner. This morning she dropped the kids off at school and made her deliveries. Her van had purred the entire time, and that pesky check-engine light was gone.

Janice dusted off her hands and lowered the washer door that released a big cloud of steam just when the front doorbell rang. Puzzled, she hurried to open it, thinking it was someone going door-to-door selling something. Most visitors knew to come in the carport door.

A deputy stood on her small front porch. "Good afternoon, ma'am. I'm here about some noise complaints in the neighborhood and some vandalism reports." His smile had the same appeal as a velociraptor's.

"Oh, I've not heard any noise from anyone around here, but it's good you came by. My friend had her tires damaged—"

The deputy interrupted her with a sardonic laugh.

"You misunderstood me, ma'am. The complaint is about you, your house, and your kids. Raising little delinquents, I suppose."

Janice reared back in confusion. "Noise? The kids are in school during the day, and the last one goes to bed at nine every night. There's no noise coming from my house at all hours."

He made a clicking sound with his tongue and assumed a patronizing tone. "Well now, that's not what I've been informed, ma'am. I'm afraid I'll have to issue a citation. First offense is five hundred dollars."

Janice blinked at him. "Five hundred dollars! I don't even have an extra fifty dollars!" She shook her head in disbelief. "No, no, there has to be a mistake."

"No mistake. You can pay up now or at the courthouse." He gave her a smarmy grin. "I tell you what. I'll reduce the charges and tear up the ticket if you pay me half in cash right now. Two-fifty buys you out of this ticket."

Janice thought for a panicked moment. "I might have a hundred in my cashbox for change when I go to the festivals, but I don't think I can come up with two-fifty."

The deputy frowned. "I'm giving you a good deal here."

Janice grew more flustered. "I know, officer, but I just don't have extra money."

The man huffed and his face flushed red. "Give

me what you've got, and I'll come back another time for the rest." He shook a finger in her face. "You fucking better have it, or I'll double the charge."

A child's high-pitched voice came from behind her. "Mommy? Why is a policeman here?"

Janice turned to see Ollie standing in the door between the living room and the kitchen. He had his favorite blanket in his hand and only one sock on. The oddly named Zeus sat on her haunches beside the child with her head cocked to the side. "He's just checking on us, sweetheart. Go find your other sock and put it on your foot, yeah?"

The boy looked down. "I have on a sock."

"Yes, you do, and it's a nice sock, but you have two feet, don'tcha know."

Ollie grinned and scampered off.

"The money?" the deputy growled.

Janice got her cashbox from the top of the refrigerator and opened it. Without counting, she placed all the money in the man's greedy hands.

He tipped his hat and gave her a shit-eating grin. "Nice doing business with you. Keep the noise down, or else I'll have to come back more often."

Janice held back the tears and nodded at the younger man. Her gaze darted to the man's lapel, and his name burned into her memory. Lewis Canter.

———

Janice was still shaken up by the encounter with Lewis and had trouble concentrating the rest of the afternoon. The money bothered her, but even more so the noise complaint. The neighborhood was a bit rundown, and a lot of older folks lived there, but no one had said squat to her about her kids being unruly or too loud when they played outside. In fact, Gertrude said she loved watching them from her back window. Gertrude was pushing eighty-something and rarely had any family come visit her. Sometimes, they shared a coffee in the morning as Janice set up her kitchen from breakfast mode to baking mode.

Janice had gone over to see Gertie after the incident to ask about the noise complaint. The old woman had blinked and demurred it wasn't her that called. Nor did she know anyone else around their area who might have had a problem.

It was still on her mind when she picked up the kids and brought them home. A Crock-Pot of stroganoff bubbled on the counter, and the dining table was covered in homework and dinner dishes when she heard the familiar rumbling in her driveway. The sound sent sparks through her middle. Was this the noise complaint? Boots's motorcycle?

She fisted her hands at her sides as she opened the carport door and stepped outside. The engine was loud, but no louder than the truck Bob down the street owned.

Boots parked his bike and turned off the purring motor. He lifted a bunch of her containers from the saddlebags and walked up to her, but the smile on his face disappeared as he took in her expression. "What's wrong?"

Janice didn't speak. She simply moved forward into his arms. Boots dropped the containers and wrapped his strength around her. The night air had a bite to it, and his body gave off heat that warmed her. *Uff-da*, what she wouldn't give to have this every night.

"Baby, what happened? Kids okay?"

"Kids are fine. Just had a bad day."

He held her for a few minutes, and she greedily absorbed all she could from him for that brief time. She stepped back after letting him go and pulled herself together. "Thanks for bringing these back to me. It helps a lot."

"No problem. Now tell me what's wrong."

"Nothing for you to worry about. I'm fine."

His face grew hard. "You don't look fine."

She wanted to tell him about the deputy's visit. She really did, but she was afraid he would do something about it. This relationship with Boots was too new, and she had no intention of starting trouble for him or the club. His intense eyes patiently waited for her answer.

She tried to play it off again. "Just a bad day. That's all."

From his skeptical frown, she could tell he didn't buy her story. "You do know you can talk to me, right? If you have any concerns or fears, please don't hesitate to tell me. I can't fix anything if I don't know what the problem is." His eyes darkened and his thick brows came together. "Has someone bothered you, Janice?"

The ominous tone of his voice revamped the fears in her belly. Not for herself though. She had no doubt Boots would never hurt her. No, her fears were for him. If he did something to retaliate against the wayward deputy, what would happen to him if he got caught? She was fully aware he had a record, although she didn't know the extent of it, only that he was currently on probation. If he went back to prison, would she stand by him?

Yes. Yes, she would. If she truly acknowledged her feelings toward this powerful man, they were that she loved him. It was not in her nature to abandon those she loved, and Boots would not be the exception. She took a breath and smiled at his tight face. "I'm fine, Boots. It was just a bad day. They happen from time to time, don'tcha know."

He might have pressed her further, but Opal chose that moment to come home. Her car's headlights flashed as she pulled into her spot. Walgreens shirt was wrinkled as she tiredly got out and came around the parked van. "Starting to rain a bit. I didn't see snow yet. Whose bike is—" Whatever she had to say next was stopped as her eyes took in the tall biker. "Oh. I'm… um… sorry for interrupting."

"No problem. I was just leaving," Boots said to the nervous woman. "I have to work at the bar tonight. Rail is taking Gretchen to some concert up in the cities, and he needed some extra hands to keep order. He's doing a great job leading the club, but he also needs to take care of his old lady."

Janice's heart softened. It was good of him to give Rail and Gretchen time to be a couple. Janice understood that need completely.

Boots turned and directly addressed Opal. "Camo is my brother, and he told me you've been having a hard time. He hasn't shared any details, but I want you to know, I'm proud of you. Being a working mom isn't easy, and I think you're doing a great job."

If she melted any further, she'd be a puddle of liquid on the concrete floor. *I don't care if he's been to prison. He is a good man.* "Be careful. The roads might be getting slippery."

His eyes came back to her, and his mouth cocked into a half smile that sent her heart pounding in another direction. "I'm always careful, sweetheart, but I just found the place I want to be, and I'm not giving it up without a fight."

He left with a nod to both ladies and strode to his bike. Janice watched a moment as he started it and pulled away.

Janice took in Opal's drawn face under the pale yellow outside light and frowned. "Are you okay?"

The young woman shook herself to wake up. "Yeah, I'm good. Rough night."

As they entered the house, the kids had finished their homework and begged for some TV. Janice waved her hands and gave them orders. "Plates in the sink. Homework in your backpacks, then one show before bathtime."

The table got cleared and the backpacks loaded before the kids started arguing about what to watch. Tad waded into the fray and herded his siblings into the living room. Pearl was in her bouncy seat on the floor, and Opal bent to pick her up for a cuddle.

Janice relaxed and let her oldest boy handle things. Her shoulders drooped a bit when she could finally let the tension out of them. "*Uff-da*. Bad day here too. I have to adjust the budget for an unexpected bill."

"A new bill? What kind of new bill?"

Janice hesitated, but since Opal contributed to the household economics, she had to tell her about the incident. "I'll explain, but you have to keep it between us. I don't want the kids or Dutchmen to know about it. If they did, I'm afraid they'd do something that could make things worse or get someone hurt."

Opal opened a cabinet with one hand and took out a plastic tumbler with a faded My Little Pony character on the side. She filled it with water from the tap and leaned against the counter. Pearl cooed and tried to grab the cup. "What happened?"

Janice sighed and squared her shoulders. "I had a visit today from Deputy Canter. He claimed there was a noise complaint in the neighborhood and that I had to pay a five-hundred-dollar citation. I checked with Gertie, and she said she didn't know about any complaints. I had kids in the house and didn't know what else to do but give him what money I had."

Opal stopped drinking as she coughed and choked. "He… he… was here?"

"Yes. He said he'd take two-hundred-fifty in cash to rip up the ticket, but I only had maybe a hundred in my cashbox. He got mad about it, but he took what I had and said he'd be back for the rest. I don't know where I'm going to get an extra one-fifty to give him when he comes back. You know how tight our money is these days."

Opal's face had drained of all color, and a fine tremor made the water in the cup slosh around. She clutched Pearl to her, and the baby let out a cry of irritation. Janice's concern changed from where she would find the money to Opal's reaction. "Uff-da, Opal, you should sit down before you fall. If it's the money, don't worry. I'll just have to make some extra rings this week. Are you sure you're okay?"

Opal poured the rest of the water out and placed the cup next to the pile of plates. "I'm… I'm… good.

I'll see what I can save from my next paycheck to help. Maybe he won't be back?"

"Mama! Ollie and August are fighting!"

Janice straightened her back. "We'll deal with it, if it happens. The baby ate well earlier, but if you want to give her a bottle, there are some made up in the fridge. Go take some time to be with her while she's little and cute."

She walked into the living room to break up the fracas, and all other thoughts or worries were put on hold.

CHAPTER
TWENTY-THREE

The transformation of Mama J into Janice had changed something in Opal. She'd seen firsthand what a new haircut and a little makeup had done for her friend. The happiness and confidence boost in the older woman gave Opal a satisfaction she'd never had before. Her skills brought joy to someone else's life, and she found a fulfilling pride that she had a hand in it.

Camo had remarked on it when he came to pick up Opal and Pearl for a day at the mall. "Mama J looks fantastic. I'm proud of you, baby. You really made a difference."

The outing was a new experience for Opal. Never before had she been out in public with a baby stroller and a man at her side. Sure, she spotted a number of covert glances from people, but she didn't spot any sneers. It didn't seem like people were looking at

Peebles the club whore. If anything it was Camo in his club colors that attracted the most attention. A few of the women might even have showed envy of Opal and her position.

Many stores had already started the Christmas season with decorations and early sales.

"I love the holidays, but I hate seeing Christmas come before Thanksgiving. Let the turkeys have their day before putting up lights and reindeer cutouts," Camo mentioned as they passed a sparkling tree.

"I feel the same way." Opal smiled as Camo pushed the stroller so Pearl could get a closer look.

The baby gurgled and giggled her way through the stores, charming the sales staff everywhere they went. Camo bought them dinner and a stuffed toy for her, but otherwise they simply strolled and talked. Opal found herself opening up to Camo in a way she'd never done before. He was considerate and thoughtful to her and Pearl all evening. He listened to her and actually allowed her to finish her sentences before answering or asking a question of his own. That was a real change for her, as most of the men she'd known only gave her token attention before pushing her back on the bed or opening their pants for a blow job.

The car seat was a tight fit in his truck, but he didn't complain as he drove them to his place. His house sat in one of the older neighborhoods close to downtown Red Wing. It was an area in transition.

Some of the homes were remodeled and upgraded already, and by the looks of them, more were in the process.

"I've taken out the old fuse box and rewired the whole place," Camo pointed out as he opened the front door for her to enter. "Boots helped me a lot since he knows more about it than I do. Put in a new heat pump too. I tore out the old carpet and put down hardwood with a matte finish. I like it better than shiny."

Opal took in the house and its new coat of paint. "It's really beautiful."

She meant it too.

He showed her the rest of the house and described his vision for the final renovations. His plans for the three bedrooms, installing a second bathroom, taking out the cracked linoleum in the kitchen and replacing with tile—he'd spoken about all of it with ambitious reverence, as if he couldn't wait for it to happen.

She loved it all.

Three bedrooms, two on one side and one on the other, lay at the top of the steps. The biggest one was obviously his, and he'd thoughtfully outfitted one of the smaller ones for a baby. A crib was scooted against the wall, and an antique four-poster bed sat in the middle. He carefully laid a sleeping Pearl on the pink-and-yellow sheets. The baby sighed and curled up in the new spot, wrapped in her favorite blanket and worn out from her busy day.

"I borrowed the crib from my sister, and the bed came from my mom's house. It's old but still sturdy."

They settled on the couch with drinks, and Camo clicked on Netflix. He leaned back into the plush cushions of one corner and pulled Opal close to his side. She rested against him as if she belonged there, laying across his chest, and hearing his heartbeat under her ear. A sense of contentment grew in her belly as Camo's hand stroked up and down her shoulder and arm. *Is this what it means to be loved?* she wondered as she drifted until the movie credits rolled in front of her sleepy eyes. The day had been the best one of her life.

Camo shifted under her, dispelling her musings and returning her to the here and now.

"You still with me, baby?" his voice rumbled under her ear.

"Yes, I'm here. Don't wanna move though."

His laugh was low and hit her right in her belly. "I don't want you to move, either, but we can't stay here all night. The room we put Pearl in is made up for you too. Come on, let's go."

He leaned forward to stand up, forcing her to get up too. He took her hand and held it to his back as he led them up the narrow stairs. "I'm sure you'll be comfortable in here. I'll be across the hall if you need anything."

Opal bit her lip as disappointment flared inside her. "I thought we'd be sleeping together."

Camo took both her hands, his thumbs stroking over the backs. "Please don't take this wrong, 'cause I'm really trying hard to do this right. I don't want you to feel obligated to me in any way. Dinner, shopping, the car—anything I do for you and Pearl is just that. For you and Pearl. Not some gimmick to get you to sleep with me as payment or something. I want you to feel safe with me, always. Tonight, you have your own place and I have mine. When we get to the point where we're both ready, you'll be in my bed, and I'll make sure you never regret being there."

Opal's eyes stung. "You've been so good to me. Better than anyone I've ever been with. I… I… I don't know how to handle it sometimes. I keep expecting something to go bad or like I'm gonna wake up and find out it's all a dream."

Camo lifted her hands to his mouth, whispering, "You'll get there, sweetheart. I'm a stubborn man and a determined one, but I'm also patient. I'm here to stay."

He leaned in and took her mouth in the tenderest of kisses. His lips lightly danced over hers, trailing sparks along her spine. She moved in to get closer, and he deepened the kiss, slanting his head to take her more fully.

Opal fell into herself as his tongue came out to trace the seam of her mouth. Her middle clutched as unfamiliar sensations flared. Desire. A true desire bloomed inside her. One that had never really happened before despite all the men she'd been with.

His body was solid against hers. Unyielding but supporting, with a gentleness that made her heart ache with wanting things she never thought she'd have. Her mother's gravelly words echoed in her head.

"You want a man? You gotta learn to suck cock really good. That's the only way to get one an' keep him."

Camo blew that lesson apart. He'd given her so much already and offered more. It was almost too good to be true, but the physical evidence was in front of her. He was here, and he wasn't moving.

She could feel his arousal against her stomach, and she ached to touch him. It actually hurt. Maybe it was real. It felt real, didn't it? Maybe this was her chance at a long life of happiness with a man that loved her.

Opal imagined herself standing at the precipice of a canyon. She'd seen pictures of the big one in Arizona and hoped one day she'd get to go see it. She took a breath and stepped over the edge. "Camo, I don't want to wait. I'm ready now."

His hazel eyes gazed deeply into hers as if weighing her words. "Baby, if I make love to you tonight, this is it. There's no going back. I'll be claiming you as my old lady and you'll meet my family over the holidays. If this goes where I want it, you'll be wearing a rock by the spring and a band by the summer. Are you sure?"

"I'm surer of this than I am of the sun rising tomorrow morning. Please don't make me wait longer."

He watched her a moment longer before leading her away from Pearl's room to his own. The wood floor creaked a bit, but the baby stayed asleep.

Camo's bed was a full queen with plain navy sheets and thick matching comforter. The folding doors of his closet were open, showing some work clothes hanging, plus a bulging plastic garment cover that Opal guessed contained his old military uniforms. The dresser held a few knick-knacks on one side and a pile of socks on the other. The room was somewhat messy, but it didn't give the aura of being dirty.

"If you change your mind, it's okay. It won't make a difference to how I feel about you." Camo's arms circled her from behind, and he placed a gentle kiss on her neck.

Her answer was simply to turn and kiss him.

That's all he needed. He carefully undressed her, stopping her hands when she tried to do it. "No, baby. I want to unwrap this gift all by myself." He kissed each part of her that appeared. Her nipples tightened into points as he stroked them with his thumbs. When he lifted one to his mouth, she let out a breathy mew. Never had she been touched with loving hands, and she was quickly learning the difference. He knelt in front of her to unfasten her jeans and pull them to her ankles. She balanced herself with her hands on his shoulders as he drew one foot free and then the other. She was sure her panties were damp, and if they weren't, his mouth would make them that way. His hot breath reached her through the thin cloth as he pressed kisses to her mound. His hands came to her hips, and he peeled the fabric down her thighs.

Anticipation coursed through her as he parted her sex. Her mouth opened, and she inhaled sharply at the warmth of his tongue on her swollen clit. A smoldering heat radiated out from her sex as he stroked over her with gentle precision. His explorations were unhurried and thorough, stoking the fire into a blaze. When he drew her tender bud into his mouth, it was an act of worship, not a means to an end.

Opal felt her knees grow weaker with every pull of Camo's incredible mouth. Orgasm was just on the horizon, and it would be her first in some ways. The first she'd not given to herself. The first she hadn't faked because it was expected. The first that happened with genuine feeling. She wasn't ready to call it love. Yet.

Her channel pulsed and flooded as she tipped over the edge. Her cry of satisfaction startled her, as she hadn't planned it. She leaned heavily on Camo's shoulders, her fingers digging into his flesh, and he kept his mouth on her, drawing out her satisfaction until she almost collapsed.

Her eyes grew wet when he scooped her up and laid her on the bed. His shirt barely made a sound when he reached behind his neck and pulled it off. The short hair on his head mussed a little, and he smoothed it back with both hands. He opened the nightstand drawer, and she heard the familiar crinkle of a condom packet.

Opal spotted several scars on his wide chest: a long thin line across his ribs, a puckered one near his shoulder, a jagged V on his hip. She remembered he had been overseas during his army days and in more than one combat situation. This was a man who put his life on the line to protect his fellow soldiers. He'd come back to the States an unsung hero and had to fight his way through addiction. Now, he helped others fight theirs, including her. He became part of an MC brotherhood, and she knew for a fact that he would go to the mat for any of his brothers. His mother and sister could count on him to be in their corner anytime they needed him.

And he was here for her, making those same promises.

Opal's eyes widened as Camo moved over her. The concentration in his face sent her heart pounding hard enough that she was sure he could hear its rhythm. Doubts assailed her, and she placed her hands on his shoulders, half pulling him to her and half holding him away.

"You okay, baby?" he asked in a husky voice. He rested his weight on his elbows and forearms as he hovered close.

"Yeah, it's… I… I haven't been with anyone in a long time."

"Since Rebel."

He made this as a statement, but she confirmed it like it had been a question. "Yes."

He shifted his hands to frame her face. "Baby, if this is not what you want, I can stop. Just tell me."

"I want you, Camo. I'm…."

"Talk to me, sweetheart." His tone was low and gentle as he lowered his head to kiss her lightly.

"… I…."

"Talk to me." He kissed her again.

"Um… I… do… um…."

"Opal, talk to me."

It might have been the use of her name or the easy directness of his words. Opal had no doubt he would stop if she asked him to, but she was scared that if she did, he would get off her and leave. She couldn't bear that.

"Eyes, baby. Look at me." He stroked a thumb over her cheek. "Do not do this because you think I expect it or that this is something you have to do for me as payback. Trust me, Opal, I have no expectations but to make you feel good and make me feel good in the process. You need to be all in, baby, otherwise I'm just getting my rocks off and using you to do it, and that's not acceptable to me at all."

Tears shimmered in her eyes, and she could feel them building. Her legs were spread under him, his hardness resting against her still-pulsing clit. She was in her most vulnerable position, both physically and emotionally. "I want this with you, Camo, I promise. I'm just… I'm really scared."

"Of what, baby?"

"That you'll figure out I'm not good enough for you." Her words came out whisper light. "That you'll leave me."

He lifted his head and set his beautiful eyes on hers. "Opal, I've been waiting and wanting you for a long time, even before you were with Rebel. Watched you with other men, and couldn't stand it. If I approached you then, I'd have just been another man in your bed, but now I've got you in *my* bed, in *my* arms. Something I never thought would happen, so no way am I going anywhere."

He shifted himself, and Opal gasped as his penis slid heavily down over her clit to rest at her entrance.

"Again, baby, you need to be all in, 'cause I promise you I am."

Her breath hitched, and she opened herself. "All in, Camo."

His hips moved forward, and the broad head of his penis pressed at her softness, smoothly penetrating and filling her slick channel. What he lacked in length he made up for in width, and she gasped at the tight fit.

When he was fully seated, he directed her gaze to his. "You good?" His breathing was heavy and his muscles hard with tension under her fingers.

"Yes, I'm… oh!"

He pulled one of her knees up and out. His hard dick slid out and surged back in at a different angle. It stroked something inside her that felt good. Real good. She gasped and clutched at his shoulders, digging her fingers in hard. He gave a little smirk at her reaction.

"Bingo, baby, but you get the prize."

He stroked that same spot again. And again. And again.

Opal tried to control her breathing, but he was pulling sensations from her she hadn't known she was capable of feeling. She found herself moving with him and wanted to move faster, but he kept the pace maddeningly slow.

Her past experience was vast in some regards, but it had taught her very little. Her virginity had been lost in the back of a car when she was sixteen to the rough thrusts of a boyfriend that told her if she loved him, she'd give it up to him. He dumped her shortly afterward, telling her she was boring and didn't know what she was doing. Opal decided the key to keeping a man was more than just good blow jobs.

She had to please them, focus on their pleasure, and give them what they wanted, whatever it was. She would scream and shudder as if in the throes of great passion, and they loved it. But they never stuck around. Rebel was the only man so far to stake a claim on her. His favorite was fucking her hard and fast from behind. He got off more when he'd bent her over in public. She had felt more like a receptacle than his old lady, but if that's what it took to keep him happy, she did it.

Camo shattered every preconceived idea she had. He kissed her over and over as he moved inside her, drawing more from her with every stroke. She strained against him, not quite knowing what she was looking for. Her middle was coiling tighter and tighter, and her fingers dug into his skin for the second time.

"Camo!" she gasped. "I'm... I...."

His eyes were dark as he held her gaze. "Yeah, baby, that's it. I got you, sweetheart. Let it go. Let it happen."

The dam in her belly suddenly broke free, and pleasure she'd never known before rushed through her body. It was overwhelming, and she couldn't stop her eyes closing or the cry that came from her throat. Wave after wave washed over her, erasing any control she thought she should have. Camo buried his face in her neck and let out his own shout of completion as he pushed as deep as he could inside her, his hard flesh pulsing as he filled the condom.

For a few minutes, all she could hear was the sound of their lungs gulping for air. Camo had given her most of his weight, and his breath sawed past her ear. His somewhat softened cock still nestled firmly in her body, and the musky scent of sex wafted over them.

Gradually, his breathing slowed. "You okay, baby?"

She took a shaky breath. "Yeah, I'm okay."

She felt him smile against her neck before he raised his head and kissed her. "That was beautiful, sweetness."

She burst into tears and turned her head away from him. He slid out of her, and she rolled into a ball.

"Opal, baby, what's wrong? Did I hurt you?"

"No… I…. It's not you…. I…."

He gathered her into his arms, fitting his front to her back. She didn't fight him. She just kept crying. "I'm sorry, Camo…. I'm…."

"Honey, it's okay. I got you. It's okay."

He repeated the words over and over until her deluge of tears subsided. His patience was astounding. Opal was sure any other man would have gotten fed up with her outburst and left in disgust.

Camo stayed and kept holding her and trailing his fingers over the skin of her arm. He kissed her neck before his lips settled near her ear. "A moment ago, I was feeling really good. I came hard in my woman after she came hard. I didn't expect to make you cry. If this is going to work, we need to communicate. What happened, baby? What did I do wrong?"

She shook her head. "You didn't do anything wrong. It was beautiful. So beautiful. I've never had that before."

She felt Camo jolt in surprise. "Are you telling me you've never come before?"

She sniffed at the need to explain. "I've had orgasms, but not with a man inside me. I've just… well… done my own."

He parroted her words. "You've never orgasmed with a man inside you."

She sniffed. "I know that sounds crazy, but it's true. I'm a pretty good faker, or at least no one said they could tell."

"You're kidding me."

"No, Camo, I'm not."

"Oh, sweetheart," he started as he dragged her around to face him. "Seriously?"

She tried to pull away again, but he wouldn't let her. A shard of pain pierced her heart, and she wanted to cry again. "Don't make fun of me."

"No, baby, that's not it. I'm not making fun of you. I'm just surprised no one has ever given that to you before. I have to say, I'm sorry for that, but pleased as hell I got to be the first. I don't know what those other assholes did for you, but for me, there's nothing better than feeling my woman come around my dick when I'm buried deep inside her and knowing I made that happen."

Something let go in Opal's chest. She hadn't realized the constriction until she breathed deeply and freely. Emotions flooded her senses and made her dizzy. The strange new feeling that budded inside her had to be love. She recognized it from the way she felt when her tiny baby girl was placed in her arms. This man held her the same way with tenderness and utter devotion. Whatever fears she had dissipated, leaving behind a certainty that she was where she belonged. "I'm really your woman?"

He nipped at her earlobe. "Yeah, honey, you are. I'll keep using condoms if you want, but if you have ideas on other birth control, I'd really like to go ungloved. I already told you, I don't like sharing, and that includes myself. If you're my woman, I'm your man. I don't want anything between us when I make you come again."

She wiggled against him. "Do you think you can do it twice in one night?"

He laughed out loud and rolled her onto her back. "Let's find out."

CHAPTER
TWENTY-FOUR

Janice pulled into the gas station and let out a sigh over the fact that she'd made it before the gauge collapsed below the E. She'd pushed the limits hard this time and was afraid she'd gone too far. She dropped the kids at school and made her deliveries. She'd made an extra stop today, as the library was hosting a children's story time and fun day that included lunch and play time. Ollie and Augustus would have four hours of entertainment that didn't include smashing Play-Doh into the shag carpet or breaking crayons into smaller and smaller pieces. Flipper usually greeted her at the Harbor restaurant, but today, only the cook and kitchen personnel were around. She finally noticed the gas gauge on her way back across the bridge and swore softly at it. *"Worst decision I've ever made to wait and fuel up first thing in the morning,"* she muttered as she remembered her forgotten bedtime vow.

Cort's Quickstop sat just over the bridge into the town. The older man was friendly and sometimes gave the kids candy when she had them with her. Today, everyone was in school or at the library, and Opal and Pearl had stayed over at Camo's last night. Janice wanted to get back home as fast as possible so she could get some housework done that she usually couldn't do when little bodies occupied every space. The library offered half-day care today in addition to the story time, and she planned to take advantage of the four completely free hours.

She pulled the hose out, swiped her card, and anchored the nozzle in the gas opening. The digital numbers flew by as she waited. A hot burn crept over the back of her neck, some premonition that something was wrong. She took in the numbers as they danced around. The reflection on the screen of two people exiting the store caught her eye, but she couldn't see much more than that. They walked around the side of the store, and a moment later, Janice heard an engine rev. The pump clicked off, and she replaced the nozzle in the holder as the machine spat out a thin receipt.

Janice pulled the perforated paper free and stuffed it into her wallet. The uneasiness increased as she opened her van. She didn't need anything in the store and had already paid for her gas, but something drew her to the glass doors of the small building. Her heart sped up as she approached and reached out her hand to grasp the handle. The front door had a cartoon paper turkey in a pilgrim hat wishing everyone a Happy Thanksgiving taped to the glass. Janice took minimal note of the decoration as she pulled the door back. The store bell tinkled, merrily announcing her entry. It felt surreal. She had no reason to be in that store at that time, other than some weird compelling sensation that she needed to go inside. Fear had her heart clutching, and she wanted to turn around and run back to her van. Instead, she stepped over the threshold.

The place was ransacked. Shelves had been dumped on the floor, bags of chips and snacks stomped on and torn apart. The coffee pots had been smashed, and brown liquid dripped from the counters to join the spreading puddle below. The glass in several cooler doors showed exploding spiderweb cracks from where they'd been hit. Everywhere she looked, something had been broken or ruined.

"Uff-da," she breathed, taking in the random destruction. "Cort? Are you here?"

A moan came from the back of the store. She stepped over the piles of garbage and spotted a body curled up on its side.

"Cort! Oh my God!"

The man moaned again. His face was bloodied,

and one eye was swollen shut. He held his middle with pained care.

Janice squatted down next to him and placed a hand on his shoulder. "Hold on, Cort." She wasn't sure that Cort had heard her as she pulled out her phone.

"Nine-one-one. What is your emergency?" a female voice articulated.

"I'm at the McGlaren Quickstop on Main St. Someone beat up Cort McGlaren, and it's bad. Can you send an ambulance?"

"Police and rescue are on the way."

Janice answered the other questions the operator asked as she mentally rearranged her day. The Quickstop had been around for decades. She couldn't remember a time when Cort hadn't been behind the glass counter. His wife, Agnes, helped run the store, along with two of their teenage grandsons. They were a kind and generous family, pillars of the community. Who would do such a thing?

Railroad. She needed to call Railroad and let him know what happened. Cort had been a friend to the Dutchmen MC when most people shied away from the club.

Janice scrolled to Rail's name and hit dial.

"What's wrong?"

No greeting of *hi* or *how are you?* from the President of the MC. Janice supposed it was warranted, as she never called Rail unless something bad happened. "Cort McGlaren's store has been robbed and vandalized. Whoever did it beat him up."

"Fuck! Are you in the store now?"

"Yes. I'm here with Cort. The police and ambulance are on the way."

"Goddamn it, get out of there! Whoever did that might come back!"

Janice bristled. "I'm not leaving Cort lying on the floor in his own blood." Sirens sounded in the distance. "They're almost here."

"I'm on my way." Rail disconnected before Janice could respond again.

Minutes later, two deputies showed up with the paramedics right behind them. They went to work on the old man immediately while one of the deputies took her to the side.

"I'm Officer Milton Tarnaski. Can you tell me what happened here?"

Janice described her encounter with Cort as well as the two people that ran off. "I didn't hear them or see anything specific, like what they were wearing or even if they were men or women." She couldn't get enough air in her lungs, and she gasped for breath. Her body flashed with heat, and her heart pounded hard, threatening to tear through her chest. Her eyes blurred and her head suddenly went dizzy. She swayed on her feet. "I'm sorry, but I think I'm—"

A pair of hands came to her shoulders from behind, and a hard body braced against hers. "I've got you," a low voice rumbled in her ear. Two fingers came up to press at the pulse point in her neck. "You're having a panic attack, baby."

Boots was here. The thought settled her like nothing else would. He was strong, solid, and wouldn't let her down. Out of the corner of her eye, she spotted Rail and Duke as they spoke with Tarnaski. Their stances were stiff like opponents sizing one another up, but they looked determined to maintain a truce.

"Deep breath, hold it, then let it out," Boots rumbled again. "Close your eyes. In through your nose and out of your mouth. Count to four."

Janice followed his direction, concentrating on the tone of his voice. The soft, low timbre resonated in her head. Her heart slowed and her vision cleared. "Thank you. I'm okay now. How's Cort?"

"They got him stable and into the ambulance."

The departing sirens faded as several officers moved around, taking pictures and collecting evidence. Boots didn't let go of her as Rail approached them, followed by Duke. His lips pressed into a grim line as his eyes darted to Boots's hands on her shoulders. "They don't think anything is broken, but they'll get X-rays at the hospital. The deputy is sending people to tell Agnes what's happened, but I don't trust anyone but us right now. This shit's getting out of hand, and Tarnaski didn't like it too much when I told him he needs to get his fucking house in order. He won't say it out loud, but we all have a good idea who did this." His eyes softened when he spoke directly to her. "You okay, Janice?"

Janice. First time Rail's called me that and not my usual nickname. "Yes, I'm fine."

He looked up at Boots. "Follow her home to make sure she gets there safe and stay there. Flipper can cover at the marina. Chapel tonight after closing."

Boots made a noise of agreement. He turned his dark eyes on her van. "You good to drive, or do you want me to make arrangements?"

She looked down at her shaking hands and clenched them hard to make them stop. "I can drive." A quick glance at her watch told her she didn't have a lot of time. "I have to pick up the kids at the library first."

Rail gave a sharp nod. "Duke, call Flipper and tell him to get his ass over to the marina. Janice, you get your kids and get home. We'll take care of things here."

"Rail, I—"

"Take the help, baby," Boots intoned in her ear. The warmth of his body brought comfort, and she wanted to relax into him despite having an audience.

Rail continued to frown. Perhaps it was Boots's possessive position or the attack on Cort, probably a little of both, that accounted for his sour mood. "Any reason you need me to call Nutter?"

The idea startled her. *Nutter? Why on earth would I need him here?* "Uff-da, no. I don't think he would be much help. I really need to go get my kids."

Boots's hands slipped from her shoulders, and one of them fell lower to clasp her palm. "You're still too shaky to drive. I'll take you. Duke, see to my bike, yeah?"

"You got it, brother."

Ollie and Augustus were excited to see Boots driving the van, and they babbled the entire way home about it, strapped in their car seats.

"We got baloney sammiches and cookies that look like little flowers with holes in the center."

"You can put them on your fingers and eat the petals first."

Boots glanced back at them in the rearview mirror as he pulled smoothly into Janice's driveway. "They still make that kind? I used to eat those when I was a kid."

"You were a kid too?"

"You like cookies?"

Boots let out a laugh. "Yes, I was a kid and I liked cookies. I still like them."

"Mommy makes the best cookies. Better than the flower ones."

Boots laughed again as he turned off the engine. He shifted in the seat to face Janice, but he spoke to the boys. "You have the best mommy, so of course she makes the best cookies."

Janice felt her face flame with a combination of embarrassment and pleasure. "*Uff-da*, I'm so far behind. Let's get in the house. I've got work to do, and you boys have messes to make."

The slow cooker was bubbling away as they entered the kitchen. The kids ran screaming into the living room, and a few seconds later, a rattling crash was heard as they emptied a bin of blocks onto the floor. Janice lifted the lid of the round appliance and expertly stirred the contents. "Taco night again, I'm afraid. It's our easiest and our favorite, don'tcha know. You want to stay for supper, or do you have to leave?"

The invitation rolled off her tongue easily enough, but she expected him to decline as he always had.

"I don't have any plans. I'd love to stay."

Her stomach flipped over and danced. Opal appeared in the doorway, dressed in her work uniform and carrying a fussy Pearl in her arms. "I heard you come in. Everything okay?"

"Boots, come see our room!" Ollie crowed and tugged on the big man's arm. "Then you can see Charlotte and Lily's room. An' Mommy's room. We can't show you Pearl's room 'cause we're not 'posed to go in there."

Boots chuckled and allowed the two boys to lead him down the hall. "We'll be back."

Janice retold the morning's events as she bustled around in the kitchen, pulling out ingredients and large mixing bowls. Opal teared up as she placed an irritable Pearl in the tabletop bouncy chair. "Cort always treated me well, even when I was with the club."

The baby let out a cry, and Opal picked her up again. "I have to get to work, but I hate leaving her when she's feeling bad."

"Teething?"

"Yeah."

"I can handle it. I've been through enough of those nights. There's some baby Tylenol in the medicine cabinet that will help. I think there's an icy ring in the fridge door, but if not, grab one at the store on your way home. They are magic."

Opal sniffed as Pearl quieted for the moment. "I don't know what I'd do without you, Mama J."

A finger of pride touched Janice's heart. "Oh well, we mothers have to have each other's backs, don'tcha know. Despite what the men think, we're the ones who hold the world together."

A familiar crash reverberated down the hallway. Janice gave the passage a wry look. "Even when our kids are tearing it apart. That was the second block box getting dumped on the floor. At least it will give them something to do for a bit." She dusted her hands and moved to take the baby. "You go do what you have to do. I've got this handled." She settled Pearl expertly against her rounded bosom.

Opal picked up her purse and keys. "You sure? I can call in sick, or something."

Janice gently rocked the baby on her shoulder. "Keep your sick days for when you really need them. I promise I'll call if I think something is really wrong."

The reluctant younger woman left with worry written all over her face, but Janice's calm assurances helped.

After the painkiller kicked in, Pearl settled back in the bouncy chair and watched while Janice bustled around the kitchen.

"*Uff-da*, I'm so far behind!" She didn't want to think about why she was behind, but the vision of Cort's bloodied face came to her anyway. Her hands came to the counter, and she gripped it hard. "Oh, my."

Two warm arms came up behind her. "I got you, baby."

"I was too late."

"You were perfect."

"Maybe I could have stopped it."

"Maybe you could've gotten hurt too. What's done is done. We'll do what is needed and move on. Cort is in good hands, and you were a part of making that happen. Cry, scream, throw shit around if you need to get it out. I'm here to catch it all."

She did. She cried into his shirt, clutching at him

like he was a lifeline. He took her weight and let her have the time she needed.

"Mommy? Can we have some juice?"

"I'll take care of it." Boots went to the fridge and pulled out two boxes. "Need help with the straws?"

"We can do that part."

For the rest of the afternoon and evening, Boots was there. He played with the boys, drove her van to pick up the other kids from school, helped her move things around in the kitchen, and simply added a calming presence to the house. He even held baby Pearl as she fussed.

Rail called with updates on Cort. Janice was able to get caught up enough by dinnertime. The kids laughed and joked at the novelty of having a man sit at the table with them. Tad had a big smile on his face as he conversed with the new/old guest. Janice recalled the promise Boots had made to her oldest son about staying for dinner one night. Did she dare hope this would become a pattern?

By the time the kids were in bed, she was able to get her house back in some order and get off her feet. Boots joined her in the living room.

"I need to go, baby. Rail's having a chapel meeting, but he needs me to see to the bar. You okay for the night? I'll come back later if you need me."

She wanted to tell him that she did need him. She needed his shoulder to lean on. She needed his strength to hold her up. She needed his kindness to her and her children. "Thank you for everything today. Go do what you have to do."

He leaned in as if it was the most natural thing in the world and kissed her. "Sweetheart, know that if it's ever in my power, someday, I will not be walking away."

Janice swallowed at his comment. She thought of several things to say, but instead, simply nodded. "We're fine here and Rail needs you."

After he left, she sat on the sofa and folded another load of never-ending laundry and tried to concentrate on that task rather than dwell on the man who constantly invaded her thoughts. *Dare she hope for a future with this man? Was it possible?*

CHAPTER
TWENTY-FIVE

THE WEATHER HAD TAKEN A MAJOR DIP, AND THE COLD air bit at her face as Opal made her way to her car. Not even the thought of frost in the morning dampened her mood. The instructor called her name in front of the class and gave her high accolades for her color project. She was proud of the multi-layered balayage she'd worked on for her model. The colors were subtly blended and looked so natural, it was hard to believe they weren't. Another student's model looked like a skunk with the stark black-and-white striping.

Even better than doing well in class, she had Camo. Never had she imagined a man to be so kind and thoughtful. Even though their work schedules were tough, he made time to see her every day, whether for a few minutes or a few hours. He spent time with Pearl and proved he could be trusted with her care. Last night, Opal had stayed with him all night again, and he'd made love to her with exquisite precision. His mouth, his hands, his body—everything just as beautiful as the first time they came together.

The shiver down her spine had more to do with the memory of him sliding inside her than it did with the cold. He had texted her earlier to wish her well in her class tonight and ask her to call when she got home.

This is what it's like to be in love, she mused as she unlocked her door. Camo was so good with Pearl, cooing and playing with her. The baby girl grinned and babbled anytime she spotted the biker coming for a visit. At first, Opal was afraid her daughter would become too attached. The little girl would be heartbroken should this new relationship go south. Those fears slowly evaporated like morning fog as time moved on and Camo stayed.

The beams of her headlights cut through the dark as she drove slowly over the frozen road. Tonight's class had been the last one before Thanksgiving break. She had thought to spend the Thursday and Friday at home, but Camo had invited her and Pearl to go to Wisconsin to meet his mother and sister. She talked to Mama J about it early that afternoon when the woman was in the kitchen baking, and she had encouraged Opal to go.

"I'm so happy you found a good man. Of course

you should get to know his family. If they're as good as he is, they'll like you from the start."

"Are you sure you don't need me to help you here?"

Mama J waved her flour-covered hand. "I'm fine. This is not my first time herding children by myself, and it won't be the last. It's okay to take a little piece of happy for yourself, don'tcha know."

Opal's mind had drifted so much, she didn't notice the vehicle behind her until the flashing lights came on and the *whoo-whoop* of the siren startled her. Her stomach plummeted. "No, please—not again."

She slowly pulled over as all thoughts of Thanksgiving disappeared, leaving behind a cold dread that had her muscles tensing in fight-or-flight anticipation. It wasn't hard to recognize the shadowy shape behind the approaching flashlight. The shiver that went through her body had little to do with the cold and everything to do with the man who appeared at her window and tapped at the glass motioning for her to wind it down.

The grinning face of Lewis Canter greeted her. "Nice to see you again, Peebles. Out of the car."

I wish I could say the same. She opened the car door and got out. She was stiff and shaky. There was a faint roaring in her ears, and she hugged herself to stay upright. "Do you want to see my license and registration, officer?"

He gave a long sigh. "Peebles, darlin', you

already know how this is going to go, right? I'm going to write you a ticket that you're going to pay by sucking me off. Let's just skip all the nonsense and get to that. I'll even let you do it in the squad car where it's warm."

Opal's teeth chattered. "No. Not this time. I'll just take the ticket."

He threw his head back and gave a long evil laugh. "I like how you think you have a choice. Get your ass in my car, bitch."

Opal stood up straighter and reached for her confidence. Camo had given that to her. With him by her side, she had learned more about controlling the drug cravings, found a happy future, and had more faith in her ability to be a good mother. Above all else, she discovered what the love of a solid man was really like, and there was no way she would ever willingly betray him.

"I said no, Lewis." Her voice reverberated with a firmness that, for a moment, made Lewis blink and step back. Then his lip curled in disdain.

"You think you're hot shit because you're getting it regular now, eh?" He moved in closer and lashed out a hand to grab her shoulder. "Don't forget what you are, whore. You're nothing. I could kill you right now, and no one would care. Not even that biker loser you're fucking."

Small wads of spittle hit her face as she cringed away from him. "You're wrong. Camo loves me."

"Bullshit. No one can love a whore."

She cried in pain as he jerked her arm, nearly sending her to the ground. "Pull your jeans down and get in the back. A blow job won't pay for this ticket, but your ass will."

A pair of headlights appeared behind Lewis's squad car.

"I hope that's Thune. After I'm done, he can have a piece too."

Fear knotted in her belly at the man's sibilant hiss. He started dragging her to his car but abruptly stopped when he recognized the man coming toward them.

"What's going on here, Officer Canter?" Milton asked as he approached.

"The usual. I pulled this woman over because she was weaving on the road and I thought she might be drunk."

A pool of light spilled from the heavy flashlight in Tarnaski's hand as he pointed the beam at their feet. "Portable Breathalyzer is with me this week. I don't smell any alcohol. She have any open containers in the vehicle?"

"No sir." The gritted-out answer sounded reluctant, but Opal supposed Lewis was being truthful only because it would be easy to check her car. She gazed with unseeing eyes at Milton Tarnaski. She'd heard good things about this man, but she also had a healthy residual fear of law enforcement.

"Maybe she was weaving because the roads are getting slick. Pike is dealing with a five-car wreck on Highway 61 near Bench Street because of black ice. Didn't you hear the call go out for all cars?"

"Must be out of range or something."

Tarnaski made a grunt that sounded like he didn't quite buy the explanation. "Maybe you should go over there and help out. Now." He turned his attention to Opal. "The roads are icing up quickly, ma'am. Be extra careful and get home safe. You're free to go."

Opal bit her lip as Lewis squeezed her arm painfully with a vise-like grip. His message was loud and clear. *Keep your mouth shut, or else.*

"Th-thank you, Officer."

Her knees shook as she concentrated on walking to her car. She kept both hands on the steering wheel as she pulled off and started in the direction of Mama J's, but somehow, she ended up at Camo's house. Numb, she went to the front door. She could hear the TV broadcasting some sort of sports game, but it was like she wasn't in her own body. It was someone else who swayed on the front steps, someone else who gazed at the brass knocker, someone else's hand that rose to rap the curved metal against the door.

It was only when Camo appeared that she came back into herself. His face showed surprise at seeing her. "Hey, sweetheart. I thought you said you'd be at Mama J's tonight." Then his expression changed into concern. "What happened? Is Pearl okay?"

"I need to tell you something. Can I come in?"

"Of course, baby. You should probably text Mama J to let her know where you are."

He led her to the living room sofa and sat next to her. "Talk to me, sweetheart."

"I'm… I…." Her heart ricocheted in her chest, choking her.

He pulled her into his embrace and rested her head under his chin as the tears rolled down her cheeks. "Talk to me."

"I'm sc-scared."

"Of what?"

"That… I…."

He kissed her head. "It's okay, baby. I swear you're safe."

Safe. She was safe. "I'm afraid you'll stop loving me when you hear." Her whisper barely sounded.

He pulled her tighter into his arms, but unlike Lewis's harsh bruising grip, this one surrounded her with security and care. "I swear on my honor, baby, there's nothing in this world that will stop me from loving you. If I have to spend a lifetime making you believe that, I will do it gladly."

Her heart bloomed. He did love her. One hundred percent. No strings attached. If she should ever fully trust anyone, it was him.

She took two shaky breaths and opened up, letting out all the nasty shit she'd been hiding from everyone.

An hour later, the concerned expression on his face had morphed into a boiling rage. She bit her lip at the sight of his hard face when he let her sit up. His hazel eyes burned with fire, but it wasn't directed at her. That sense of safety continued to surround her as relief poured through her veins. Someone else knew about her nightmare and maybe could do something about it.

Camo picked up his phone from the coffee table, keeping his hot gaze on her the whole time. His thumb moved across the screen. "We need a chapel meet ASAP."

CHAPTER
TWENTY-SIX

Janice wiped the counter and glanced at her wall clock. Two more hours until Nutter came back with the kids. Ever since he discovered Boots's interest in her, he'd been coming to see the kids regularly. She wasn't so sure of his motivations, but she was glad to see him take a bigger interest. Hopefully, he would keep it up this time, but her optimism was dim when she thought of how many times he'd let her down over the years.

He's never had competition before. She giggled at her thoughts. Boots came around often and not just to see her. The big biker took an interest in Tad, and the two of them spent time working on some house projects. They recently installed the new vertical blinds that Boots brought from one of Duke's salvage jobs. Yes, they were outdated, but they were clean, the right size/color, and new to her. Ian handed them the screws and brackets, and Boots showed Tad how to measure and use a cordless drill.

"Always make a pilot hole first," he'd explained.

"Why?"

"So the wood doesn't split when you install wood screws."

"Do you have to use wood screws?"

Boots picked up a piece and held it in his palm. "It's always best to use the right parts for the right job. Wood screws have wide and deep threads to grab and anchor extremely tight. They're also tapered so they'll drill in easier, but there's a lot of pressure as the screw drills into the wood. Making a pilot hole relieves some of that pressure and makes for a better, cleaner job. Make sense?"

Tad grinned. "I get it. Are you staying for dinner?"

He had that night, enjoying her Crock-Pot lasagna and trading knock-knock jokes with the girls. He'd been so good to the kids, so good to her, that whenever Nutter said something about him, she couldn't mesh the two opposing concepts together.

"He's a bad man, Mama J. You can't trust him."

This bad man installed a dishwasher to make her life easier.

"He's not the kind of man you want around the kids."

That same man fulfilled a little girl's dream when

he found a piano from a salvage job and paid to have it fixed and tuned.

"The Dark Horses kept him on a tight leash. Even the Dutchmen are afraid of him."

He spent an afternoon working with the boys to fill in the holes the dog dug under the fence, showing them different tools and how they worked.

"If you knew him better, you wouldn't let him in the house at all."

He brought her containers back to her almost every night of the week.

Janice dropped a tab in the dishwasher and started the machine. Zeus appeared with her favorite toy in her mouth. Or rather, the carcass of her favorite toy. The stuffing and the squeaky had been destroyed already, but the canine still loved to play with the ratty, torn pile of cloth. The night she joined the family, Boots hadn't said anything to Janice about Nutter's lack of judgment. Instead, he made a special trip to go get the necessary items.

"I'm here. Let me help you."

The contrasts didn't fit together. Janice decided it was Nutter getting jealous just because someone else was interested in her. Truthfully, she was interested in Boots too. More than interested. He was on her mind constantly. The way he treated her with respect as a woman and still showed his desire for her. He seemed to understand her life and always had the right words. If she called Nutter for something, it would only be his voicemail message she got long before he would show up, whereas if she needed anything at any time, she had no doubt that Boots would step up, no questions asked.

She loved that about Boots.

She loved Boots.

Her chest loosened and warmth flooded her senses at the realization. She'd fought it with some token resistance, but she couldn't help it. The man had worked his way under her skin and embedded himself so deeply, she couldn't see a future without him in it. The trouble was, did he feel the same way? She wasn't stupid and recognized his attraction to her, but were his feelings a result of alpha male competition or were they genuine?

Nutter was definitely a competitor. What about Boots?

Her phone chirped a message, and she picked it up.

Opal: I don't want you to worry, but I had a bad night tonight. I'm over at Camo's, and he wants me to stay awhile. Maybe all night. Would you mind taking care of Pearl?

Concern for her roommate replaced her concern for the men in her life.

Mama J: Don't worry about the baby. She's asleep right now and should stay that way for the night. You take care of you.

A light knock at the door caught her attention, and Zeus's ears perked up. Only one person would come see her this time of night. The dog's nails scrabbled on the linoleum as Janice opened the carport door.

Boots stood there with several containers piled up in his arms. He glanced around the kitchen. "Where are the kids?"

She opened the door wider as he entered the house and placed the big plastic boxes on the counter. The dog danced in joyous circles around his legs.

"Nutter has them tonight. All of them. He decided to take them for a night of pizza and games." She took a breath. "I think he's trying to impress me or something. He's supposed to win me back by taking his responsibilities seriously."

Boots leaned over to scratch Zeus behind the ears. "Is it working?"

"Yes, and no," she answered honestly.

He stood up and moved directly in front of her. He smelled of cold wind, motorcycle, and man.

"The Dark Horses kept him on a tight leash. Even the Dutchmen are afraid of him."

"I'm here. Let me help you."

"How do you mean?"

Janice imagined herself at a crossroads. There was a pathway that was clear and comfortable in some ways. Evenly paved, well-trodden, no surprises, but still it was a painful one. It had moments of heartache and more to come as she continued down its route. The other path was foggy and dark. She couldn't see where it led, but it held promise. Once she stepped onto either, there would be no switching directions.

A fine trembling started in her belly. Was it time for her to decide which way to go? Boots's eyes held no answers, but she already knew her course.

"I'm happy Nutter is spending time with the kids, and I hope he keeps it up for their sake. The on-and-off-again relationship he has with them is not good. The younger ones barely know him as their father. Ian is confused by him, and Tad—well, Tad is a very angry boy that might grow into an angry man if Nutter keeps drifting in and out of his life."

She squared her shoulders. "I know a couple things for certain. My children are a big part of who I am, and I'll always be there for them. To me, my kids are a lifetime commitment, and nothing or no one will change that."

He stepped closer. Electricity sparked in the air, and the fine hairs on her arms stood straight up. "What's the other thing?"

A thrill rippled down her back. This was it. This was the moment that would change her life. "I will not take Nutter back. I care about him as the kids' father, but I've moved on. I don't love him like I used to. There's someone else I want like that."

His eyes flared. "Who?"

Energy rose to the top, filling the room with anticipation. She sensed he was focused intently on her next words with the hunger of a starving man. "I think you already know the answer."

His mouth came down on hers, and she reveled in its texture.

Timing was everything. The shit with Nutter, her aching heart, her suppressed needs as a woman—it was simply too much for her to contain anymore, and she had reached her limit. She slipped her arms up under his and across his back, and she pulled him to her. He slanted his head and took the kiss deeper in response.

Mouth to mouth, heart to heart, groin to groin, she kissed him back, letting go of any control. She wanted to be touched, needed it like she needed air. It had been years since anyone made her feel like Boots did. His steadfastness was a balm to her nerves, and she had no doubt she could trust him.

It hit her with the force of a falling star. She wanted this man in her life and would take him any way he came.

He must have sensed a change in her. His mouth moved with harder purpose, and his hands drifted to her hips to pull her in tighter. She felt his erection pressed into her stomach, and her own body responded. Her lower abdomen warmed, and she experienced something she hadn't had in a long time. Desire.

He ended the kiss but didn't move away. His breath puffed against her trembling lips as he spoke. "Is this an invitation, sweetheart?"

"I think so."

"Baby, you need to know so. You need to be one-hundred-percent sure this is what you want."

Janice's heart fluttered. No, she wasn't one-hundred-percent sure of anything in her life. So many changes and challenges had occurred over the past few years that had led her in directions she never thought she'd go. Her carefully planned future had shattered with Nutter's constant betrayals, and she'd never thought she'd be a single mom at her age. Nevertheless, this was one of very few moments she could be Janice, the woman, and not Mama J, the mother.

"Yes, I'm sure."

Boots pulled back to look into her eyes, and her belly fluttered. "You need to be very clear on what's about to happen. If I come to your bed, I'm not leaving it. You take me into your body, that means you've made your choice. I'm too old to play games, and I don't want to. I'm in this for the long haul, and you need to be ready for that."

His words made her heart jump. Part of her

wanted to dance with joy at the thought of having this man as her own. Part of her was also scared to death of this dark, unknown path. She'd loved before and got burned. Badly. But time heals, right?

"You and I will be together," he continued, his dark eyes deepening. "I'm in your life and you're in mine. We'll talk, make plans, have family dinners with the kids, take private time for ourselves, and all the other shit couples do. You need something, you'll call me before Nutter or Rail. I need something, I'll be calling you to help me. I'll be at the kids' games, school plays, and any other things they do. You'll be on the back of my bike, and you already know what that means."

Yes, she did know. She knew exactly what riding with Boots meant. A twinge of regret passed over her mind as she wondered how Nutter would take the news. Then she realized it didn't matter what Nutter thought, as he didn't have a say in her life. Not anymore. She'd been hurt plenty of times by those little darts that embedded themselves in her heart during so many years with him. She didn't want to hurt him back, but she also didn't need to let him dictate her happiness. A kind of euphoria filled her. She was free.

Boots dipped in for another kiss. "I'm going to ask again. Are you sure this is what you want?"

She'd never been surer. "Yes."

Boots had been in the house enough times that he

didn't have to ask which bedroom was hers. He led her there and frowned at the small bed as he faced her. "We'll make do for now, but a bigger bed is a priority."

Daylight streamed through the cheap blinds, and Janice wished for darkness. She held her breath as Boots faced her and reached down to grasp the hem of her tunic top. He paused and looked at her with the cloth still between his fingers. "Change your mind, sweetheart?"

She let out a long sigh. "No, not exactly. I'm not…. I've had four children."

"Yes, you have. I'm not expecting nor do I desire a tiny-waisted fairy with a thigh gap and no body fat. Bony is not my thing and never has been. I like real women with real bodies." He let go of her shirt and slid his hands down over her bottom, gripping and lifting her against himself. "First time I got a look at this, I wanted it. Big, round, juicy, magnificent." He chuckled lightly as he massaged the mass of flesh. "I could write poems about your ass, baby. I can't wait to see it naked when I take you from behind."

The flutter in Janice's stomach rose, and heat bloomed between her legs at his words. "It's been a while. I'd like to go slow if you don't mind."

"Absolutely, sweetheart."

She hated the awkward feel of the tunic whisking over her head as she raised her arms. Luckily, she'd shaved her armpits and legs recently. Not having

Nutter around much, she'd let those things go for a while, but she also felt better when she groomed herself. Standing in her plain bra and leggings, she dropped her eyes to the floor and crossed her arms over her loose stomach, wondering if this was the point when Boots would get turned off.

"Please don't ever hide from me, baby," he muttered as he placed his fingers under her chin and lifted it. His mouth molded to hers, and his tongue teased her lips open. "How much time do we have?"

"Mmmm… a couple of hours. Opal texted to say she'll be over at Camo's. Had a bad night. Pearl is asleep and should stay that way. Oh!"

The sudden release of her bra behind her back startled her for a moment, but then he filled his hands with her naked breasts, and she forgot to be self-conscious. A moan slipped out of her and into his mouth as his thumbs circled her tight nipples. They moved over the tips, flicking and lightly scratching, and the sensations shot straight to her clit.

How long had it been since anyone touched her like this? So many months. No, more like years since she had a man want and admire her. The last few couplings with Nutter had happened so long ago and were more like obligations than acts of love.

"Lay back, sweetheart." He guided her down to the bed and sat next to her. "This is the way it's going to go. I plan to play with these beautiful tits until I have you squirming, then I'm going to go down on you and make you come with my mouth. After that I'll repeat steps one and two until you've had enough and tell me to stop or until we run out of time. You okay with that?"

"But I thought we'd… you know." She was surprised at the tremble in her voice.

"What, baby?" He leaned over and kissed a spot just above one breast.

"I thought you'd… come inside me. Um… sex." The lameness of her words bothered her, but she didn't know how else to say it.

"I don't have any condoms, sweetheart."

She bit her lip, hoping her next sentence wouldn't be a deal breaker. "You don't need them. After Augustus was born, I had my tubes tied. That's when I gained a lot of weight, and…." Her voice trailed off.

"And what?" He placed more kisses, moving closer to her nipple.

"That's when I think Nutter lost interest in me. Because I couldn't have any more babies."

"Nutter's a fool. Let's kick him out of this bed while I show you how interested *I* am."

"Okay. Ah!" She gasped as his mouth reached its target. Boots sucked the nipple into his mouth and pressed it against the roof. Janice arched her back, pushing more of her flesh into him. He groaned and continued laving the tight bud until she thought she would go insane. He finally released her only to suck the other nipple inside his hot mouth. Mewing sounds filled the room, and she realized they came from her. Breathing became harder and heavier, and he switched leisurely from side to side. She found herself running her fingers through his thick hair, marveling at its softness. He groaned again at her touch.

When he finally pulled back, her nipples were puckered and red from his attentions. "Beautiful," he growled as he reached for the elastic band at her waist. "Raise your hips, baby."

With one long pull, he took off her leggings, underwear, shoes, and socks. "You ever shave here?" he asked as he spread her legs and settled between them.

"Not really, I—*uff-da!*" Electricity shot through her as his tongue made contact with her already pulsing clit.

"Don't ever do it. I like it the way it is. I'm going to make you come now."

It didn't take long. He held open the flesh of her sex and teased the sensitive bundle of nerves. There was nothing she could do to stop the avalanche of sensation that flowed from her pussy. She gasped and cried and writhed under him as he brought her to the pinnacle and without hesitation, pushed her over. She slapped a pillow over her face and screamed into it as her body lost control and the promised orgasm crested over her. A second wave closely followed the first, and it was almost more than she could take.

"Boots!" she gasped, her body wracked with spasms of pleasure. "Please, I need you inside me."

"You sure you want to go ungloved this first time?" His voice was hoarse with his own need.

She was ready to beg. "I trust you. Please."

She didn't have to wait long. Boots quickly stripped, and she got her first look at his fully naked body. The tattoos were still menacing, but they decorated one of the most masculine bodies she'd ever seen. His chest was wide and tapered to his hips. Between his legs, an enormous penis hung hard and heavy from a nest of thick wiry hair. He called her beautiful, but in truth, he was the beautiful one.

He knelt on the bed between her legs and leaned over. The heat from his body drifted over her as he brought his mouth down for a kiss. She tasted the tang of her own body and barely felt the head of his hard penis before he pushed it inside her welcoming body. Yes, she'd had four children, but it had been a long time for her, and he was a large man in every sense of the word. She inhaled sharply as the delight of being filled again washed over her. This wasn't just sex. It was a binding between two people. An act of commitment she had craved so long, she forgot how it was supposed to work. It didn't matter if her body wasn't perfect. It didn't matter that she had a lot of baggage in dealing with a deadbeat ex. It didn't matter that she had no money and struggled to make ends meet. This man accepted her, the children, and all the flaws she had in her life. He too brought his own troubles, and she had no problem letting him in.

Could this be the love I've always wanted at last? Is it selfish for me to still want that?

"I'm here. Let me help you."

Boots kissed away the tears she hadn't known she'd made. "Did I hurt you, baby?"

"No, I'm...." She had no words to describe the euphoria that bloomed inside her at the thought that this was it. This was what she'd been waiting for all her life. "I'm wonderful."

"Good." He smiled and shifted his hips. "Now, let's make it better."

Janice bit her lip as he withdrew and pushed in again, letting every inch of hardness drag along her channel. *Uff-da*, it felt so good! He varied his movements from slow and exquisite to hard and fast, drawing gasps and cries from her. She moved with him, rising up to meet his thrusts with her own, clutching at his shoulders and stroking his back. His back muscles flexed under her fingertips, and he groaned his approval of her touch. Over and over again, he kissed her as he made love, murmuring against her mouth how beautiful she was and how good she felt. He drove her higher and higher to that same pinnacle, and this time, he hovered there with her before plunging them both into satisfaction.

For Janice, it was the most intense and intimate experience she'd ever had. More tears flowed down her cheeks as she came down into absolute bliss. Boots moved in and out of her while the last of their orgasms faded, leaving behind a contentment few people could claim.

He rained tiny kisses over her face and lips. "I hope you're feeling as good as I do, baby. If you don't, I need to step up my game."

She gave a short laugh. "Your game is awesome. I wouldn't change anything about it."

He laughed too as he lifted himself up and regarded her with a big smile. "Oh, I don't know about that. We'll do some exploring. Some different positions, more oral, maybe some bondage if you're willing. I'm not really into the anal thing, but I'd try that with you if you're into it."

Her face heated up at his words. "I'm not sure about all that, but, well, maybe."

He leaned in for another kiss. "We have all the time in the world."

A premonition stuck in her head. All the time in the world. Did they really?

He pulled his softened dick out of her and stood up from the bed. A bone in his back popped, and he let out a mild groan. "I'm getting old, Jan. I hope you're good being with a codger like me."

"There's a few miles on me, too, don'tcha know. I prefer to think of myself as classic instead of old."

He threw back his head and laughed. "I think of you as perfect. I'm gonna get a washcloth and clean you up. I bet I can make you come a few more times before—"

His phone buzzed from the back pocket of his discarded jeans. He picked it up and read the text. His entire demeanor visibly changed from one moment to the next. Gone was the happy, teasing man, and in his place was someone else. Someone who was cold and unreachable.

"What's wrong?" she asked as she sat up, clutching the comforter to her naked breasts. Her skin had pebbled under the loss of his heat.

"Rail called an emergency chapel. He wouldn't do that unless something's happened." He turned his charcoal gaze on her, and her shiver was only partially because of the room's temperature. There was menace in those dark depths that was not directed at her, but it sent chills down her spine nonetheless.

He noticed her sudden rigidity, and his threatening expression lessened. "I need to go. Nutter's probably on the way with the kids right now. I'll call you later, and we'll figure out how we'll handle everything, yeah?"

"You bet."

He leaned and placed a gentle kiss on her lips that was so contradictory to his menacing stance just seconds ago. "I meant every word, sweetheart. I will not let you go."

She wanted to tell him she loved him, but with all the emotional upheavals, her personal worries, the issues between him and Nutter, and whatever was happening with the Dutchmen at the moment, it wasn't the right time. She gave him the next best thing she could. "Me either. I trust you."

Five minutes later, he was gone.

Ten minutes after that, the kids arrived in a wild cacophony. Nutter didn't come inside.

Janice sorted them into their nightly routines. The youngest two boys bathed first splashing around the tub together, while the girls brushed their teeth. Then they switched places. Ian and Tad did their own baths separately while Janice read Curious George to the boys and Clifford the Big Red Dog to the girls.

Tad read for himself, but occasionally, Ian still wanted his mom to read to him. Thankfully, tonight he pulled out his copy of 5,000 Awesome Facts about Everything, and Ian settled in his bed with a Harry Potter book from the library. Janice did her best to smile and talk with her kids at bedtime, but throughout this normal nightly occurrence, her mind was peppered with thoughts of Boots. Her body still hummed from his lovemaking, and she easily recalled the feel of him as he slid inside her. Then the text changed all that and he became, however brief, someone different. Someone she wasn't sure she wanted to know.

"The Dark Horses kept him on a tight leash. Even the Dutchmen are afraid of him."

She quietly sat on the sofa with the nightly basket of laundry and turned on the TV for light and muted the sound as to not wake the kids. As her hands automatically folded and stacked, her brain wouldn't stop churning out the same question over and over again. *Why?*

CHAPTER
TWENTY-SEVEN

Rail sat at the head of the conference table, his face set in an angry frown. The other Dutchmen came in one by one and sat in silence, waiting for everyone to show up. The cryptic two-word text and the hour when it was sent had every member on edge.

Rail: Chapel. Now.

Camo also displayed extreme anger. Rage, Boots would say. The man's posture made him appear ready to explode. Duke came in and settled in his appointed spot. Spider, Nitro, and others randomly entered, some with irritated looks on their faces and some with quizzical ones.

The chair creaked under Boots as he sat back to wait. Nutter was the last to arrive. He shot Boots a venomous look before taking his place.

Rail rapped the gavel once. "I talked to Cort earlier today. He's still critical but stable. Said that one of the men who beat him and trashed his store was Mark Thune."

Duke cursed. "Fuck me sideways and up the ass. Thune is a deputy and hangs with Canter."

Rail inclined his head. "There's more. A lot more. Everyone knows my wife is deaf, and there are people who tend to talk shit around her because they think she doesn't understand or that her disability makes her stupid."

Boots nearly laughed aloud. Gretchen was one of the smartest, toughest women he knew, and anyone who thought otherwise was a fool.

Rail smirked a little. "In case you don't know, she can read lips pretty well. She met with the people who run the Flora Jones Home of Grace for their quarterly update at a restaurant in Lake City last week. John Macaffee was sitting catty-corner to her table with a couple other men. She had a bird's-eye view of him and his buddies. She told me he was amused at first as he kept winking and blowing fake kisses at her, more to irritate and be an asshole. You guys know Gretchen's not easily intimidated by that kind of shit, and she didn't give Macaffee any atten-tion until she saw him say, 'set another fire soon.'"

The entire room came alert.

"The fire at the Bait and Tackle? It was ruled acci-dental," Nitro started.

Duke's growl interrupted the younger Dutchmen member. "John Macaffee is the guy who used to hang with Canter at the clubhouse back in the day. He was there when Iceman beat the shit out of Minute and kicked him out permanently."

"He's also an officer in the Lake City Police and works as a volunteer firefighter." Rail leaned his elbows against the worn table. "Gretchen watched him as covertly as she could. Macaffee made reference to the store and a repeat performance if the old man didn't start paying up."

"Thune was in Randy's last week, getting his fucking free food and another fucking envelope. Randy asked me if there was anything the club could do since the law won't." Duke spat. "Hell, it's the fucking law that's doing this shit."

Grim murmurs went around the table amongst the bikers. Rail rapped the gavel for order. "Camo has something to share." He nodded at the younger man.

Boots observed Camo's fisted hands where they rested on the table. He expected it to be bad before he even spoke.

"I found out earlier tonight that son-of-a-bitch, Canter, has been harassing Opal. Following her home from classes, threatening her with bogus tickets and forcing her to give him blow jobs. She refused to get on her knees tonight, and the fucker tried to make her get in his car. Tarnaski showed up before he succeeded."

The volume around the table increased. The Dutchmen partied wild, drank hard, smoked a little weed, and fucked women freely. However, a long time ago, the past president, Iceman, made it a hard-and-fast rule that the club women were to be respected. If a woman wanted to fuck, have at it. If not, find someone else, but don't ever force a woman to do something she didn't want to do. Every man there remembered Opal as Peebles before she decided to turn her life around. Every man there also admired her for doing just that. Their collective instincts to protect the club women, even a former one, activated.

Camo continued. "Canter also tried to shake down Mama J. Opal said he came to her house with some bogus claim about a noise complaint. Fucker made her give him every dime she had in the house before he would leave."

If every man in the room was angered over Opal's treatment, the rage that now rolled through the air put that emotion to shame.

"What the fuck!" Nutter exploded out of his chair, and it fell over backward with a sharp crack.

"Goddamn motherfucker!" Duke kept his seat but was no less vocal.

Other men cursed and pounded their fists or

slapped their hands on the table. Rail's gaze came to Boots.

If fury had a name, it would be his. Boots stayed seated. If he moved, it would be to go find Canter. If he did, then no one else would ever find Canter again.

Rail pounded the gavel until the head flew off and rattled across the table. "Everyone, shut the fuck up and sit your asses down!"

Nutter picked up his chair, cursing the whole time, and slammed it in place before planting his ass in it. "So, what the fuck are we gonna do about this shit?"

"We guard and escort as much as we can. Neither Opal nor Mama J is left alone if it can be helped. Spread the news around that those women in particular are under Dutchmen protection. Our name still carries weight in this town, and if anyone thinks we're weak, it's time for them to learn different."

Rail's eyes met Boots's again. He raised an eyebrow at the former Dark Horse member. Boots gave a single nod at the implied question. Rail inhaled deeply and let out the breath slowly. "Getting free cigarettes and hot wings is one thing. Arson, assault, extortion, and rape puts this shit on another level. As far as we know, there's at least three bad cops, and there might be more. I'm thinking of that little shit who tried to throw his weight around on the pier when Nutter and Boots had their fallout. We've stayed out of it so far, but that cancer is spreading, and it's touched us directly. I think it's time we cut out that tumor at the root."

"Canter." Duke's single word was a statement, not a question.

"Canter," Rail confirmed, his eyes still on Boots. "I didn't want to go there and prayed like hell we wouldn't have to, but fuck me, I think it's time."

Nitro whispered, "What's he talking about?"

Duke let out a long breath similar to Rail's and followed the president's line of sight. He didn't need a crystal ball to figure out what Rail had implied. "Fuck me."

CHAPTER
TWENTY-EIGHT

Opal was exhausted but happy that her last exam was over early, and she thought she'd done a good job. If all went well, she'd be graduating this time next year with her full cosmetology license. She spotted the light flakes dancing in the air when she left the campus parking lot. The skies heralded a coming snow that was supposed to be thick. Road crews were already out preparing the roads and gearing up to clear whatever built up overnight before the usual morning traffic. The heating system was running great now after Boots worked his magic. She hesitated before driving away, but she didn't want to wait for another half hour for whoever Rail had assigned that night to follow her home. She dashed off a quick text to Camo to say she was leaving the school now and would be home soon.

Opal kept the wipers moving to dust the flakes from her windshield. Home. Such a small word for a big concept. Four letters that meant she had a place in this world, and it was a good one.

Life was good, and it was getting better all the time.

The flashing lights from the car behind her killed her happiness in a millisecond. Her fingers clenched the steering wheel, and her belly twisted into knots. *Please, no. Not again.*

Her phone sat on the seat beside her, and she quickly swiped it and touched the speed dial for Camo. The car behind her let out several *whoo-whoops*, and she glanced at the blinding lights in her rearview mirror. The vehicle was right on her bumper. A whimper rose in her throat as she pulled over. She didn't have time to see if Camo answered, but she didn't hang up and set the phone between the seats.

More snow swirled in the headlights as the dark figure of Lewis Canter approached her car. Opal swallowed to keep her gorge from rising as she rolled down the window.

"Well, now, Peebles. Nice to see you on this wintry night. License and registration." His smile was friendly, but it didn't take much to see the evil in his eyes. The last time he stopped her, Tarnaski showed up and inadvertently saved her. She hoped she would get that lucky this time.

Opal handed over the two documents. Her license was up to date. So were her registration, inspections, and insurance. She made damn sure she was following the exact speed limit, and if anyone checked the recorded time stamp, they would see it.

"Step out of the car," he ordered.

Opal glanced once more at her phone lying face-down between the seats before complying. "Please, Lewis, I—"

"That's Officer Canter, cunt," he snapped. "Take off the jacket."

"Why?"

"Because I said so. I need to make sure you don't have any guns or other weapons on you."

She tried again. "Officer…"

"Are you noncompliant?"

Another whimper escaped her lips as she unzipped the heavy parka. He snatched it from her hands and tossed it into the front seat of her car. Her shiver had nothing to do with the cold. She forced herself to breathe slowly as he examined the documents with disinterest.

"Seems like everything is in order this time." He reached up to click off his body cam. "That is, except for that broken taillight."

She wrapped her arms around herself. "I don't have a broken taillight."

Lewis took three strides and swung the heavy flashlight. She jumped and let out a little scream as the cover to the light shattered, adding red glitter to the thin white blanket of snow.

"You do now. This is a major infraction, Peebles. I'll need a more thorough payment now to cover this one and the last one. Take your pants off and bend over."

Opal's eyes burned with tears, but this time they were angry ones. "No. You want to ticket me, go ahead. I'm not fucking you."

Pain exploded on the side of her head, and she fell to her knees. Blood filled her mouth, and she spat red into the snow. He'd struck her with the flashlight, and her head rang woozily from the sharp impact.

"You'll do what I fucking tell you to do, cunt," he snarled as he seized her arm and forced her to her feet. She staggered once before he pulled her arms behind her and clicked handcuffs tightly around her wrists. He reached around to her front and squeezed one breast until she cried out in pain. "Fucking whore, Peebles."

He shoved her against the car hood, and she stumbled. He pulled open her jeans and yanked them down to her thighs. The sudden cold against her skin revived her awareness. She screamed and struggled, determined to fight him as best she could. "No! Stop! Don't touch me!"

His reaction was to grab her hair and slam her face into the car's hood. She heard her nose crunch before the pain hit her. The ringing in her ears got louder, and her vision started to gray. Lewis kept his legs against the backs of hers to hold her in place.

"Stupid bitch. Only good for one thing. Fucking cunt."

He spread open her buttocks, and she vaguely heard a hawking noise before a warm wad of spittle hit her anus. She tried again to push him away, get him off her before he raped her. He was too strong. "Think you're a lady, like you deserve some respect? You're just a whore, Peebles. A whore who takes cock up her ass."

She felt him press against her ring of muscle, and she arched away, tightening against his intrusion. He pushed harder. She cried out in desperation once again, "Stop!"

Then, suddenly, the painful pressure was gone. He was no longer behind her, and without his body holding hers up, she started sliding to the ground. Two hands caught her and lifted her to her wobbling knees.

"I got you."

Camo! she sobbed in her mind as the man whose name she didn't know pulled her jeans back into place.

"Boots, grab his keys, will ya?"

A jingling sound cut off abruptly, and the stranger turned her gently to unlock the cuffs. "Hang in there."

"Where's Camo," she tried to say, but her lips

were too thick to make the word come out right. Both eyes had swollen shut, and her face throbbed with pain. She could only breathe through her mouth now, and the wheezing noises she made muted any other sounds outside of her head. She still made out some words as well as the thudding sounds of flesh hitting flesh.

"I'm a fucking officer of the law!"

"You're a fucking rapist."

"She's a goddamn whore. Asked me to do her."

"Asked you? *Asked you*?"

More fighting sounds and cries of pain came to her ears.

The man spoke next to her. "I'm Nitro. Used to be an EMT in another life before I moved here and joined the Dutchmen. There's a lot of blood on you, and it looks like he hit you in the head. That how your nose got broke?"

"Doh, Ee zmasht it id."

"I'm going to set it before it swells any further, yeah? Hold still."

Her face had gone numb at this point, and she barely felt him shift her nose back in place. She still couldn't breathe through it.

"Did that asshole… get inside you?"

Opal didn't know how she was supposed to cry with her eyes already swelled up. "Ee tried. I fawghd'em and he didn' ged me. I fawghd'em off."

"Can you hang on just a few more minutes, Opal? Just stay with me, yeah?"

A gun shot rang out, along with loud curses and yells of caution.

"Fuck! Did he get you?"

"Winged me. He got Camo."

Oh no! Did Camo get shot? Please God no! The cold started to seep into her consciousness, and she shivered. Sleep. She wanted sleep so bad, but she had to know. "Werz Cambo? Id he okay?"

Other voices joined the surrounding discord.

"Tie it tighter."

"Shit, that's bad!"

"Fucker got away."

"Not for long."

"Get her phone. Damn smart to call and leave the line open."

"Stay awake, Opal. We'll let you sleep soon."

It was Duke's voice that spoke to her now.

"I'll dri-ee, bud I godda ged homb and take care of by liddle girl." She slumped against Duke and hoped Camo would understand. "Imb zo tired. Werz Camo?"

Duke didn't answer. "The ambulance is on the way. Someone will call Mama J about Pearl. We got this covered."

"Pleez don' ged id trubble."

"We got that covered too."

She heard several sirens blaring off in the distance. The sound grated on her raw nerves. "Werz Camo?" she asked again.

Duke held her closer and didn't answer.

CHAPTER
TWENTY-NINE

Lewis was frantic. His eyes darted around while he whipped his car through the quiet neighborhood. Blood crusted his lip and nose where what's-his-name tore into him. Camo? Yeah, Camo. Lewis had grabbed for his gun as the biker punched him, and fired blindly. Camo jerked and fell, and out of the corner of his eye, he saw Boots get hit as well.

Boots was after him. He was sure of it. The bullet only grazed the man's upper arm. It might be a good thing it did, as Lewis didn't know how he was supposed to explain killing a man for interfering with a traffic stop. Fuck, if Camo died—

"Fucking cunt," he swore viciously. The memory of Peebles laughing at him and teasing him when he failed to penetrate her so many years ago came to his mind. She'd been on her back with her legs spread wide, and he came all over her stomach before he made it to her pussy. She'd giggled at the sight of his cum on her stomach and dubbed him Minuteman. Her amusement had humiliated him in front of the club he desperately wanted to join, and the subsequent beating the then president, Iceman, gave him put the final nail in the coffin of him ever becoming a member.

"Stupid bitch!" he screamed and pounded his hand against the steering wheel of his patrol car. This was all her fucking fault. Hers and Tarnaski's. Thune and he had started with simple shit. A carton of cigarettes here and there. Free dinners at Randy's. A little money now and then. He was owed those things, right? For protecting their dumb asses. So what if he asked for more? A cop's pay was shit, and the extra those store owners and businesses gave him were like tips. Thune, Macaffee, Stevens, Pike, and he *deserved* that money.

Then that asshole down in Lake City got the idea he was going to blackmail them 'cause he had security camera footage. Fucker learned quick when his placed burned to the ground. Cort McClaren thought he was hot shit and could stop payment. He learned too after Thune beat the shit out of him and told him they'd do the same to his wife after they took turns with her. The old man kept his mouth shut to Tarnaski and the other goody-two-shoes on the force.

Snow was coming down heavier now, and the roads were getting white. Thick flakes fell through the frigid air, and he turned on the wipers. That fucker, Boots, had been on his bike, right? Dumb fuck probably had no other vehicle, and riding a bike in this weather was dangerous. Lewis had no doubt, though, that the big biker would come after him. No way would a man like Boots let him go after getting shot.

He refused to think anyone would care if he fucked Peebles up the ass. "Fucking whore isn't worth the effort."

A single headlight flashed in his rearview. Lewis felt a cold lump of ice freeze in his gut. Boots was coming after him. *Boots was coming after him!*

"Goddamn motherfucking hell!" he screamed.

The motorcycle would have more trouble on the roads in this weather than his car. He could get away as long as he paid attention. There should be enough time for him to escape, but a man like Boots would keep coming until he caught his prey. A quick glance at his surroundings helped Lewis form a plan in his head.

"I'm done playing, asshole."

He gunned the vehicle, and it slipped a bit, but he kept pushing as fast as he dared and pointed the car in a familiar direction.

CHAPTER
THIRTY

Janice hung up and let out a small whimper. She had to be quiet since the kids were asleep, but all she wanted to do was cry. Duke didn't say much, only that Opal had been attacked and would be at the hospital for a while. He didn't fill in any details, just that she was hurt pretty bad, and would Janice please take care of Pearl.

As if that were ever in question. Janice had never refused to take care of a child in her life and certainly wouldn't start now.

Zeus entered the living room and stretched her lean body in a doggie bow. Her mouth opened in a long yawn, and her pink tongue curled up. She sat up and regarded Janice with odd eyes and cocked her head to the side.

"You need to go out?" she asked the dog softly,

already knowing the answer. "It's snowing, so you'll have to be quick."

The puppy gave a short whine and pawed the air as if saying, *I get it.*

Janice slipped her sockless feet into her sneakers and grabbed the leash. "Make this the last time tonight, yeah?" Zeus yipped, and she shushed the eager canine. "Keep it down."

She didn't bother putting on a coat as she only planned to be outside for a few minutes. Zeus, however, decided to take her time as she sniffed at the front yard bushes.

"*Uff-da*," Janice muttered as the cold crept up her bare legs. She shivered in her thick robe and admonished the puppy. "Please pick a spot and pee already."

A car with flashing blue lights careened and slid as it turned the corner into her street. Someone in her neighborhood must have called nine-one-one for an emergency. Janice hoped it wasn't Gertrude who was in trouble. She was shocked when the car jerked violently and skidded into her yard.

At first, she thought the car simply hit some bad ice, but then a man erupted from the driver's side and lifted his hand. "Don't fucking move, bitch!"

Janice froze at the sight of a gun barrel pointing at her. Lewis Canter. He never came back for the rest of the money he claimed she owed, and she hoped this wasn't his way of collecting. As he approached, he staggered some, as if in pain. His face was bruised, and rivulets of blood had dried on his cheeks from his nose and mouth. Spatters of it stained his uniform. Lewis's eyes were wild, unfocused, and there was a sneer of contempt on his face.

She forgot about the falling snow, the puppy, her cold skin. Her only thought was what future would the children have if she died?

She dropped the leash and Zeus scrambled under a bush, excited about the unexpected freedom. She barked and started digging. Janice didn't say a word to Canter but raised her hands in the air.

"Why are you doing this?" Her voice cracked and trembled.

The crazed man jeered at her. "Why am I doing this? Ask your fucking club. They wrote me off as useless years ago, and look at me now. I got all the power I need with this badge. People give me whatever I want and do whatever I want. Fucking Dutchmen think they own this town? Not anymore." He slapped his chest with his free hand. "*I* own this fucking town!"

Janice kept her mouth shut and stood still as Lewis approached. Her heart pounded so hard with fear, she thought it would break free from her chest. Zeus growled from behind, but Janice's eyes remained focused on the gun pointing at her chest from not two feet away. The man was crazy, and if he fired at this range, there was no way she would survive it. She hoped someone would find her body before the kids woke in the morning. She didn't want them to see her that way.

Her knees nearly gave way at the thought. She locked them into place, determined to keep some sort of control. "Please, Officer C-Canter. I have kids that depend on me. Please don't take me away from them."

Lewis ignored her. "Fucker thinks he's some sort of badass. Thinks he can fuck with me. Let's see how brave he is when he finds his whore bleeding out." He sighted down the gun and closed one eye.

A rumble echoed in the distance, and the deputy's aim dropped a fraction. A single tiny spot of light appeared down the street. The sound was very familiar as she had heard this same bike on many, many nights.

Boots! she thought. Relief flashed through her and warred with the knowledge that he wouldn't get there in time. If Lewis chose to pull that trigger, she'd be dead before Boots reached her.

She should have realized how depraved the deputy's mind had become. "Well, well, well. Seems lover boy is here. Just in time to watch his old lady take a bullet or three."

Zeus growled again.

"Officer—"

"Shut up!" Lewis screamed. Flecks of spit flew from his mouth. The gun wavered but stayed trained on her. He turned his head to watch the slow progress of the bike as the round headlight got closer. The low purring of its engine cut through the air, making the wait for its arrival more agonizing.

Janice stiffened herself against the inevitable. When Boots got here, she would die. Oddly, her body relaxed, and she no longer felt the bitter cold. The club she tried so hard to leave behind would take care of her kids. Rail and Gretchen would step in, and if Boots survived tonight, he would too. She had very little legacy to leave behind. Maybe enough insurance to bury her, but that was about all. The house had been a gift and would be the only real thing of value. That and her love. She hoped the kids would remember her. Tad would take it the hardest. He was such an angry boy, and even though he was starting to come out of his shell more, her death would take away all the progress he'd made so far and then some. Tears were pouring down her cheeks, and she thought of the pain her children would go through in the coming days. She asked the universe to take care of her kids and braced herself for the impact she was sure was coming.

The bike cut off abruptly and silence fell. Small ambient noises touched the background. The bike creaked lightly as it rested on its kickstand. Snow crunched softly as Boots dismounted. Flakes of ice pattered against the dark house, and the growls of the pup who still crouched in the bushes punctuated each step the big man took.

"Ever been to Europe? France is my favorite place to visit." Boots spoke in an easy voice, as if holding a casual conversation over coffee.

Every nerve in Janice's body suddenly fired up into awareness. That cool calm in his voice covered something dark. Something hidden deep in this man she loved. Something she'd not heard before, or at least never acknowledged. Something she hoped never to hear again. Her muscles tensed until they screamed.

Lewis snorted. "What the fuck are you talking about?"

"I studied literature in college with the idea that one day I'd be a professor. I was on my way to becoming a scholar, if you can believe that. My master's thesis would have been on nineteenth-century French poets." Boots pulled at the fingers of his black gloves.

"You're giving me a fucking history lesson?"

"Victor Hugo, Jules Verne, Arthur Rimbaud, Paul Verlaine."

Lewis's face grew red with frustration. "You're fucking crazy."

"My absolute favorite was Charles Baudelaire. He wrote a book of poetry called *Les Fleurs du mal* or the Flowers of Evil."

Janice kept her stance and focused her eyes on

Lewis, but Boots's lilting voice captured her attention. Dread settled in the pit of her stomach as she listened to his voice. He sounded as if he were in a lecture hall instead of a yard with snow falling. It made him more sinister than if he'd been yelling curses and threats.

He made a show of tucking the gloves into a side pocket of his jacket. "Decadent work. Some eroticism. Disgust toward evil within oneself and an obsession with death. His work was so controversial, several of the poems were banned for being indecent."

"Why the fuck are you still talking?" Lewis's voice didn't have the same bite as it had a few minutes ago.

"Much of his work focuses on the concept of man's suffering as it relates to original sin. Do you know what that is, Lewis?"

"Now you're giving me a fucking Bible lesson?"

"It's not sex like a lot of people think. It's the rejection of God's moral authority. Adam and Eve started it when they ate the fruit from the tree of knowledge."

Lewis tensed with every sentence Boots uttered. Cold trickled down Janice's spine that had nothing to do with the weather. Boots was too calm. Too precise. Too relaxed. He didn't speak like the man who had held her in his arms or tutored Tad with his schoolwork. There was an undertone to that easy voice that held a menace she couldn't identify. This man was dangerous. Deadly dangerous.

"I've always considered Cain to be the true original sinner. There's nothing worse in this world than to kill one's brother."

"Stay away from me." Lewis's voice shook, and Janice saw the loose gun shaking in his hand. She held her breath and hoped the man didn't pull the trigger accidentally.

Boots stopped moving, and silence ensued. The pressure rose around them, and Janice felt a scream build up in the back of her throat. She swallowed it.

"Trust me, baby."

Lewis's red face shone with sweat, and his breath puffed rapid and hard. "What the fuck do you want?"

Boots didn't react to the frantic yell. He seemed to grow bigger, and his face darkened and changed, twisting into something unnatural. His voice lowered to a growl as he recited,

> *"Je suis la plaie et le couteau!*
> *Je suis le soufflet et la joue!*
> *Je suis les membres et la roue,*
> *Et la victime et le bourreau!"*

Cold raw fear pierced Janice's heart, freezing the blood in her veins. This was Boots as his most elemental self. The part of him he'd tried so hard to leave behind. The specter called back up from his past to be in his present once more.

"What the fuck does that mean? Who are you?" Lewis's hoarse scream cut through the tension, and she felt her stomach roil.

Boots / not Boots grinned.

"I am the wound and the dagger!
I am the blow and the cheek!
I am the members and the wheel,
Victim and executioner!"

Later, Janice would think back and go over each step in her mind. The tiny details that flew by in rapid sequence. She would recount and repeat them over and over to person after person until she wanted to collapse into a ball of tears. She still wouldn't know which happened first or how those few seconds unfolded. All she would remember was a blur of movement.

Zeus burst from her hiding spot and bit into Lewis's thigh with a bloodthirsty snarl. The man screamed in pain and swept the gun against the dog's head, tearing himself free and knocking the puppy to the ground. Zeus yelped and lay still. Lewis's voice cut off abruptly as he clutched at the knife buried in his throat. Janice hadn't seen the throw, just the protruding handle. Blood poured from his mouth as he tried to speak, and a surprised look crossed his features. He raised the gun, and a second knife flew through the air, hitting him in the shoulder. The gun dropped as his arm went limp. He coughed and blood splattered from his lips onto his uniform. A third knife buried itself in his midchest, and he stumbled backward to the ground. Gurgling noises came from his mouth as he continued to choke on his own blood.

Boots moved to stand over the dying man.

"I'm the vampire of my own heart
One of those utter derelicts
Condemned to eternal laughter,
But who can no longer smile!"

Janice started quaking and couldn't stop. Boots's words sent shards of ice into her belly. Her feet froze to the ground, and she was unable to move at the sight of Boots watching the writhing man as he bled out his last breath. The biker's face showed no reaction. No anger. No remorse. No pity. Nothing. A dead expression. The sheer lack of feeling made her horror more acute.

"Mom?"

It was Tad's watery voice that spurred her into action. She whirled around and dashed to the corner of the carport before the boy could come any further. Thankfully, he'd only come to the edge and hadn't gotten far enough to see anything in the front yard. "Go back inside, sweetheart."

"What's going on? Where's Zeus?"

Blue lights flashed across the house as several vehicles arrived.

"Zeus is outside. She's… had an accident. I'll go check on her in a minute. Please, go to your room."

"Is she hurt?" The child's question came with tears.

"I don't know. I have to go look. There's some stuff I have to go do, and I need you to stay in your room."

"But, Mom…."

Boots appeared at the edge of the carport. "Do as your mother says." His tone and appearance had reverted back to his normal self, but Janice still tensed and placed herself between him and her son. Boots noticed and his face dropped. "There's going to be a lot of activity for a little while. I know it sucks, but you'll get an explanation after everything calms down."

Tad sniffed. "What about my dog?"

"I'll take care of her. She'll be fine."

"Did a car hit her?"

Boots hesitated. "I promise someone will talk to you later. Right now, you need to be the man of the house and take care of your siblings. You trust me?"

Tad nodded and sniffed. "Okay. Remember, you promised."

"I'll remember."

The boy shuffled back into the house. Janice turned to Boots and swallowed her trepidations. Her hands were shaking. Hell, her whole body was shaking, but she had her children and her household to take care of, and therefore any personal breakdowns had to wait until later. "Are y-you sure Zeus w-will be okay?"

"She's moving around. Rail, Duke, and Nutter are on the way. One of them will take her to the emergency vet."

Janice's body continued to shake violently.

His tone changed. "Go get your coat, baby. Milton is here now and will need to talk to you. Best to do that out here where Tad or any of the other kids can't hear you."

Her teeth chattered as she spoke. "You're worried about T-T-T-Tad?"

"Yes." He stepped toward her, and with a sharp breath, she stepped back. His face reeled in shock for a moment followed by an expression of sadness so deep, it was as if he himself had been stabbed. "I'm worried about you, too, baby. I'm sorry, Janice. I'm so goddamned sorry you had to see that. That you had to see *me*."

He was interrupted when another car with blue lights showed up, along with an ambulance. Milton came up to them, his eyes darting as he looked around, taking in the scene. He gave a long sigh. "I need to go by the book and get statements from everyone, but I'm pretty sure I already know the outcome."

Janice turned stiffly to go into the house. "I'll make a pot of coffee for everyone."

"Stay here and I'll do it," Rail insisted as he walked up, followed by Duke. "The faster you get this part done, the faster we can settle everyone down."

An hour later, Milton had everyone's version of what happened. The paramedics hadn't even tried to revive Lewis. The handle of the throwing knife still protruded from his throat as they zipped up the body in an oblong plastic bag.

Milton shook his head as Lewis's remains were loaded into the transport. He turned back to Boots and gave a long, tired sigh. "There are times I hate my job. I was so damn proud to become an officer of the law. For thirty years, I've followed it to the letter and kept myself accountable to the citizens of this community who trusted me to keep them safe." He nodded at the departing ambulance. "We had suspicions about him and his buddies and started an investigation, but we couldn't find enough proof. Cort called me to come see him, and the next thing I know, he's in the hospital with tubes running all through his body and a permanent case of amnesia. There's no doubt in my mind that Canter was a part of that."

He shook his head and sighed again. "I've tried to be a good cop all my life, and it pisses me off when the job I love gets shit on by people like him. Pisses me off more that I have to do this because of that useless fucker." He turned reluctantly to Boots and stood up straight. "Boots, I'm afraid you're under arrest. I wish like hell I could let this go, but if I did, I'd not be the officer of the law I swore to be."

Another dart pierced Janice's heart. So many of them had hit her over the years, one more shouldn't have made a difference, but this one burrowed deep. She cut off a sob and pressed her lips together so tightly they hurt.

Boots nodded in acquiescence. "I understand." He turned and placed his hands behind his back before being asked. Milton snapped metal cuffs around his wrists while he recited the Miranda rights.

Tears poured down Janice's face. She didn't bother wiping them away.

"Motherfucking hell," Duke swore, stomping in circles in his agitation.

Zeus whined as if sensing the discord that permeated the air.

"I'll get the legal shit started and post bail as soon as possible," Rail stated as Boots was escorted to the police cruiser. "I don't know how this will turn out, brother. You could be looking at some serious time if this goes bad. Maybe worse."

Boots grunted. "I realize that. I still wouldn't change anything. If it came down to my life or hers, I'd cut my own throat. Maybe this is the price of atonement for all the sins of my past. I've committed plenty of them, and this is how I pay."

"It would be best if you exercised your right to silence," Milton advised. "Don't say anything around me that would get you in deeper. Let's get this shit done."

CHAPTER
THIRTY-ONE

That night was the longest of Janice's life. Sleep eluded her until her eyes felt gritted up with sand. Nutter had taken Zeus to the emergency vet, and the dog would be there overnight. She texted Rail and got few answers. There was only one of him, and he was trying to cover all bases. He let her know that Opal was at the hospital. Duke was with her and would bring her to the house when he could.

Railroad: She's hurt and will need some help.

Mama J: Where's Boots? What's happening to him?

Railroad: I'm at the jail. Can't talk now. I'll call you later.

That was hours ago.

Then there were the kids. Most of the time, they

could sleep through tornados, but with the sirens, lights, and the activity from the people crawling all over her property, there was no way they could stay in bed. After Boots was taken away, Janice wandered into her kitchen and found Tad handing out juice boxes to sleepy, confused children.

"Mommy?" Lily came up to her, rubbing her eyes and reaching out her arms to be picked up. Janice leaned down instinctively and lifted the little girl to her bosom. Ollie copied his sister and clung to her side like a barnacle.

"Thank you for helping and being so brave, Tad." Her voice was hoarse, as if she'd been screaming for hours. Maybe she had and didn't know it. Her mind whirled in so many directions with so many questions, it had gone numb. Zombie-like. She felt on the verge of collapsing and would have but for the crowd of tiny bodies around her. Leaning on her. Depending on her to be strong. She swallowed the knotted ball of emotions that stuck in her throat and tucked it away to untangle later. Right now, she needed to be Mama J. Janice could wait.

All of them ended up in a tangle on the living room floor with every blanket and pillow in the house. The TV played a cartoon movie, and a pile of empty juice boxes and cookie crumbs covered the floor. That was how Nutter found them. Janice was sitting with her back against the sofa, surrounded by dozing children who crowded as close to her as possible. Her feet and legs had fallen asleep under the weight of the kids seeking comfort from the only steady source of it in their lives.

Janice looked up at her ex with tired red eyes. "If you're here to help, that would be nice. If you're not, then just leave. I don't need any more to deal with tonight." She gave a rough laugh. "This morning."

Nutter shifted from foot to foot, but he ultimately kept his mouth shut. He easily lifted the two little girls from their curled-up positions on Janice's legs and carried them to their beds. Tad roused enough to frown at his father, but he too stayed silent as he poked at Ian. They got up just as Nutter came back to carry the two smallest boys.

Janice's back cramped and her feet prickled with a thousand needles as they came back to life. She winced as she stiffly rose from her position. She almost lost her balance, but Nutter appeared and steadied her.

"Thank you," she muttered as he helped her ease to the sofa.

"Kids are all in bed. I checked on Pearl. She's making fussy noises, but she's still snoozing for now."

Janice glanced at the sky through the front bay window. A cold winter dawn was creeping up, heralding more snow and a dark day. "She'll be up soon, wanting to be fed. I'll go...." She fell back on the cushions as her legs gave out.

"Stay here. I'll take care of it when she wakes up." Nutter stood over Janice as he spoke in a low tone. "I promise I'm not gonna fuck anything up. I'll stay and take care of the kids as long as you need me. Duke's got Opal and is on the way."

She nodded tiredly, unable to speak. Her kids were safe. Her house was quiet. She could think for a minute or two before the next round of responsibilities started, but she didn't want to. Not yet.

Boots.

Tears formed in her eyes, and her heart bloomed in pain. "Do you know what's going on?"

Nutter shook his head. "Not all of it. I'm not exactly in Rail's good graces these days." He huffed a laugh. "I don't think I'm in anyone's good graces right now. He said you were by yourself with the kids with all this shit going down. I came as soon as I could."

"Did he tell you to come?"

"No. He told me to leave you alone, but I thought you'd need me. You'd need someone since...."

She finished his hanging sentence. "Since Boots got arrested."

"Yeah."

The sound of an engine caught their ears as it pulled into the driveway. A few minutes later, Duke knocked softly and entered. He carried a sleeping Opal in his arms. She had thick white bandages on her face and head, and Janice inhaled sharply at the sight.

"She's out cold from painkillers. Good thing too. It's gonna be rough when she wakes up."

Nutter closed the kitchen door. "Camo?"

Duke's mouth screwed up tight, and he shook his head, unable to vocalize an answer.

"Fuck. Her room is back here. Baby's still asleep, so try to keep it quiet, yeah?" Nutter directed.

After Duke disappeared, walking sideways down the hall, Nutter turned to Janice. Raw pain showed on his face, calling to her nurturing nature and giving her the focus she needed. She closed the space between them and wrapped her generous arms around the big man. He clutched at her and lowered his head to her shoulder. Grief poured from him as he shook and cried.

"I'm so fucking sorry. For everything. All the shit I put you through. All the women. All the times I let you down. I'm so goddamn sorry."

She stroked his back but didn't comment. Forgiveness would come eventually, but she wasn't ready to give it yet. So many other thoughts crowded her head. So many other needs that she had to fulfill for herself before Nutter's could be met.

She had to stay strong—just a little while longer.

Duke came back and jammed a hand over his weary face. "Mind if I make some coffee? I think I could drink a whole pot just myself. Shit's hit the fan big-time, and it's gonna cover everything."

"I'll get it." Janice bustled to her kitchen where she could find everything at her fingertips. The familiarity of making coffee helped to calm her raging nerves. She might seem like she had it under control on the outside, but inside, she was a churned mess of total chaos. "Duke, I'm tired of the bullshit. Please tell me what's going on?"

Duke sat heavily on a counter stool and leaned on his elbows with his head hung low. "Yeah, I think you need to know."

Janice held her temper when she heard about Lewis Canter stalking Opal. The threats and actions taken against Cort and Randy. The suspected arson in Lake City. The club trying to stay out of it as well as protect everyone. Opal's attack that evening and her injuries. The ultimate ending to the night when Boots threw that first knife into Lewis Canter's throat.

"He wanted to leave that shit behind him and start a new life. A new direction." His red eyes rose to meet Janice's wet ones. "He was so goddamn happy, planning a future with you. We drew up blueprints to pop the top and expand this house, build more bedrooms for the kids, add in another bathroom or two, that sort of shit. He never wanted you to see that part of him." He sat back. "You need to be ready,

Mama J. This is probably going to go bad for him. Real bad."

Janice disregarded the tears flowing down her cheeks. She didn't need a mirror to see her blotchy face and swollen eyes. "Why? What part of him?" she asked in a hoarse whisper. She wanted to hear the answer, and at the same time she dreaded it.

Nutter spoke up. "Boots did the jobs no one else wanted to do in the Dark Horses. He was the enforcer, torturer, and when necessary, the executioner."

Pain struck her heart. "He's killed other people?"

"Yeah. The ones that deserved it. Like when Musicman's daughter was raped by this asshole from her job. Boots made it go away. Poof!" Nutter raised his hands and flared his fingers as if performing a magic trick. "The Dark Horses said he could beat a man bloody, and his heart rate never went up. Never broke a sweat. No one knows what he did with the bodies. They're just gone, as if they never existed. He didn't do anything without a reason or an order, but when he was called into play, that bastard could be colder than Iceman on a bad day."

Duke sat back with a bitter laugh. "That's only the small shit. The big shit happened before he became a Dark Horse. All that fucked-up crap will come back on him, and he'll have to deal with it all over again."

Janice brushed at her eyes and sniffed. "What are you talking about?"

Duke fisted his hands. "I can't."

Janice lost it. "Don't you fucking do that to me. My son almost saw someone die tonight. His dog is at the emergency vet with a broken leg and a fractured skull. Boots…. Boots…. He's my old man."

Nutter jumped at her words, but she ignored him. "Duke, you need to tell me everything you know. I deserve that."

Duke's face dropped. "You're right, but it's not my story to tell. You need to go see him."

"I will, but give me something," she demanded.

"Janice."

"Fucking tell me!"

Perhaps it was her loss of control, or maybe the F-bomb that rarely, if ever, fell from her lips. Duke took a huge breath and gave it to her. "Boots was set to become this big-time academic guy when he was younger. Smart, educated, fucking brilliant. Then there was an accident on his family's farm, and he went to prison for it. Ruined his career before it got started. The charge was manslaughter. He killed his brother."

CHAPTER
THIRTY-TWO

Boots paced inside the small cell, unable to settle. Rail assured him they would take care of things for him, but he expected the club would drop him like a hot potato. The Dutchmen had built a hard-won reputation in the legit world, but it was far from solid. Any scandal could topple their work to ground zero. Therefore, distancing themselves from him and the events of this past night would be in their favor.

He couldn't blame them.

His biggest regret was Janice. Janice with her bouncy curls, gorgeous wide ass, and her beautiful generous nature. Surely, she would never want to see him again. He thought his dark side was gone forever, purged with the disbanding of the Dark Horses, and his past sins paid for with his life's forfeitures. He thought he'd already atoned when he lost the career he loved. Then again when his parents died, and his family's legacy was sold to a land developer. His rage and bitterness manifested him into a man who was capable of such violence, and the world of the Dark Horses provided a much-needed release. Bullets, blood, pain, torture—he was good at it. Perhaps that was why he admired Iceman of the Dutchmen MC back in the day. Both of them could cut a man's throat, dispose of the body in such a way it would never be found, then go drink or fuck until the sun rose. Carmen would clean the blood from his cut or his clothes, and never said a word to him, not that he cared.

But with Janice, he did. He cared what she thought of him. Cared about what Tad and the other kids thought of him. Fucking hell, he just *cared!*

He was too scared to say the word love. If he admitted to that, his heart would shatter.

A clanging noise interrupted his thoughts, and he paused his pacing. Milton appeared with a set of keys and unlocked the cell. "Visitor to see you. I'm putting you in the interrogation room. Up the stairs to the left."

"Lawyer?"

Milton shook his head. "Nope."

"Don't you think I'll try to escape?"

"Nope. Not when you see who it is."

The room was small and plain. Only a cheap wooden table and two plastic chairs added any color to the dirty beige walls. Janice turned her head to face him when he entered.

His heart thudded. "I didn't think I'd be seeing you again."

Her manner was cool, but there was something more in her eyes. "Why not?"

He swallowed the saliva that had gathered in his mouth. "After you saw me, saw what I'm capable of, I figured you'd be done and walk away."

She cleared her throat. "I'm still here. I… um…. Duke told me some things about you."

The strength left his knees, and he sat heavily in the chair. Grief hit him, sharp and exquisite with its cutting edge. "You know."

"I know what he told me. What I don't know is your side."

He wasn't sure what he was hearing. "What are you saying?"

This wasn't a place where she had to talk to him on a telephone through a glass wall. She reached across the table and took his hands. "I can't believe the man who came with me to my son's soccer games, brought me a dishwasher I sorely needed, came to me anytime I needed help, is an unredeemable bad one."

He dropped his eyes to her hands where they held his. Short nails, strong fingers, firm from hours of kneading dough—these were hands that comforted children, helped friends, touched a lover. Hands that held him now.

"I come from a big family. All of us worked the farm, and I learned early how to fix engines, basic construction, and other skills. There was always work to be done, and I sometimes wonder if that's why my parents had so many children. We were never particularly close, but Jarrod was by far the worst one. We fought constantly. Argued all the time. He was a year younger than me, and we never got along as kids. Never."

His eyes stayed on their combined hands, but he was focused somewhere else. His hands started to shake with a fine tremor. "I was the only one to go to college and do something different. I was in grad school at the time and had my whole life planned. Professorship, research grants, history lectures. Most of my other brothers worked other jobs at other farms and came back once in a while. A couple of my unmarried sisters stayed at home, but Jarrod never left the farm. I'm sure it was because he had nowhere else to go. He'd started drinking a lot when I was doing my undergrad. He never had any real ambition growing up, and I've wondered if his alcohol abuse came from jealousy of me and my escape from farm life. Long story short, my dad got sick, and my mom couldn't handle the workload. She needed help and called me to come home."

He stroked his thumbs over her fingers, watching

how the skin moved over her knuckles. "I took a leave of absence from the university to go help my parents. Jarrod hated me being there. Lots of snide remarks, little digs about my love of literature instead of cows and farming. Picked fights with me anytime he could. I was in the yard, working the chaff cutter one night, trying to finish the massive job by myself. He was supposed to help me but never showed. I'd been at it all day, and during that time, my irritation with him festered. To put it bluntly, I was pissed as hell at him."

He paused to swallow. "I'd taken the safety shield off the machine to get more material in the hopper so I could finish the job faster. Jarrod came in and started in on me. He'd been drinking all day with his buddies somewhere and not helping anyone else either. I was tired, hungry, and thirsty, and so damn mad, it didn't take much for me to give him the fight he was looking for. I don't remember who threw the first punch, but I remember we went at each other pretty hard. Our sister, Marilynn, came to check on us and he tried to punch her. I shoved him away."

He stopped, his vision clouding as the memory of that night assailed him. "I forgot about the cutter."

Janice's gasp slashed through him, like the teeth of the farm machine that tore away Jarrod's arm. He could still hear the screams of pain, smell the copper tint of blood in the air, see his other siblings as they ran to the work yard and tried to stop the flow from

Jarrod's mangled body. Nothing helped. Boots closed his eyes as he recalled the horror in his mind when the fingers of Jarrod's remaining hand pointed straight at him and named him as his killer. One by one, his other siblings turned away from him in anger and disgust, even Marilynn.

"I had no money for a lawyer, so I had to use a court-appointed one. He didn't try to get an accidental death ruling but got me a plea bargain for manslaughter instead of murder. I'm not sure how that's better, as no matter what, I lost everything. My degrees, my friends, my family." Tears he didn't know he was shedding dripped from his eyes onto the entwined fingers on the table beneath them. "Prison changes people. I had to learn quick how to survive, both physically and psychologically. I saw men who had nothing to live for and didn't care who they hurt in the process. No feelings. No remorse. No humanity left. Animals treat each other better. There are things that happened behind those bars I will never share. I can't."

He took a breath. "When I got out, I discovered both my parents had died, and the farm was gone. Sold for a housing development. None of my brothers or sisters would speak to me and told me to never contact them again. I was angry, bitter, and pissed at the world for what I thought it had done to me. It was that rage boiling inside of me that made me join the Dark Horses. They made me welcome, and I found a niche in their club. Something I was good at. Something I didn't care about. Again, there are things I did for the club I will never speak of. They are over."

A shuffling in the hall caught his ear for a moment. "A couple of years ago, I had an epiphany, so to speak. I was back in prison, this time for a misdemeanor, but because of who I am and my past record, I was put in gen pop with murderers and rapists. A lot of them were repeat offenders back for the second and third time. No hope. No reason to change. I was in my bunk one night and vowed that wouldn't be me. I asked for forgiveness and promised I'd atone for every sin I'd committed. The next day, I was told I qualified for early release. Rail came to get me, offered me a job. Now, here I am. Back where I started, and I'm scared I'm being drug down that black path again."

He finally raised his watering eyes to meet Janice's equally wet ones. "I wanted so fucking bad to have a life with you. I was ready for it. Ready to fight for it. It's likely I'll go back to prison, and I can't ask you to stay with me. It's too much, and you do not deserve that. Your kids don't either. I know you're here to break it off with me, and you're right to do it. The price of my atonement is to let you go, but please know this. All this time, I've loved you, and no matter what happens, I'll never stop."

Janice had stayed across from him as he purged

himself with words. She didn't let go of his hand once to wipe the wetness from her cheeks. When she did speak, her voice cracked. "Boots, I didn't come here to break up with you. I came here to thank you."

His belly clenched up. "What?"

"You saved my life. You probably saved Tad's life too. And Zeus's. There is no more to pay. You've already atoned."

She released his hands, only to get up and move around the table. She slipped into his arms like she belonged there. A perfect fit. He was crying openly now, not caring if anyone saw him. It was cathartic. Her strength as she held him tight brought him hope. This. This feeling was worth fighting for, and he would not go into that good night quietly.

The door to the room flew open, and several people walked in. Milton led the way, followed by a grinning Rail and a woman who he happened to know had some rather intimate tattoos under her tailored clothes.

"I hate to break up the party, but we have some business to discuss." Bella slammed down a briefcase on the table, then smiled shark-like in her lawyer power suit and heels. "Nice to meet you Boots, aka Caleb Ambrose. I'm Isabel, your attorney."

EPILOGUE

"MOM, CAN WE GET IN THE WATER NOW?" THE WHINY cry came from Lily, who was dressed in her yellow-and-pink swimsuit. Charlotte had decided her favorite color was powder blue, and the fights over who got what had all but stopped.

Janice had her head inside the giant cooler. "Wait for one of the adults to go with you." She pulled out a handful of Capri Sun pouches and handed one each to Ollie and Augustus. "Want one?"

The girl took the offering and punched the straw into the top. "What about Tad? Can he come watch us?"

"Tad is helping pitch the tents. You can go watch him first, and then ask if he can watch you in the water after he's done. Only up to your knees though. If you want to go all the way in, you have to wait. Deal?"

"Deal." The little girl skipped off, yelling for Charlotte to come with her.

Janice stood up and felt her shoulder cramp. Before she got her fingers on the bothersome spot, someone else pressed into the knot and began massaging it loose. Boots leaned down and kissed her neck, taking a second to nip at the flesh behind her ear. "Tents are done, baby. I can take them if you want."

"Sounds good to me. I'll be down in a bit with some waters and snacks. Supper won't be for a few hours yet, and wearing them out would be a good way to get them to sleep tonight."

His hands snaked down to grab double fists of her bottom. "I have other reasons to wear them out so they'll sleep. Why else did I get four tents and an extra pillow for you to bury your face in when I make you come?"

"Won't you need an extra pillow too?"

He growled and nipped her again. "No need. I'll have my face buried somewhere else."

She laughed even as the now familiar tingle started low in her belly.

The trial hadn't even made it to court. Isabel had wiped the floor with the prosecutor at the pre-trial hearing. She brought sworn statements from witnesses that saw Canter shoot Camo, stated the fact that Boots too had been shot, and displayed hospital pictures of the assault on Opal.

Compounded with the fact that Janice had feared for her life and that of her son while being held at gunpoint, it all pointed to a solid self-defense plea. Isabel proved to be just as deadly a vampire in the courtroom as she was as her club character when the prosecutor tried to get Boots convicted on a probation violation for having throwing knives concealed on his person. She twisted rings around him, proving that the laws cited did not apply to these knives, nor were they longer than four inches at the blade. Boots found himself a free man.

The investigation into Lewis Canter's side hustle revealed a network of cops working extortion angles and involved in harassment. Thune, Macaffee, and several others were awaiting their own trials, and it was predicted that they would all be put away before the summer was gone.

Nutter finally realized he wasn't going to get his Mama J back and moved on. Since he was not going to stop collecting as much pussy as he could, he elected to get the vasectomy that was long overdue. Janice was nice enough to take him to and from the surgery and bought him four bags of frozen peas. She didn't even laugh when he exited the doctor's office, walking stiffly and slowly, although she smiled rather widely.

Mimi signed over custody of Ollie and Charlotte to Janice but kept the other little boy. Janice wondered what the kids would think years from now, knowing they had another half-sibling in the world, but there wasn't much she could do about it.

The marina had expanded as had the Harbor Bar and Restaurant. People had been flooding the Dutchmen-owned business for a while because of their connection to the big cult trafficking bust a couple of years ago. The steady flow hadn't abated, and the club finances were well in the black. Rail had floated the idea of opening up another bar further down the river in Lake City or Wabasha. Duke had scouted locations and mentioned he'd be into it so he could be closer to his old lady, Penny.

The one bad spot was Camo and Opal. His death had left a devastating hole in her heart and her life. Many nights Janice sat with her as she healed from her injuries, holding the grieving woman and rocking her as she would any of the children. Opal cried for days, the pain of the loss unbearable. Baby Pearl was the only person to keep the young woman from going completely insane. It took a bit of time, but Opal got herself together and made some firm decisions.

A few weeks ago, Duke and Nitro packed up Opal's life and helped her move to a new one. One of the other students, Kimmie, had some cousins in North Carolina in a small town called Bryson City. A local shop had some openings for a hairdresser and a nail tech. With Opal's glowing school record, her instructor's recommendation, and Kimmie's support, she'd gotten the job. The news was tearfully shared one night while Janice and Opal sat in the living room with the ever-present laundry basket.

"Are you sure? You'll be all alone with no help, no family, no support. It's a big decision and a big leap of faith."

"Kimmie will be around, and I'll have Pearl. There's nothing left for me here in Minnesota. I think…. I think Camo would be okay with it."

Janice inhaled a big breath of the clean lake air as she recalled the conversation. She had heard from Opal several times. The younger woman was settling in at the salon and had already made friends with the owner and some other local ladies. Janice wished her all the happiness in the world and hoped she would find it someday.

Life was good. Great, even. Her own business had grown after she'd moved it to a brick-and-mortar building and partnered up with two other bakers. Mama J's Old World Treats, became simply Old World Bakery and Treats. She worked hard there on a daily basis, but she could still take time off to be with her family on the camping trip Boots promised to her kids.

Boots. She never thought she'd wear a property patch again, but she had one that said, "Property of Boots." It was on the back of her jacket that was sitting in the closet at home, ready to be pulled out when the cool weather started again. Boots had designed the new upstairs into four bedrooms plus a den area, so the four oldest children had their own space. Ollie and Augustus, despite their constant bickering, didn't want to be separated, so Boots made them connecting rooms on the first floor in the area furthest from the main bedroom. This gave Janice and him the privacy they needed.

She grinned. She still stifled her cries of pleasure in a pillow or Boots's shoulder, often both, nearly every night of the week.

Boots walked into the water along with the laughing kids. They squealed and splashed him as he splashed back. Zeus jumped in with them and bit at the water with happy barks. He wore old cutoffs jeans instead of swim trunks and kept a black tank on his torso to keep his shocking tattoo covered. It was too elaborate to do any big changes on it.

"Do you want me to look into laser removal?" He had asked her one night after they'd made love.

"No, honey. It's in the past, and you don't need to go through any more pain because of it."

He'd smiled at her answer before rolling her onto her back and showing her how much her words meant to him.

Her nipples tightened as she thought about that moment, and a little thrill shimmied down her spine, settling between her legs. Her man had some serious stamina.

Later that night, they sat around a crackling fire, setting marshmallows on fire and making s'mores.

Supper had been little more than toasting hot dogs on long forks. They had the kids make up their own foil packs of ham, cheese, potatoes, peppers, and onions, and let them cook in the fire until done. They thought it was loads of fun, and Janice liked the easy clean-up, saying, "No dishes to wash, don'tcha know."

She looked across the family circle to watch as Boots sat with Tad, showing him how to sharpen a stick with a knife and talking to him. Her oldest child had let go of his anger and was now in a better place. He had a man in his life that had stepped into the role of mentor and teacher with ease, and it showed in the boy's attitude. Ian was also opening up more and set to follow in his big brother's footsteps.

A sense of well-being filled Janice. This is the family she'd always wanted. Happy, fulfilled, satisfied, comfortable—all the adjectives she could think of to describe her complete contentment. A year ago, she never thought she could have this life. She gazed through the shimmering smoke at the man who helped make that dream come true. As if he could feel her eyes on him, Boots peered back at her, winked, and mouthed, "*I love you*" to her.

She smiled and whispered it back to him.

———

I hope you've loved reading my Dutchmen MC. I've had such fun with this series. I have two other series for you to check out—Dragon Runners MC and MacAteer Brothers. If you're wondering what's next, be sure to join my publisher's newsletter or follow me on social media.

ACKNOWLEDGMENTS

Life doesn't always come with happy endings. It can get complicated and messy in a heartbeat. This is a big reason Nutter and Mama J don't get back together in this story. Not every couple can survive infidelity, and divorces happen every day. But I couldn't leave Janice hanging, so I found her a hero, however unlikely he is, and gave her a happy ending. I'm partial to hardworking single moms, as I've been one. Every single mom out there deserves all the happiness life can give them.

So why did Camo have to die? I debated over this plot point a lot and almost scrapped it to let him live and give Opal her happy ending too. The hard truth is people also die in this fictional world, and in this case, Camo became the sacrifice. I know, it sucks, but I promise Opal will get her own story in a different series and find love again.

Big thanks to everyone who helped me get this book done. First look, Demmarie Borland, I appreciate you taking me on. Beta readers McKinley Hellenes Krantz, Keeley Catarineau, Paula White, and Jamee Thumm, I love getting your honest feedback and suggestions. Kristin Scearce, thank you for your reminders and keeping my butt on task. Lori Gries, Donna Pemberton, Becky Johnson, and all the Hot Tree people, I love y'all bunches for taking a chance on me and helping me grow in this fantastic world of writing.

ABOUT THE AUTHOR

Thanks for reading THE PRICE OF ATONEMENT: DUTCHMEN MC, BOOK FOUR. I do hope you enjoyed Boots's and Janice's story. Opal's story will continue with another book in a different series. I appreciate your help in spreading the word, including telling a friend. Before you go, it would mean so much to me if you would take a few minutes to write a review and share how you feel about my story so others may find my work. Reviews really do help readers find books. Please leave a review on your favorite book site.

Don't miss out on New Releases, Exclusive Giveaways and much more!

Join my newsletter: HTTPS://WWW.MLNYSTROM.COM/CONTACT

Visit my website for my current booklist: HTTPS://WWW.MLNYSTROM.COM/

I'd love to hear from you directly, too. Please feel free to email me at melody@mlnystrom.com or check out

my website HTTPS://WWW.MLNYSTROM.COM/ for
updates.

facebook.com/authorMLNystrom
twitter.com/ml_nystrom
instagram.com/mlnystrom
bookbub.com/profile/ml-nystrom

ABOUT THE PUBLISHER

Hot Tree Publishing loves love. Publishing adult romantic fiction, HTPubs are all about diverse reads featuring heroes and heroines to swoon over. Since opening in 2015, HTPubs have published more than 300 titles across the wide and diverse range of romantic genres. If you're chasing a happily ever after in your favourite subgenre, HTPubs have you covered.

Interested in discovering more amazing reads brought to you by Hot Tree Publishing? Head over to the website for information:

WWW.HOTTREEPUBLISHING.COM

9 781922 679383